BLOODY KINGDOM

THE CRIMSON CROWN BOOK I

KAYLEIGH KING

BLOODY KINGDOM

Cover Design: Cat at TRC DESIGNS
CopyEditing : Ellie McLove at MY BROTHER'S EDITOR
Proof Reading: Rosa Sharon at MY BROTHER'S EDITOR
Formatting: Cat at TRC DESIGNS
Beta Reading by G. Rivers, A. Ayala, C. Imb & Bre Books

ISBN: 978-1-7359304-2-8

BLOODY KINGDOM

THE CRIMSON CROWN BOOK I

KAYLEIGH KING

For the ones who still believe in
fairytales

Close your eyes and picture the sun
That's what it felt like to love her; warmth.
-Atticus

PLAYLIST

The Night We Met - Micky
Blood Sport - Sleep Token
Three White Horses - Andrew Bird
The Watchmaker - Woodlock
The Garden - Woodlock
I Can't Lose You - Isak Danielson
Love You Better - The Haunt
Bittersweet - ARCHIS
Rival - Ruelle
Destroyer - Of Monsters and Men
Woke Up Dead - Kyla La Grange
Contaminated - Banks
My House – PVRIS
My Blood – Echos
Dancing After Death – Matt Maeson

PROLOGUE

Silas

"That's her, sir?" my employee asks from the driver's seat, sounding skeptical of my choice. "She's the one you want?"

She's the only one walking down the street without an umbrella or hiding beneath one of the shop awnings. She doesn't look remotely fazed or bothered by the sudden downpour. Instead, she lets the rain soak through the strands of her long golden hair and drench through the thin fabric of her revealing tank top.

She tilts her head back, exposing her slender throat as she lets the rain fall on her pretty face. I sit like a piece of stone, forcing myself to stay put at the sight of her easily accessible neck. Centuries of iron-clad control slipping at the sight of her jugular.

"She isn't what I *want*," I bite out between clenched teeth. "You know this, I don't want anything to do with her, but she's perfect for what *he* needs."

My driver sits there silently for a minute, but I hear his heart rate pick up the longer he stares at her. He wants her, who can blame him? She's beautiful. "She's reckless, walking these streets at night alone like this. She might get herself killed before you're even able to get your hands on her."

He's right, why she'd be walking the streets of New Orleans alone is beyond me. I know for a fact she's smarter than that. Word will get out soon that she is untouchable, under my protection, and no one dares defy me. It's a death sentence.

"This needs to happen as soon as possible," I order him, not once able to drag my eyes away from her. She pauses beside a man slouched against a wall with his head bowed dejectedly. Most people would have walked right past him, but not her. She digs in her bag and hands him what looks to be a granola bar of some kind. Her expression holds no judgment or distaste. Just a soft smile and kind eyes, a warmth I swear I can feel from almost a block away radiates off her.

This unyielding kindness is what made him choose her.

"I want her brought to me by the end of the week." My voice sounds stiff even to me. "Make it happen."

"I'm on it."

She comes to a stop at the street corner, checking both ways before crossing the dark road. Before she steps off the sidewalk, her eyes glance at my dark car and hold. As if she can see me sitting in the back seat, she stares directly at me. If I had a heartbeat, I wonder if it'd be pounding loudly right now.

Grinding my teeth and scowling at the woman I know will end up being more trouble than she's worth, I nod my head at my driver in the rearview mirror. "I've seen enough." Finally, I tear my eyes off of her. "Let's go."

It won't be long before my control is really tested, and she's standing before me. She may have run from her past life, but I'm dragging her into mine.

Welcome to my bloody kingdom, Quincey Page.

CHAPTER 1

I thrive in chaos.

Chaotic energy and bustling noise invigorate my soul and keep my mind occupied. When it's quiet and still, that's when the demons I've avoided start creeping out of the cages I've trapped them in. Too much time spent pondering my thoughts, and life is never a good thing. If I do that, I'll fully grasp what an *epic* dumpster fire my life has become. And I don't need that kind of self-realization, regardless of what those self-help bullshit books my friend Lucy buys but never reads say.

I'm more than happy living in my beautiful la-la land, thank you very much.

Is it the healthiest way of coping with things? No.

Am I going to keep doing it? You bet.

Until the shambles of my life fully implode and I have nothing left, I'm going to keep moving forward and continue to find peace in the chaos.

"I don't care what life event is happening, I will never wear a tiara and a tacky, glittery sash," Lucy declares as she pours another pitcher of beer for the rowdy group of frat boys that scream '*tourists*'.

The customer across from me takes her freshly made gin and tonic before handing me a few bills in return. "What are you talking about?" I ask my best friend as I turn around, not understanding her left-field comment.

"I'm talking about the gaggle of bleach blonde airheads that just took up residence at the other end of my bar." She rolls her eyes, jutting her thumb in the direction of the girls I'm just now noticing. Sure enough, the one in the middle is wearing a sash that says it's her twenty-first birthday, and a cheap plastic tiara sits lopsided on her head. All the girls wear beads around their necks, even though Mardi Gras was over two months ago. "I'm embarrassed for them."

Smiling, I shake my head at Lucy. "Come on, can't you remember a time when we saw the magic of this city?"

"No, I always thought it was a dirty shithole full of drunks and bad drivers." Lucy snatches a credit card out of a man's hand when he waves it obnoxiously at her from across the counter. She shoots him a dirty look but closes his tab anyway.

"When did you become so jaded, Luce?"

"I turned twenty-one and decided pretending everything was sunshine and rainbows was exhausting." Lucy smirks at me over her shoulder. "I'm much happier since I've taken on the role of bitter bitch."

"I could add some sunshine to your life, sweet cheeks," a voice slurs from the other side of the bar. Turning, I find one of the frat boys standing across the bar top, a sloppy grin on his face.

Flicking her dark hair over her shoulder, she smiles slyly at him. To anyone else, the smile would come across as inviting, sultry even. But I know Lucy too well. I know that smile means she's about to ruin this guy's night.

"Walk away now, dude." I grimace at him. "You've been warned."

Lucy's hand flies up, shushing me. "No, no. Let's hear what he has to offer." She leans across the sticky wood counter, pushing her ample tits up, showing off her cleavage in her tight leather top. "I'm curious, baby. You think you could add some sunshine to my life?"

"Maybe not to your *whole* life, but for the night? Hell yeah." The kid smirks confidently.

Poor baby, he has no idea what he's in for.

"You think you could take me home? Rock my world?" She trails a finger across the counter as she bites her lip.

"I know I could." The guy puffs his chest out.

Lucy tilts her head. "Do you want me to tell you how I see our night going?"

"Yeah, sweets, tell me all the nasty things you want me to do to that rockin' bod."

Ugh. Douchebag.

The smile on Lucy's face grows, the evil gleam in her eyes shining brightly. "Okay honey, this is how I see this going. You'll take me home, and we'll barely make it through the door before you start pawing at my breasts like a middle schooler. You'll kiss me, my guess is you'll use too much tongue and you'll taste of stale alcohol and whatever fruity-flavored vape you've been hitting all night. I'll push past it because I'm horny and it's been a minute since I've gotten laid. A girl has needs after all."

I have to cover my mouth with my hand to hide the smile growing on my face.

"Once we finally make it to the bedroom, you'll rip off that cute polo and your khaki shorts, then you'll climb on top of me. You'll make it four thrusts before you're seeing Jesus. You'll then roll your sweaty body off mine and promptly pass out from the copious amount of alcohol you've consumed. I, then, of course, will have to pull out my handy-dandy battery-operated boyfriend to finish the job."

I'm hardly holding back the laugh that is bubbling up in my throat as I watch this exchange. The more Lucy talks, the more the man's face falls as the realization that he's made a grave mistake sets in.

"So, what do you say, *babe*? Let's skip all that shit and you just let me go home alone to my vibrator in peace," Lucy asks him with a tone that is dripping in false sweetness.

The frat guy's face is now red in anger and embarrassment. Glaring at her, he bites out, "You're a bitch."

Smiling happily, Lucy salutes him coyly. "We all gotta be good at something, sport."

"I'm going to get you fired," he vows, shouting over the loud music.

Lucy tilts her head back and cackles. "I would honestly love to see you try."

I can't help it, the laugh I've been holding in finally escapes and I double over in hysterics as I watch the poor man stomp away.

One of the few good things to happen in the past couple months is that I was reunited with Lucy. I was away from her—*from home*—for five years. Sure, we talked on the phone all the time and she visited me once in Boston, but it wasn't the same. Now I work with her *and* live with her. We're together more than we are apart.

"You're so mean, I love it." I wipe away the tears that fall from my eyes from laughing so hard. "He just thought you were pretty and wanted to make your night better," I jokingly pout, like I'm truly offended on behalf of the frat boy.

"I don't want men to think I'm pretty, I want them to be scared of me and leave me the fuck alone," Lucy shoots back.

"You're in the wrong industry then." I gesture around the bar and at the clothes we wear. St. Sin is a club here on Bourbon Street, the waitstaff and bartenders wear more revealing clothes than some strippers. I've worn tank tops longer than the leather dress I'm currently wearing. My new attire is a far cry from the modest medical scrubs I'm accustomed to wearing, but I was desperate for a job and Luce has the manager wrapped around her finger. She just batted her eyelashes and

Ray hired me on the spot. It's not like I don't have experience serving alcohol, I started pouring drinks for my mother at the age of five.

Plus, Ray said I was *'pretty enough',* and it didn't matter if I knew how to mix a drink since looks are all he cares about anyway.

He's a real southern gentleman.

Lucy slips around me so she can grab a bottle of vodka off the glass shelf behind the bar. The shelving unit goes all the way to the ceiling; a sliding ladder sits off to the side so we can climb and reach the bottles at the very top. The entire thing is backlit by gold LED lights, matching the black and gold theme of the club itself.

"I bitch about this job a lot, but we both know I was never meant to sit behind a desk or save lives like you."

Saving lives like me. This makes my stomach knot and guilt shoot through my body. Lucy knows why I abruptly left my job as a trauma nurse in Boston, and it wasn't because of my ability to save lives. Quite the opposite, actually.

"I have no idea what else I would rather be doing, than this."

I wish Lucy could see that she was meant for greater and bigger things, but as long as she's content working as a scantily clad bartender, I'll support her. Bartending was never my goal either, but I need the money. *Bad.*

The pay and tips I make here are just keeping me afloat. I'm going to have to figure out quickly how to make some extra cash. Barrett will be here soon looking for his monthly payment and I don't even have half of it socked away.

I thought I had escaped the disaster that was my father when I moved away five years ago, but it appears that even in death, he's fucking with my life.

Thanks a lot, *Dad.*

I inherited a lot from my dad, like my blonde hair and blue eyes, but I also inherited his mountain of gambling debt. Of course, he didn't owe money to a bank. No, Ronald Page borrowed money from fellow criminals. When he died, his two hundred-thousand-dollar debt was transferred to me. And Barrett Gallo always collects. The gun he waved in my face when he informed me of my new financial situation confirmed that.

"Q, where'd you go?" Lucy shakes my arm, drawing me out of my thoughts.

"What? Nowhere, was just thinking about something." I brush her off nonchalantly. Lucy doesn't know about the debt, and I plan on keeping it that way as long as possible. She would try to help, and I don't want her to be in danger because of me.

Noticing I've balled my hands into fists at my side, I slowly unclench them and try to relax. Forcing an easy smile, I turn around to check on the customers sitting at the bar. *Fake it till you make it and all that jazz, right?*

"Well shit! Look what the cat dragged in!" Lucy's voice suddenly rises above the loud music as she hurries around the bar to greet someone.

I turn just in time to watch as she flings her arms around a man I don't recognize. St. Sin is considered high-end, and anyone who is anyone in this town is a frequent visitor here. Because of this, Lucy knows everyone and is privy to a lot of gossip. If there is anything going on in this city, Lucy will know about it.

I've been away for so long, I have no idea what's going on anymore. There isn't any time or energy left in me to care about the town's secrets anyway.

The man barely catches Lucy as she launches herself at him. He must be really special if Lucy has this kind of reaction to seeing him. The last time she was this happy is when she picked me up at the airport after I ran from Boston two months ago.

"Shit!" he grunts, but the smile on his face tells me he's okay with my friend clinging to him like a toddler. His big hands hold her thighs when she wraps them around his waist. "Give a guy a warning next time."

"Duke! Where have you been?" Lucy slaps at his chest in annoyance. "You said you were going to be away for a month for work, but it's been over three."

Putting her back down on the ground, *Duke* runs a hand through his messy, dirty blond, longish hair. The wavy strands curl around the nape of his neck and fall forward into his face, even though he just pushed it back. "The boss had me out of state working on some stuff for him," he answers vaguely. "But don't worry, he's got me working on something here, so I'll be around for a while."

As if he can sense me standing there watching the scene, his head turns in my direction, a friendly smile on his face. Nothing about this man's appearance is intimidating other than maybe his tall stature and clearly built body, but I've been around long enough to sense the hardened edge in him. I don't know if it's because his easy smile doesn't reach his eyes or what, but I can tell he's hiding a part of himself.

Aren't we all, though?

"Oh, right!" Lucy gestures at me and then back at Duke. "Duke, this is my best friend, Quincey. You've heard me talk about her before. She just moved back here a couple months ago after abandoning me for five years."

"*Abandoning*?" I mock. "Such a drama queen."

Duke reaches across the bar to offer me his hand. "The nurse, right?"

I just barely hold back the cringe as I shake his hand. "Yep! Or, well, I *was*. I'm no longer practicing."

Being a nurse was something I always strived to be. I worked my ass off in high school to make the grades to get into one of the top nursing schools. Being a nurse—*helping people*—became my whole identity and now that I don't have that, I have no idea who I am or what I'm doing. Telling Duke I'm no longer a nurse feels wrong, even if it's the truth.

"Did you give it up completely? Or just taking a break?" Duke presses as he slips into one of the free barstools across from me.

I shake my head quickly. "I don't see myself going back to it. Turns out that saving people just wasn't in the cards for me." That's not the full truth, but he doesn't need to know that.

It turns out that those vile words my mom used to spew at me while she was wasted as hell are true. I never was one to put any stock into her '*readings*', thinking it was the ramblings of a drunk, but actually seeing the events she swore would come true happen, persuaded me to change my outlook on things.

Duke here doesn't need to know that my "*psychic*" mother warned me that my touch would eventually turn deadly. Hell, I've barely told Lucy.

"Do you miss it though?" Duke lays his arms on the bar top as he leans in closer so we can hear over the loud music.

I hesitate to answer, not really liking talking about my failed career. "Yeah, I miss it. I always thought it was my calling, but I'm just moving on to better things." I wave my hand around the crowded club.

Duke laughs. "You've moved on to a better uniform, that's for sure." His eyes wander over my tight dress, making my skin warm.

"Hey!" Lucy scolds, backhanding his shoulder. "Don't be pervy, she's my friend."

He gives her a smirk and slowly looks her over. "Would you rather I be pervy with you?"

"*No*." She rolls her eyes.

Someone waves at me from the other end of the bar, and I quickly excuse myself to grab them another beer. When I return to Lucy and Duke, their heads are bent in a private conversation.

Clearing my throat to grab their attention again, I ask, "Duke, what is it that you do?" He asked about what I do, it's only fair I get to ask, right?

Duke shrugs his broad shoulders. "I just run odd jobs for a local business owner. Sometimes I run errands for him around the city, other times he sends me out to check on his different ventures outside of the country. Depends on the week and what kind of mood he's in."

"Well, *that* wasn't vague as hell or anything." I chuckle.

"You're lucky, that's more than most people get." Lucy places her hand on his upper arm and gives him a playful shove. "I have my theories, but *I* don't even know who he actually works for."

The pointed look she gives him doesn't go unnoticed, and it makes me think Lucy knows more than she's letting on.

"Luce, leave the poor man alone. If he's going to keep up that allusive, mysterious air of his." I gesture with my hands around Duke's frame. "Then he can't go around telling you all his secrets. How else would he keep you interested in him?"

The appalled look on Lucy's face is priceless. She can claim all she wants that she wants men to leave her alone, but deep down, she's a hopeless romantic.

Glancing at the ornate gold-trimmed clock mounted on the far wall, I nod at Lucy. "I'll finish up here, it's going to start slowing down in the next hour anyway. Why don't you two go catch up?"

"What?" Lucy frowns. "I'm not going to leave you here alone. There's still a lot of people in here."

"Lucy, I've got this." Lucy has been the person to get me through the past couple of months. Without her, I'd be jobless and homeless. The least I can do is cover for her for an hour or so. "Go have fun, go get into trouble like we used to."

Prior to moving away, Lucy and I were the epitome of troublemakers. We were young and dumb, believing the laws and rules didn't apply to us. We are lucky that we made it out of our teen years alive.

Lucy looks between Duke and me, the internal battle she's having with herself written across her face. Finally, she points a finger at me. "Fine, but you have to promise to call me when you leave. I don't like you walking the streets here alone, I don't know how many times I have to tell you it's a bad idea. We'll talk on the phone until you make it home."

"I have the Taser you gave me too."

Duke stands from the barstool, his big arm wrapping casually over Lucy's shoulders.

"Good." Lucy nods once, blowing out a long breath. "Call me if you need anything."

"I've got this," I repeat. I may not have a lot of the shit in my life under control, but I know for a fact I can handle bartending alone for a little while.

CHAPTER 2

Quincey

I'm dead on my feet by the time I stumble out the back exit of the club. It's just my luck that five minutes before closing, a rowdy group showed up. By the time I served each of them and they all left, I worked almost an hour longer than I planned.

My feet are killing me from standing all day in these black pumps and my stomach is all but screaming at me for food. The last time I ate was breakfast, and it's close to one in the morning now.

Absentmindedly, I reach for the granola bar I had put in my bag a couple days ago. It's only when my fingers can't find the snack that I remember I gave it to a homeless man the other night. It's okay. He needed it more than I do anyway. He'd been sitting out in the rain for God knows how long, huddled up under one of the awnings to avoid getting soaked. I didn't have an umbrella or any cash on me to give him, the only thing I had to offer was the peanut butter-flavored granola bar.

Even though I don't mind walking in the rain, I'm thankful for the clear sky tonight. The need to let the rain cleanse me of my problems isn't as strong as it was the other night when I walked down Bourbon Street with my face tilted toward the downpour. People watching me probably thought I was crazy or just another drunk bystander.

Locking the back door with my key, I turn and trek down the dark alley. Cutting between the buildings is always the fastest way to Lucy's small apartment a couple blocks away. My body is so desperate for sleep and food that shaving a few minutes off my commute is worth the sketchy walk.

Pulling my purse higher up on my shoulder and tucking it tighter under my arm, I march forward. The farther I get away from the bars and nightlife, the quieter it gets, but the louder the thoughts in my head become. The music and constant bustle of the club drowns them out, but each night when I leave, the unwanted thoughts start screaming at me until my head pounds.

I don't see a light out of the dark tunnel I've suddenly found myself in. I don't know how or when I'll be able to acquire the kind of money it will take to pay off the debt. The salary I had as a nurse wouldn't have come close to covering it. The logical thing would have been to go to the authorities about Barrett threatening me, but he knew that would be my first recourse. The night he showed up at my door in Boston, gun in hand, he showed me pictures of both Lucy and my mom, proving to me if I step out of line, they'll be the collateral.

As much as I hate my mother, I still don't want to risk her life like that and there was no way I was going to risk Lucy.

Barrett would know, too, if I tried to tell the cops. Since I've been back, I've felt the eyes on me, his little spies watching my every move. Just the other night while I walked in the rain, I saw the dark SUV sitting there alone on the street. It was blacked out, but I knew someone was in there watching me. Their gaze made my skin burn and the tiny hairs on my body rise.

The sound of a trash can being knocked over behind me brings me back to the present. I hold back the startled yelp that threatens to escape my lips and push forward, walking as fast as I can manage in the heels I wear. Silently cursing myself for forgetting the pair of flats I usually change into after my shift at home this morning. *I'm an idiot.*

I didn't want to bug Lucy while she was with Duke by calling her like I promised I would. I've walked these streets alone before with no problem, tonight shouldn't have been any different, but the sudden sound of footsteps behind me tells me I was wrong.

Glancing over my shoulder, I spot the hooded figure following after me.

Maybe they're just following the same path home? I try to reason, to settle my nerves, but when I cut down another alley and the person follows behind, the alarm bells start going off in my head, screaming *danger*.

Trying my best to stay calm and push down the fear bubbling in my stomach, I quicken my pace until I'm jogging. The sound of my heels clicking against the cobblestones echoes off the walls of the alley.

My hand digs ungracefully through my purse, looking for the Taser or my cell phone. Everything my fingertips brush against isn't what I'm looking for. I scold myself for filling the bag with such useless items. Just because I have a large bag doesn't mean I need to stick everything I own in it. Not the lesson I should be learning right now, but it's the lesson I'm fixating on. *Did you really need to put the worn paperback in here, Quincey? Not like there is downtime at the bar for you to read, dumbass.*

Looking behind me once more, I find that my follower has also picked up their pace. If I have any hope of outrunning them, I need to lose the heels. The streets and sidewalks of New Orleans are notoriously filthy. The idea of running barefoot through these alleyways is wildly unappealing, but getting away from the person behind me is my main priority.

Slowing down just long enough to bounce on one foot at a time, I pull the pumps from my feet, tossing them to the side for someone to find later on. Without the shoes hindering me, I take off at a dead run, ignoring the sharp bite of gravel and debris digging into my soles. I try my best to not be disgusted by the warm, dirty puddles I step into, the liquid splashing up the back of my exposed calves.

Lately, I've been thinking a lot about dying, mainly because I knew I'd never be able to pay off Barrett in time, not without selling a kidney or robbing a bank. I thought there was a bullet out there with my name on it. Not once did I think I was going to be ambushed in an alley and attacked, but the stomping footsteps gaining on me make me think this might be my untimely end.

My legs burn and my heart slams against my chest, adrenaline pumping through my veins. I'm so focused on keeping up my pace and finding my phone in my bag, that I'm not watching for the obstacles in front of me. I don't see the rusty piece of metal leaning against a trash can before my ankle catches on it, catapulting me forward. Pain radiates from my hands and knees when I land, skidding across the pavement. My ankle burns and aches, I don't know if the liquid I feel dripping down my skin is from the puddles I've splashed in or my own blood, but I don't have time to check. My bag, holding all my belongings, is splayed across the ground, the contents all over the place.

My fingers reach to collect my things on instinct, but the approaching footfalls behind me spur me back into action. Cursing from the pain in my extremities, I clamber back to my feet and continue my escape. I'm moving slower than before, the damage to my ankle making me limp.

In horror movies, you always question the girl who trips and falls, screaming at the television for her to get her shit together, and run. I know I've done that before, even going as far as to laugh when they tripped. Now that I'm in this position, I'm not laughing.

It's not so funny when *you're* the dumb blonde in the slasher flick.

Hobbling toward the end of the dark alleyway, I feel a sliver of relief. I'm just feet away from a relatively busy street. Someone will be out here who can help me.

I just barely round the corner of the brick building, stepping only one foot on the main street, when fingers tangle in my long hair and I'm ripped backward with so much force, my neck cracks.

My world spins and I desperately try to keep up with the sudden and fast pace at which I'm hurled backward. The scream I've been fighting since I saw the hooded figure coming after me, crests from between my lips, but only the softest squeak escapes me before a big hand slams painfully down on my mouth, silencing me.

"You're fast, I'll give you that." His voice is deep and his breath reeks of cigarettes. Dark beady eyes scan over me as I struggle beneath his hold. Spinning me, the man presses his entire body to my front, effectively pinning my back to the building. "Yeah, baby, keep fighting me. I like it when I get to collect the feisty ones."

An angry sound comes from the back of my throat before I sink my blunt teeth into the fleshy part of his hand.

"Fuck! You bitch," he hollers as he pulls his hand from my face. He glances at his hand once, checking for damage, before his fist connects with my cheek with such force I taste blood and see spots.

I've never been hit before. My parents were a lot of things, but never abusive. My eyes burn, tears threatening, but I force them to stay put. Instead, I spit the blood in my mouth at his face and tilt my chin up defiantly. I can fake a brave face better than anyone; I've been doing it most of my life.

His hand clasps around my chin and jaw, fingers digging punishingly into my face. "I was told to bring you in alive, but he said nothing about bringing you in without bruises," my attacker seethes. "He won't be happy about it, though. He likes a pretty face. You're useless to us if you're damaged."

My head attempts to jerk to the side in hopes of loosening his hold on me, but this only makes his fingers tighten on my face. Marks will, without a doubt, form from his rough treatment. "I haven't done anything to you!" I cry. "Let me go!"

He chuckles. "You're right, you haven't done anything to *me*, but you owe my boss a shit ton of money."

Money?

The debt. Fuck.

"I have five more days!" I try to bargain. "The monthly payment isn't due today—I still have time to get it to Gallo." There's no way I'll be able to earn or find four thousand dollars in five days, but he doesn't need to know that.

"Mr. Gallo isn't a patient man. He's decided he's no longer interested in your little payment plan." He moves in closer to my face, so close his hot breath whispers across my throbbing cheek. "You'll repay your debt a different way."

For a split second I'm confused, but when the realization of what he's saying hits me, dread like I've never felt bubbles in my stomach. The fear turns my veins to ice and my throat constricts to fight back the nausea rising.

"*No*." My voice is just barely a whisper. "Please, no."

He skims a dirty finger down my face. "You're going to make him so much money. You've got that innocent, doe-eyed look about you. Men eat that shit up like it's candy." His tongue swipes out, licking along the side of my face. "Sweet like candy too."

I push and shove against him, but still, he barely moves. I hate feeling weak and defenseless. I've never been one to rely on others to save me. The best thing that came out of my mom and dad's horrible parenting is that I became independent—self-sufficient—at a young age. I can take care of myself, but I can't save myself right now. He's bigger and he's stronger. The alleyway is dark, devoid of light, making it so no one can see us back here.

As a last-ditch effort, I fill my lungs with air, preparing to let the biggest scream of my life loose, but the air deflates from my chest quickly when the blinding headlights of a large vehicle illuminate us. It takes me only a second to realize it's the same black SUV as the other night.

The sound of a door opening fills the space, and a dark shadowy figure emerges from the car. Dread joins the overwhelming emotions swirling through my body. The man joining must be another one of Gallo's henchmen, here to aid in collecting me. Or so I briefly think, but the look of confusion and then worry in my attacker's eyes tells me differently.

The new arrival's face is hidden by the brightness of the headlights. I can't make out any of his features other than his large silhouette.

"Are you lost?" the man holding me spits at the new man. "This doesn't concern you. I recommend you get back into that fancy car of yours and mind your business."

The silhouette's head shakes slowly. "I recommend you let the lady go."

That voice... Something about it is so familiar.

"Why would I do that?"

"You're already not making it out of this dirty alleyway alive," the new arrival answers, a slightly amused tone in his voice. Almost as if he knows something the rest of us don't. "There's no need for you to make your last seconds more painful than they should be."

"What in the hell are you rambling on about?"

"You have your hands on something that doesn't belong to you," the shadowy figure calmly states. "And you're going to pay for making her bleed."

My attacker's head tilts back, a sardonic laugh escaping from between his dry, cracked lips. "That's where you're wrong. Her pretty ass belongs to my boss."

A low, ominous snarl fills the alleyway, bouncing off the brick walls surrounding us. My eyes dart around the space, looking for the source, but I can't find anything. The sound dies off and is followed by a quick *whoosh*.

Something moves behind the man so fast my eyes can only see the briefest blur. I check that the man standing in the headlights is still there, and I find he hasn't moved an inch.

"Not anymore," a haunting voice resonates from somewhere in the shadows. The voice sends chills down my spine and goose bumps spread across my skin.

Abruptly, my attacker's black eyes go wide, and an almost inaudible gasp escapes him. His hand that hasn't once loosened its grip on my face slowly slides off my jaw as he stumbles backward.

He staggers away, his hands tearing at his chest. Following his movements, I find the white T-shirt he wears under his dark hoodie is growing dark, deep crimson blood blossoming from a wound.

When did he get hurt? *How* did he get hurt?

On pure instinct, I shift forward, ready to help the man, but as my shaking hand reaches for him, I pause. He gasps and gargles on his blood while his eyes meet mine. He can't speak, but I see his silent cry for help written across his face. But still, I stay frozen in place. My touch won't save him anyway.

I still don't move as he falls, landing harshly against the stone ground. I don't look away as the blood pools around his body and his chest grows still.

In pain and on shaky feet, I finally slowly start backing away from the deceased man. Movement to my left jerks my head in that direction. The large silhouette moves toward me.

"Please," I beg, holding up my hand to halt him. "Please just let me go, I won't say anything."

He doesn't stop, his steps only become more purposeful as he stalks closer. "Sorry darlin'," his smooth southern voice drawls. "I can't do that."

Finally, his face comes into view and my whole body turns to stone, halting in my sluggish escape. "*Duke*?" Lucy's friend comes into view; his ruggedly handsome features are pulled tight, almost pained. "Duke, what are you doing?" I stammer.

I back away from him, farther down the alleyway. My ankle and face are screaming at me in agony, and my heart slams against my chest. The adrenaline pumping in my veins makes my whole body shake.

"I'm not going to hurt you, Quincey." Duke raises his hands, showing me they're empty, void of any weapon. "Please don't run."

"I don't believe you." I shake my head, causing my hair to stick to my sweaty and bloody face.

I know he's expecting me to do it, I'm almost positive he saw it in my face before I moved, because when I spin away from him, he lunges at me. By some miracle, I evade his grasp and sprint down the alleyway again.

"Quincey!" Duke calls after me, but I still don't stop.

I'm so focused on Duke behind me and getting as far away from the dead man as I can, that I'm not paying attention to where I'm going.

My body slams against a body that feels as if it's made of stone. Strong hands grip my upper arms before I can stumble back and fall. My yelp of surprise dies on my tongue when I'm instantly pulled tight against a hard chest. With wild, unfocused eyes, I tilt my head to take in the new man's face, but all I can make out in the shadows are the sharp angles of jaw and cheekbones.

"Who—" I start to ask, but the rest of the words never come because the sharp bite of a needle in my neck silences them. My vision becomes hazy and my limbs heavy as the drug invades my system.

The hands that hold my arms shift and I feel my body being lifted off the ground. I want to scream for help, but I can't move. The darkness at the corner of my eyes alerts me of my impending blackout.

"Want me to take her, boss?" I hear Duke ask, his voice sounds like he's a hundred miles away.

"No," the man who's holding me answers, his chest vibrating against me when he speaks. "I'll take care of her. Deal with the body, Duke."

Why is this happening to me? is the last thing I think before my world goes dark.

CHAPTER 3

Silas

I can't remember the last time I saved someone, taking lives is so much easier than saving them. There was a second tonight where I considered letting Gallo's man scoop her up and take her off to God knows where, but unfortunately for me, I need Quincey Page alive.

He needs her.

He could have had anyone, but he was adamant it had to be her.

That thought makes an angry growl build in my throat and my hands scrub harder at the blood caking my fingers. Punching your fist all the way through someone's chest isn't the cleanest endeavor, but I wasn't thinking straight. The scent of Quincey's blood filled the dirty alleyway and made my control slip momentarily. The sweet scent—almost like vanilla—spurred the beast inside of me on.

The water in the sink turns from dark crimson to pale pink before finally running clear. With an exhausted sigh, I reach for the soft black towel the maid left folded on the counter for me.

I wasn't supposed to be there tonight. Duke promised me he had it handled, but I found myself ordering my driver to take me to her bar. When I discovered she'd been left to walk home alone again, I'd taken off on foot tracking her, the voice in my head I usually elect to ignore encouraging me to find her. Good thing I had listened since Duke was fucking late.

While her unwarranted positivity and courageousness is admirable, it's also wildly thoughtless. She knows the dangers of these streets, yet she elects to pretend they do not exist. I know the dangers better than anyone—I'm the biggest threat in the shadows after all.

"Boss?" Duke's voice comes from behind me, and I meet his eye through the mirror in front of me.

"Is she awake?" I question as I slip off the ruined, blood-stained dress shirt I wear.

Duke scoffs, his blond head shaking. "There was enough sedative in that syringe to take out a two-hundred-pound marine. The girl's going to be out a little while longer."

I toss the shirt into the trash can before making my way into my vast closet. I would prefer to take a shower before changing into a fresh suit, but I don't have the time. "Did the doctor check on her wounds?" Even without the overwhelming scent of her blood, it was clear to me she was injured in her attempted escape. Her face was already starting to bruise on the drive to my house.

"She's been bandaged up and given a tetanus shot." Duke leans against the doorframe, his arms crossed in front of him. "They gave her a dose of strong antibiotics as well, just in case bacteria got into any of her open wounds."

"She ran through the French Quarter with no shoes on, of course, she was exposed to bacteria," I say dryly. "Humans and their weak immune systems." I don't remember what it's like to worry about things like disease and germs—it's a foreign concept to me at this point.

"We aren't all invincible like you, Laurent."

"Pity." I finish fastening the last of the buttons on my black dress shirt.

"She's asleep in the guest room in the west wing like you instructed." Duke steps out of the way, letting me pass him. As usual he's unfazed by the stern look I give him. If anything, he finds amusement in my irritation. "She has more fight in her than I originally thought." His lips twitch. "She looked so docile when we were watching her, but when push comes to shove, I think Quincey is going to push back. Are you prepared for that?"

I pause at the door, hand on the handle before turning to look at him over my shoulder. "You don't think I can handle a tiny, angry, human?"

Duke just shrugs. "I'm just saying, you've been bent out of shape and not acting like yourself since you agreed to bring her in. I've never seen you put your entire hand through someone's chest before. That was bloody. Maybe a little gross." Stuffing his hands in his worn jeans, he shuffles a few feet forward. "I'm just asking if you can keep it together while she's here. I've taken care of a lot of bodies for you, hers is one I don't want to drag into the swamp."

I have him pinned to the wall behind us before he has a chance to say one more thing out of line. Holding him by the throat, a foot off the ground, I remind him who the fuck he's dealing with. "I've been lenient with you, Duke, because usually I don't mind your company. You're smart, good at your job—overall an asset to me, but at the end of the day, you're still replaceable. Keep that in mind the next time you question me or my control." Duke is strong for a human, but his efforts to free himself are futile against me. "It's true. I don't want her here, but I made a promise a long time ago and I plan to follow through with it. That means I need her alive."

Even as I say the words, I know it will be easier said than done to keep my control intact with her in my space—my home.

"No one will harm that woman again." I've made sure of it. "Let alone me. I don't intend on spending any more time with her than necessary. Not" —my hand grips his neck tighter to drive my point home— "that I have to answer or explain myself to you, Duke."

Without a second look, I release him. The sound of his large body hitting the ground echoes behind me as I exit the room.

She sleeps soundly in the middle of the large bed. Her ankle is bandaged, and the tan skin of her face is marred with angry purple marks. The doctor filled me in when I arrived at her room. The wound on her ankle has a couple stitches in it that will need to come out in a week or so, but other than that, she'll just be in some mild discomfort for a few days.

Overall, she's lucky.

Well, she would be considered lucky if she'd actually made it away from the alley a free woman. Instead, she just traded one monster for another more ruthless one. I'm sure I should be experiencing a level of guilt for forcing someone like Quincey into my world, but for reasons that may be selfish, I need her here. If it means sullying her in the process, so be it.

Duke was right. The sedative she was given was not meant for someone her size. She's been sleeping for the past hour since I entered her room. From my spot by the window, I watch her chest rise and fall steadily. Her heart combined with the wind outside are the only sounds that fill the vast room.

Quincey looks younger than her twenty-four years while she sleeps. The innocence I knew already existed in her is even more prevalent in the way her pale pink lips pout and quirk from her pleasant dreams. How someone put in her situation still has enjoyable dreams is beyond me. Her sleep should be filled with nothing but nightmares. Her life itself is a nightmare right now and I'm her new monster under the bed.

When her eyelashes flutter and her eyelids slowly blink open, I freeze in place, hoping the shadows conceal me for just a moment longer. Her eyes slowly scan the room, confusion pinching her features.

I know the second she remembers the events that took place today because her heart rate spikes and she flies into a sitting position in the bed. Her blonde hair, the strands still caked with blood and grime, whip around her shoulders.

Instantly, a pained expression crosses her face as she holds her head in her hands. "*Shit*," she groans.

Deciding to not prolong the inevitable confrontation, I step away from the window into her view. "I wouldn't recommend moving so fast, you took a blow to the head when you were attacked."

Her head snaps up and powder blue eyes filled with panic clash with mine. Her skin pales and a small gasp escapes her parted lips. "Who—" she stammers. "Who the hell are you?"

I take a step forward. Quincey instantly backpedals farther up the bed until her back is pressed to the headboard of the canopy bed frame. Just like she did with Duke in the alley, she holds up her shaking hand, silently begging me to stay back.

Not one to take orders, I stalk closer to the bed.

Her eyes dart to the door. "Where's Duke?"

"He's here," is the only information I offer.

She nervously licks her lips, wincing when her tongue brushes the cut that now resides there. "Why am I here?" Quincey questions. "What do you want from me? Money?" She shakes her head. "I don't have anything to give you."

I bark out a cold laugh. "I'm well aware of your financial situation."

She's already cost me a pretty penny.

Quincey presses against the headboard even harder, as if that extra inch of space between us will do her any good. The poor girl has no idea who she's trapped in a room with. "Then you know I have nothing to offer you." She pushes her hair out of her face. "I have *nothing*."

The way her eyes dart between the door and me doesn't go unnoticed. She's not as sly as she thinks she's being, I know what she's planning. It's foolish, but once again, her bravery knows no bounds.

"That is where you're wrong, Quincey Page." I come to a stop at the foot of her bed. Cocking my head, I eye her with a bland stare. "You have something I need."

Her body goes rigid, the muscles of her throat shifting as she swallows hard. In a move that is shockingly fast and agile for a human, she springs from the bed. Even with a wounded ankle, she's quick as she flies across the room. The white T-shirt the doctor changed her into rides up her legs as she sprints toward the door.

With an exasperated sigh, I look to the ceiling and count to five to calm myself. I stay put even when I hear the turning of the door handle and her bare feet pound down the hallway. She can run as much as she'd like, but unfortunately for her, she's not getting very far. It doesn't matter how much of a head start I give her, she'll never outrun me.

Ten seconds, that's how long I let her have before I fly after her. I'm behind her in less than a second. The scream she lets out as my arms wrap around her middle is loud enough to wake the dead. My sensitive ears ring from the high-pitched noise.

"Stop screaming," I order. "It's such an unpleasant noise." The cries are cut off when I abruptly lift her over my shoulder. Her legs kick and thrash, her hands beat on my lower back. "That's enough of that," I grumble, clamping my arm around her thighs, locking her in place.

"How did you move so fast? Put me down!" Quincey growls, her hands never letting up from their assault on my back. "What the fuck is wrong with you?"

"More than you'll ever be able to understand."

I march back into the room I intend to be hers for the foreseeable future. Unceremoniously, I toss her back onto the king-size bed. I bite back a smirk as she lands in an ungraceful heap.

Like an angered kitten, she turns on me, teeth bared. "I don't know who you think you are or who gave you the right, but you can't just kidnap me and then manhandle me!"

In a flash, I'm towering over her, my arms caging her in on the bed.

Her chest heaves just barely an inch away from mine. "You're wrong again, Miss Page. I have every fucking right. You see, five hours ago I forfeited a large sum of money to obtain such rights. It is now my *right to* hold you here as long as I see fit. It is now my *right* to manhandle you however I desire. It is now my *right* to do whatever the fuck I want with you because that little debt of yours? It's been paid." I lean in close, so close the vanilla scent that clings to her suffocates me. "You no longer owe Barrett Gallo." My voice is just a whisper. "You owe me."

Her heart pounds against her chest, the erratic beat filling my ears. "Why the hell would you pay my debt?"

"Isn't it obvious?" I question. "I want you indebted to me."

Her eyes harden and she inches close to me. "Then you're an idiot."

Caught off guard, I narrow my eyes at her. I've never been called an idiot before. Most people—aside from Duke and two others—are too afraid of me to say such things. "Excuse me?"

"You're. An. Idiot," she repeats slowly as if she's talking to a child. "I was never going to be able to repay Gallo, how the hell am I supposed to repay you?"

"I don't believe I said I wanted to be repaid in money." This close to her face, I spot the freckles across the bridge of her nose. Sweat builds at her temples from the fear surging through her body.

"You want me to repay you in what, *sex*?" Quincey's face hardens, chin tipping defiantly. Her slender arm points at the far wall before she vows, "I'll jump through that window before I become a whore for you."

I recoil from her, quickly putting space between us. "Let's get one thing clear, I will never share a bed with you, Miss Page." I adjust my now rumpled suit jacket from my brief interaction with her in the hallway. "After tonight, you'll barely see any of me."

She sits up straighter on the bed and eyes me warily. "I'm *so* confused."

Sighing, I place my hands behind me and take in the disheveled girl in front of me. She's been in my home for less than two hours, for the majority of that time, she's been drugged and unconscious but I'm already tired of having her here.

The reason that she's here flashes through my mind and I resign myself for what's to come. "You were a nurse back in Boston," I start. "I'm in need of the skills you possess."

Quincey frowns, eyes flicking over my frame. "Well, buddy, I hate to be the bearer of bad news, but I'm retired. I hung up the stethoscope and scrubs a few months back. Besides, you seem more than healthy to me."

"You wouldn't be working on me, Miss Page." No, I have no personal use for a nurse. "There is someone else that requires your assistance."

Quincey pushes off the bed, standing to her full—*short*—height. "Well, that's a shame, there goes my plan to stab you with a scalpel." She mockingly pouts her bottom lip before returning to scowling at me. "I'm no longer working with patients, I'm sorry—no wait, you know what? I'm really not." She crosses her arms tightly against her chest. "Now that this is settled, let me go home."

"Miss Page, there seems to be a misunderstanding here."

"No shit."

"You seem to believe I'm giving you the option to work for me." I shift to stand in front of her, just in case she gets any ideas of running from me again. "You either work for me as a nurse, or I will send you back to Gallo to be used as nothing but a warm cunt for them to abuse." My hand clasps her chin, my finger lying over the bruises already there. "Do I make myself clear?"

The brave face she's been wearing starts to slip. She's breaking in front of me, the defiance in her eyes is melting away and her jaw wobbles under my touch as she fights back tears. *Good*. She'll be so much easier to deal with if she realizes she's lost this battle.

"I can't," she whispers.

"You can," I snap. "And you will." My hand yanks roughly away from her face, making her head jerk. "Follow me to meet your new patient."

CHAPTER 4

Quincey

I'm fucked.

Royally and completely fucked.

Not in the good way that makes your toes curl and your vision blur. I'm fucked like a pig is at a slaughterhouse. No way out and my fate inevitable. At least for poor Wilbur, it's relatively quick. I, however, feel like I'm on the slow march to death as I follow behind my mysterious captor.

I know he was there tonight. I recognize his voice from the alley. While it's as smooth as it was when it came from the shadows, now that I know who it belongs to, it's less appealing.

This man is *scary*.

He's not scary in the way he looks, no, the man looks like he walked off a runway in Milan. His dark, haunting features would capture the attention of anyone. The scary part of him is the intimidating energy coming off of him. It wraps around you until you feel like you're asphyxiating on it. For Christ's sake, in one night he's killed *and* kidnapped someone.

This man fears no one. No, he's the one people fear.

My mind wanders back to the look of horror on Gallo's man's face as he bled out from the ghastly chest wound. I still have no clue how such a wound was created. Racking my mind, I try to recall the sound of a gunshot or the glint of metal from a knife, but I come up blank. One second he was standing before me unharmed, and in a flash, his chest is pouring blood.

I've tried to fake a brave face in front of my captor, was doing okay at it too, until he told me how I'd be repaying him, and I didn't have a choice in the matter.

He stalks in front of me, not once does he look behind him to make sure I'm still with him. Somehow, he just trusts I won't wander off. It's probably due to the fact he proved earlier he's stronger and faster than me. He lifted me off the ground like I weighed nothing.

I fist the T-shirt I wear tighter to my thigh, feeling exposed and underdressed. "Can I have a pair of pants?" *Underwear at the very least. Wait... where is my underwear?* Nope. I don't want to know the answer. I probably won't like it anyway.

"Yes," he answers gruffly. "Later."

"Great. I'm going to be meeting this patient like *Winnie-the-Pooh* with my ass hanging out in the breeze," I mumble to myself under my breath, but when my captor's head turns slightly in my direction, I deduct it wasn't as quiet as I thought it was. *Oops*.

"I don't believe Ira will mind."

"Oh, I'm *so* relieved to hear that," I dryly say as I scan the dark hallways. The house—*no mansion*—I've found myself in is old. That much is clear from the original features of the home, but it's also obvious a lot of money has gone into updating and modernizing it. *My kidnapper is a psychopath with an eye for interior design*. The dimly lit lights cast shadows over the pristine décor. "It was going to keep me up at night, worried I made my kidnapper's buddy uncomfortable." I'm scared of him, I'll admit it, but I'm also *pissed* at him. I couldn't stop the sarcastic comments even if I wanted to. They're my only defense right now.

I'm so fixated on the features of the vast—*beautiful*—home, that I'm not paying attention to him walking in front of me. So, when I run into his back, I'm embarrassed of the girlish yelp that escapes me. I reach out for his arm to steady myself as I bounce off his hard as stone body, but before my hand can touch him, I recoil from him like he burned me.

His eyes narrow and his pale lips pull back in a sneer, the tips of his straight white teeth reflecting the low light. "Let's keep the chatter to a minimum when we enter Ira's room. He doesn't feel well, and your irritating commentary will not help the situation."

Once again, his features are hidden by the faint light. Seems no one in this house requires proper light to see where the hell they're going. As he blatantly glowers at me, I find myself wondering what color his eyes actually are. They're so dark in this lighting, they could be black or brown—hell, dark blue maybe? My money is on black. Black like his fucking soul.

"Are you even listening to me?"

"Don't worry your pretty little head, douche lord. I haven't missed a single thing you've said tonight. You haven't left much up for interpretation." I know exactly what my fate is and where I stand with him. I either play along or I end up as a whore to be used by Gallo.

I wish my father was alive right now so I could kill him again. Running him over with a bus and then backing over him seems appropriate right about now.

"Douche lord? I would recommend watching how you speak to me, Miss Page," his voice rumbles. The more he talks to me, the more apparent a faint accent becomes. It's as if he's spent years perfecting his American accent, but his original dialect slips through the cracks here and there. French maybe?

"Why?" I question boldly. "What are you going to do? Drug me and hold me captive? You've already done your worst." My arms cross tightly across my chest as I stare him down. My insides quake with fear, but I keep my exterior hard—strong. "Besides, it's not like you've offered up a name, what else am I supposed to call you?"

He takes a menacing step forward and I somehow manage to force myself to stay put even with the voice screaming in my head that I need to run. "If you think this is my worst, you're more naïve than you look." *Ouch*. I'm many things but naïve isn't one. "As for what you can call me, Mr. Laurent will do for now."

Laurent.

"Douche lord is more fitting." I smirk. "If it quacks like a duck and all."

His response is a low, menacing growl that sends cold shivers of fear down my spine before continuing down the hallway.

Laurent comes to a stop in front of a set of closed double doors. The way his hand pauses on the ornate glass doorknob doesn't go unnoticed, nor does the way his back stiffens and his posture straightens. It's like he's bracing himself for something.

Or someone? Who the hell is behind these doors?

After taking another second to collect himself, Laurent pushes the doors open to a room that is thankfully better lit than the rest of the house. A warm, welcoming glow shines into the hallway where I stand as I hesitate to follow behind.

I don't want to go in there. I have little to no interest in whoever is in there. I'm a curious person by nature, but I don't want to learn more about the mysterious situation I've found myself in.

"I just want to go home."

I don't realize I've spoken aloud until my captor answers me. "When your debt to me is paid in full, I'll deliver you myself to the shitty apartment you share with your friend."

There's no reason to ask him how he knows about Lucy. If he didn't already know everything about me, I'm sure the traitorous asshole Duke would have filled him in on her. When I get my hands on Duke, it's not going to be pretty. It's clear that him showing up at the club tonight was a setup to get me alone. *Asshole.*

A thought dawns on me. "Is Lucy okay? If Duke did something to her, I'm—" The panic I've been barely keeping at bay surges forward.

"Your friend is just fine," Mr. Laurent cuts me off but not surprisingly I don't find reassurance in his words. I won't believe Lucy's unharmed until I set my eyes on her myself.

A faint voice interrupts me before I'm able to tell him just that. "I told you she was a strong one, boss." The statement is followed by a fit of coughs.

My eyes flick between the person I can't see and Laurent's face. His features pinch slightly before a stone-like mask falls into place, hiding his pained look. His fingers dig into my arm as he pulls me into the room, opting to not give me the choice to enter on my own.

Smart man, as I was just thinking of running from him again. I'll get away from him and this place somehow, but now is not the time. I need to wait for him to turn his back—let his guard down ever so slightly. Surely there is a door or window I can escape through.

I'm dragged harshly into the room, the fight I put up against his manhandling is useless against his brute strength. God, why is he so strong? If it wasn't so irritating right now, I may be impressed by it.

The room is large, the ceilings over ten feet tall. A roaring fireplace sits on the far wall, windows with their curtains drawn tight sit on either side of it. I'm instantly uncomfortable by the temperature in the room. It's April in Louisiana, it's already too warm for a fire to be lit.

In front of the fire is a small seating area. On the glass coffee table sits a chessboard. A game looks to have been started but never finished. I wouldn't know for sure though, I never learned to play. I was taught to gamble, not play a classy game like chess.

I reluctantly turn my head toward the other side of the room. A hospital bed that looks completely out of place with the rest of the furnishings sits there, a side table littered with medications and medical supplies next to it. A vital sign monitor beeps steadily next to it. Following the wires connected to the monitor, I finally look at the old man lying in the bed.

Without knowing his diagnosis or prognosis, I know immediately he's in bad shape. The thought must be written across my face, because the ill man's face splits into a smile. "I don't look that bad, do I?" He laughs for a second before coughing. His bony fingers reach up to cover his mouth as he heaves.

It's Laurent who speaks first. "No, Ira, you don't. You look as strong as the day I met you." He lies. *Why*? To spare this man's *feelings*? I don't buy it.

I opt to ignore the dirty look I'm given by him as he moves closer to his sick employee. I would call Ira a friend, but I don't get the impression that Laurent has friends.

"You're a dirty liar," Ira jokes easily, his southern accent thick. "But I could use the ego boost right about now, so I'll let it slide."

How in the hell can this man be so calm in the presence of someone like Laurent? I'm convinced he's the devil in a nice suit. It's got to be whatever cocktail of pain meds they've got him on.

"You know I never lie." Laurent stops a foot from Ira's bed, choosing to not move any closer.

Ira shifts, his frail body attempting to scoot farther up the bed so he can be more in a sitting position. The poor man groans and at some point during his labored movements, one of his heart monitor sensors come loose. The alarms go haywire on the machine, beeping loudly.

My body moves on pure instinct. Years of training and education have ingrained the reflex in me. In a second, I've moved to the side of the bed. I don't even think twice about pushing past Laurent to get to the patient.

Realization of what I'm about to do dawns on me just as my fingers brush against the fabric of Ira's shirt. At the last second, I yank my hand away from the sickly man as dread wraps its cold fingers around my heart. *Don't touch him!* The confusion coming from Ira is written across his pale face as I tuck my hands behind my back, safely away from his deteriorating body.

"Don't just stand there, Miss Page," Mr. Laurent snaps at me.

Like a stubborn child, I stare blankly up at him, not making any move to fix the disconnected leads.

"Surely you haven't lost the ability to speak, you haven't shut up since you woke up." It's finally in this light I discover I was right. His eyes are as black as midnight. At least in the night sky, there's always the light of the stars. Nope, Laurent's eyes hold no light. There isn't even the glimmer of any warmth in them. They're as cold as a piece of marble.

"I told you before, Mr. Laurent." I'm pleased by how steady my voice is. "I can no longer work with patients."

"Can't? Or won't?"

"Both," I answer after a moment of hesitation. My trembling fingers run through my hair as I back away from the bed. "Look, believe it or not, I'm actually looking out for what's best for Ira. You clearly want nothing but the best for him." My eyes glance at all the high-end medical equipment. This all cost a good chunk of change. "I'm not what's best for him. I'll only cause him more harm than good."

Ira listens to me but doesn't speak, his quizzical green eyes watch me intently.

Meanwhile, Laurent looks like he's about to lose his absolute mind. If we were in a cartoon, I'm positive steam would be coming out of his ears as he glowers at me. "I spoke directly to your supervisors in Boston. They spoke of you with nothing but high regards. From what I hear, doctors used to argue and fight over whose service you were on. You were simply the best." His voice is tight, like he's trying to keep the obvious rage at bay. "So, tell me, why can't you take those impeccable skills and use them now? Fix the wires."

He's not wrong. I was good at what I did—excellent even. Calm and cool under pressure with trauma. I was able to detach when I needed but never did I let that harden me. My empathy for each and every one of my patients was always present—pushing me to do better. The desire to see each of them walk out of the hospital was my driving force.

Or at least it was… "If you talked to my supervisors, they must have told you that I quit," I say. "And if I was half as good at the job as they told you, there must be a good reason for why I quit abruptly."

"I don't care what your bullshit reason is," Mr. Laurent snaps, his hands tightening into fists at his side. "God himself could have swept down and ordered you to stop, but I would still be standing here demanding you fix these wires."

"I—"

"I want to know," Ira suddenly says, stopping my reply. "I want to know why a talented individual would walk away from a career they were clearly meant for."

"Ira," Laurent sighs frustratedly. "It doesn't matter. She's going to do it, regardless."

Ira shakes his head slowly, sucking in a shaky breath. "It matters to me, Silas. I want to know her reasoning."

My heart skips a beat at the sound of his name. *Silas*. It's fitting, and that frustrates me because his name humanizes him in my mind. It makes him a person instead of the monster who abducted me.

"Tell me, Quincey." How the hell does Ira know my name? "Why did you walk away?"

Ira's presence has the complete opposite effect on me. His voice is calming, his face welcoming. Thin gold wire glasses sit on his nose, they're slightly crooked. Deep lines sit around his eyes and forehead telling me he's spent a lot of years laughing and smiling. He's like the friendly grandpa I always wanted.

His kind green eyes beckon me to speak and I find myself willing to open up to him. The hair he has left is just a soft gray fuzz covering the edges of his scalp.

"You're not going to believe me. It's going to sound completely made up," I start.

The corners of Ira's mouth twitch like he's amused by what I said. "Try me."

"I'm cursed." I say the words as fast as possible before I lose the nerve.

"Ridiculous," Laurent—Silas—mutters beside me.

"Let her speak," Ira orders Silas. *Oh yeah, I'm liking Ira more and more by the second.* He doesn't let Silas run over him or intimidate him, and I appreciate that immensely. "Cursed? How so?" he presses further.

I hate reliving my childhood traumas but seeing as I've already found myself in a living nightmare, I might as well dredge those up too. "My mother believes she has psychic gifts. Earns all her money sitting on a corner in the Quarter coercing tourists to spend money to get their fortunes told. She swore they were real, not even behind closed doors would she admit her readings were made up. I figured out at a young age she was a fake. Her readings were nothing but the ramblings of a drunk. So, when she told me my fate, I wrote it off as more bullshit." This was a mistake on my part. "She's been telling me since I was ten that one day, my touch would become deadly. That anyone I tried to help or save would die."

Her readings are what pushed me to pursue a career in the medical field. I think a part of me was always trying to prove her wrong. That she was nothing but a con artist.

"Three months ago, every single patient I touched started dying. Doesn't matter what part I played, if I touched them, they died." The faces of the patients I lost all start filling my head. I haven't forgotten a single one of them. I drop my head, squeezing my eyes shut at a poor attempt to block out the memories. "I thought it was a weird fluke the first week it started happening, but after two weeks, I knew it was me. I was killing them." My voice is barely a croak as I force the words out.

“And this is why I can’t help you, Ira, because if I touch you, you’re going to die.”

Ira’s response is the last one I’d ever expect. Instead of the sullen expression I’m expecting, when I look at him again, I find him smiling. “Then you’re in luck, honey, because I’m already dying.”

I jerk back at his words, my eyes darting to Silas for confirmation.

Black eyes meet mine. “I don’t need you here to help Ira live, I need you here to help him die.”

CHAPTER 5

Silas

"A hospice nurse I believe is what it's called," I explain to the woman who has quickly become the bane of my existence. "You were right, Miss Page, I've already hired the best doctors—the best surgeons—in the world, but it wasn't enough to cure Ira. So now I need the best to administer palliative care during the last of his numbered days."

The grating sound of the heart monitor has yet to cease. All she needs to do is reconnect the leads to the sensors on Ira's chest. Even though I know how to do that, I'm trying to prove a point here. My demands must be met, I will accept nothing less.

Quincey looks utterly lost and confused. "I'm not a hospice nurse," she states the obvious.

"I'm aware."

"You could have picked—*afforded*—the best hospice nurses around, but instead you abduct me off the streets?" She's shrieking now, the false bravado she's been wearing since we left her room slipping.

Good, her sarcastic comments were driving me mad.

"I'm *aware*," I repeat blandly. I told Ira the same thing since the beginning, but he insisted it be Quincey. Plus, "I've found my best employees are the ones who are indebted to me. Their work ethic seems to be so much better when their lives are on the line. And I need you at your best because like I said, I will accept nothing but the *absolute* best for Ira."

"But—"

I'm quick to cut her off. "This is how this will play out. You will work here as Ira's personal nurse. You will assist him with his medical needs while keeping him comfortable. Administer palliative care. You will stay quiet, much like a child, I believe you are better seen and not heard. As it is, I've already heard you say too much for my liking." If I was capable of having a headache, I'm sure she'd have given me one by now. "This is how you will repay the two hundred-thousand-dollar debt I have paid for you. That is" —I pause giving her a knowing look— "if you don't want me to hand you over to Gallo. That option is very much on the table still."

Quincey glowers at me. "My option is either repay my debt with my body or by being a nurse for your dying employee?" He's more than an employee, but I will never tell her about the details of Ira's and my history.

"Yes, those seem to be the options you've found yourself with." Technically this is all her father's fault, but I don't bring him up.

Her brows furrow and she worries her bottom lip between her straight teeth. Why she thinks this is something she needs to think over, I don't understand. There's a clear option here.

There is no such thing as curses, she's got herself worried over something that doesn't exist, but convincing her of this would be like trying to convince a devout catholic that Jesus was never real. Plus, I don't have the time for an argument like that. Sunrise is right around the corner.

Ira is racked with a sudden fit of coughs. He wheezes for breath and bends almost in half at the severity of them. With an exasperated sigh, Quincey finally moves forward. Her hands clench and unclench at her sides for a second, before she reaches for the leads that have come loose.

The room fills with the steady sound of Ira's heartbeats when she fixes the wires. Quincey adjusts his oxygen cannula as well and hands him a tissue from the box at his bedside. After a minute, the coughing stops, and she steps away from him.

She turns to me with a defeated look in her powder blue eyes. I had originally expected to find triumph in receiving that look, but I feel an unrecognizable emotion when she looks up at me. "How is this going to work?"

"I have to live here?" She sits across from me, her still bare legs crossed tightly to conceal herself from me.

"Yes, the room you woke up in earlier? It will be yours for the time being. It's close to Ira's room." And far away from mine. "This will make it easy for you to get to him if something happens during the night."

"All I have to do is care for Ira?" Quincey presses, "There's no fine print you're purposely not telling me?"

I shift in my seat behind the desk, eyeing the clock on the far wall. Five thirty in the morning, less than an hour before the sun is up and I'm indisposed for the next ten hours. "There isn't a single thing otherwise I can think of that I would want from you, Miss Page."

I'm lying, there is one other thing I want from her.

Her wounds on her ankle, while bandaged, are still bleeding slightly. The sweet scent of her blood is filling my office and it's waking up the beast inside of me. I need to get the fuck away from her before I lunge across this wooden desk and drain her dry.

She rolls her eyes at me, something I don't typically tolerate but for some reason, I let slide with her. "What about my job at the club?"

"What about it?" I shrug. "You obviously won't work there anymore."

"How am I supposed to make any money? You won't be paying me actual money for my work here," she starts, sitting up straighter in the leather chair she sits in. We moved into my office on the other side of the house after we left Ira. This is the one and only time I'm allowing her into this space. This room along with my bedroom is my sanctuary. I don't need her tainting it. "I still need money to… *live*."

"Food will be provided by me during your time here. Anything else you may need will also be provided—*within reason*." I'm not about to go buy her luxuries. The bare minimum is what she's getting.

She sits silently for a second, but I know the reprieve of her incessant talking will be short-lived. "I want to work one shift a week at the club."

"This isn't a negotiation, Miss Page."

"Well…" She frowns. "I'm making it one. Even if this were a normal job, under normal circumstances, I would need a break. I'm not asking for a long break, just a couple hours to walk away and maybe make some cash."

Her request isn't unreasonable, but I'm not feeling in a generous mood right now.

"You will quit your job at St. Sin," I tell her, leaving no room in my voice for debate while I stand from my chair. "Tomorrow, you will be taken to the apartment you've been staying at and you will collect all your things. You will tell your friend that you will be away for some time. After that, you will start repaying your debt to me."

Her arms cross tightly across her chest and her powder blue eyes glare at me. "I don't like you."

"I've found that most don't." I smirk. "But I've also found I don't give a fuck who likes me. I care only about who fears me."

"You want me to fear you?"

Moving around the desk, I grab the back of her chair as I lean down. The way she stops breathing and her eyes widen appease me. "I don't want it," I answer lowly. "I crave it."

CHAPTER 6

Quincey

"I don't understand." Lucy sits on the cracked and chipped kitchen counter, a bowl of cereal in her lap. "You got a job, but you can't tell me anything about it?"

The traitor who shall not be named, dropped me off at the small apartment complex I've called home for the past two months a little while ago. Lucy had lost her mind on me when I first walked through the front doors, asking where the hell I'd been all night while threatening me with various levels of bodily harm. She's calmed down since but the skepticism and worry remains in her eyes as she watches me pack up. I'm still tempted to hide the knives from her though.

Duke—the traitor—is waiting downstairs for me in one of Laurent's fancy SUVs. The same kind of SUV I saw the other night when I felt like I was being watched. I don't know if I should find comfort in the knowledge that it was Silas and not Gallo stalking me. Honestly, neither

"All I can tell you is I got a job as a private nurse." Not a total lie. "I can't tell you who my employer is because I signed a nondisclosure, Luce. All I can tell you is I'll still be in town; I just won't be able to see you." Okay, I won't exactly be in town, Laurent's home is thirty minutes away. From what I saw leaving the estate, his large home with its antebellum-style architecture sits on multiple acres of land. I didn't see another home or building for miles. His driveway is surrounded by oak trees, Spanish moss hanging from the branches.

If I wasn't looking at it as my new prison, I would be drooling over the property. It's something straight out of a magazine.

"This whole thing is so weird to me, Q." Lucy waves her metal spoon at me, droplets of milk falling to the floor as she does. "Were you even looking for a nursing job? I thought you told me you were done with that for good?"

I shove the sparse amount of clothes I still own into the battered suitcase as I look around the small space. Lucy's apartment is a one-bedroom, so her living room became my bedroom. Meaning I've been sleeping on her lumpy, old couch for the past couple of months. We talked about hanging a curtain or something to create more privacy, but we never got around to it. Not that it matters any longer.

The room I will be staying in at Laurent's is bigger than Lucy's whole apartment, but still, I'd rather be staying here than in that tastefully decorated hellhole.

"No, I wasn't looking for the job. They sought me out," I tell her, trying desperately to keep it as vague as possible. The NDA I signed was no joke, I'm pretty sure I may have signed away my firstborn child in that document somewhere. Besides, as much as I don't want him to, Laurent still scares me. I wouldn't put it past him to feed me to the gators in the swamp if I broke the contract.

"What? How did they even know about you?"

One of the few good skills I learned from my parents is my ability to lie. "My boss back in Boston recommended me when she learned someone here was looking for a private nurse." *Lie like your life depends on it, because right now it does.*

Lucy gives me a look that tells me she's not buying it. "Yeah, but how did someone in Boston know—"

I cut her off. "Look, Luce, I can't pass up the offer." Nope, I'm *super* stuck. "It's only for a couple months." *Tops*. Ira's condition is only going to get worse by the day. "I'll be back pouring drinks with you in no time." I hope the smile I give her puts her at ease because it's the best I can muster right now. I didn't sleep at all last night. My body is physically exhausted, and my mind is a mess.

"Okay, fine." Lucy hops off the counter and grabs the hoodie I'd left thrown over one of the barstools. "I just want you to know that I think this whole situation is suspect and I'm not buying it." She drops down on the floor next to where I sit with my suitcase open in front of me. "But I'll play along. *For now*," she relents as she folds the hoodie and places it in my bag.

I grip the shirt I hold in my hand tightly, my fingers digging into the fabric. "Thank you, Lucy."

"You just have to promise me you'll send me a text every single day telling me you're alright," she bargains. "If you go radio silent on me, I will lose my absolute shit and we both know that's not a pretty sight."

Laurent hasn't said anything about me having access to my phone, but I promise Lucy anyway. "I'll make sure I message or call you every day." I lay my head on her shoulder and soak up the small amount of comfort my friend gives me.

While I want Lucy nowhere near Laurent, I still wish I could take her with me. The situation wouldn't be so bad if I knew I had someone in my corner watching my back. Instead, I feel like I'm walking into a wolf's den with a target on me. I don't even feel like I can trust Ira. He may be my patient, but he's an ally of Laurent's first and that instantly makes him undependable.

And Duke, well I still want to hang him up by his toes and beat him like a goddamn piñata. I cannot believe he drugged me. Yeah, the sensible part of me realizes he was just following his devil of a boss, but I still feel betrayed. I make a note to make sure Duke knows to stay away from Lucy.

It doesn't take me long to pack up my stuff even though I was procrastinating and trying to prolong it as long as possible. The hour passes in a blur before I'm standing at the door with Lucy looking at me with worry in her caramel-colored eyes. She wraps her arms around me tightly before I have a chance to say anything or do the same thing to her.

"Be safe and stay out of trouble," she whispers before letting go of me.

I'm pretty sure I'm running headfirst into trouble, is what I want to say, but instead, I say, "You too."

"Are you going to pout the entire time you work with us?" Duke finally breaks the silence after fifteen minutes of driving in awkward, heavy, air. He'd opened the passenger door for me when I'd come downstairs with my suitcase, but being the hardheaded brat I am, I opted to throw my luggage at him before climbing into the back seat.

Childish? Possibly, but I have no regrets.

"Come on, Quincey," he sighs, his eyes watching me intently through the rearview mirror. "You're only going to make this harder for yourself if you alienate everyone. I can be a friend to you if you'd let me."

I want to hit him, but my life is currently in his hands with him driving this damn car. "Friends don't drug and help kidnap people, *dick*." My fingernails dig painfully into my bare legs. I was given a pair of sweatpants to wear home this morning, but I'd changed into some ripped-up jean shorts before leaving Lucy. Little crescent moons appear all over my thigh from my nails. Slowly, I watch each mark fade. "There had to be a better way of going about this. He didn't have to abduct me and blackmail me."

"You'll learn quickly Silas doesn't do anything unless he knows he's got a foolproof plan. He leaves nothing up to fate, everything in that man's life is meticulously planned out." Duke's loyalty is clearly cemented in Silas. "He made it so you had no other choice but to say yes to him. And let's be real for a second, Quincey, you would have turned him down had he asked you nicely."

He's right. I would have turned down any job offer given to me if it meant I had to touch a patient again, but Duke doesn't deserve that validation. "I don't get the impression many say no to Mr. Laurent."

Duke chuckles. "Not if they value breathing, they don't."

My mouth dips into a frown. "You find that funny? That he kills anyone who disagrees with him?" I can't believe I'm employed by a murderer.

I finally meet his eye in the rearview mirror as he says, "No, I don't find it funny, but I do find it interesting you told him no and expressed your interest in harming him with a scalpel, and you're still sitting here breathing." Clearly Silas confides in Duke. *Interesting.* Even a man of Silas's stature needs someone to vent to. "Why do you think that is?"

"Maybe he finds me wildly endearing and enjoys my company?" I smile sweetly at him. "I've been told I'm a complete joy to be around."

"Yeah." Duke shakes his head. "I don't think Silas enjoys anyone's company."

"He must enjoy Ira's if he's gone through all this trouble for him," I muse aloud as some of the puzzle pieces fall into place. Silas has a soft spot for Ira. "In his own fucked-up way, he cares about Ira and that's why I'm still breathing. If Ira didn't need me, he never would have put up with my bullshit," I answer Duke's previous question.

Duke gives me a knowing look. "You're not as helpless as you think, Quincey. Remember you have more leverage than he wants you to think."

Frustration causes me to dig my nails extra hard into the skin of my thigh "Why are you telling me this?"

"Because I can be your friend if you'd just let me."

CHAPTER 7

Silas

I don't dream.

Haven't in centuries. I spent decades pleading with the universe to make the dreams of the life I lost stop and eventually they did. While I would like to think the universe listened to my pleas, I think it's more likely my body forgot how to perform such a mundane skill. How they stopped doesn't matter to me, just as long as I don't dream of the person I lost so many years ago.

Until today, I was met with inky black nothingness while I slept. Just the way I liked it.

And then she showed up.

For the first time in over three hundred years, I had a dream, and it wasn't about them like they always used to be. No, I dreamed of *her*. Quincey Page somehow found a way to poison my dreams.

Her powder blue eyes framed with thick lashes blinked slowly up at me, her pale pink lips parted with a gasp as my fangs sunk into the smooth column of her neck. Her blood tasted sweeter than I imagined it would. With a single drop of it on my tongue, I'd lost all control. I'd ravaged her like a starving man, taking every single ounce of blood from her. When I was done, I sat and stared at her limp body lying across the end of my bed. Those eyes of hers that had looked at me with so much life before, now dull and still. And to my dismay, an emotion I can only describe as remorse filled me to my core.

That's an emotion I haven't felt in a long time.

I'd woken up with my fangs aching painfully, my throat burning as hunger racked my body. The first bag of blood I'd consumed barely scratched the intense appetite I woke with. By the third bag, I felt more like myself and was able to leave the sanctuary of my room.

Out of pure habit, I make my way to Ira's room, intent on seeing how his day went. It's not until I'm standing in front of his open door that I remember the woman I killed in my dream would be in this room with Ira.

My hopes for a quick retreat burst when I lock eyes with her across the room. She's pulled one of the side chairs from the seating area closer to the hospital bed. She sits with her feet propped up on the end of Ira's bed, a book in her hand.

I force myself to ignore the bandage on her ankle and the red spot from where she'd bled through the gauze. My eyes trail up her exposed tanned legs to the pair of revealing jean shorts. It then dawned on me I never gave her a dress code. Everyone who works in my home is expected to adhere to certain guidelines regarding clothing.

Her shorts and casual T-shirts are simply not going to do.

She's not even wearing shoes.

"I thought you said I wouldn't have to see you much?" Quincey looks up at me briefly before returning to whatever book she's reading. "I went over twelve hours without hearing or seeing you, I was starting to grow hopeful you were telling the truth, but no surprise, I find myself disappointed."

"Not that I owe you an explanation, Miss Page, but I always visit

Ira around this time." He's my first stop after I wake for the night.

She looks at the clock on the bedside table. "Noted." Her mouth pulls into a tight smile. "I'll be sure to make myself scarce around this time from now on."

This woman… "That may be wise." Reluctantly, I move farther into the room and closer to Ira's sleeping form.

He was once a strong man. Short in stature and always scrawny, but he was stronger than people expected. *Than I expected.* That was what drew me to him in the first place, that despite what life had thrown at him, he kept his head high. He didn't let anything beat him or tear him down. I respected that most about him.

"How did your first day go?" I finally ask her since I don't want to wake Ira to ask him. The man deserves whatever peace he can get.

"He slept on and off most of it, I think all the excitement last night got to him," she answers, finally putting down her book. She sits up straight, pulling her bare feet off the bed.

"The pain meds they've got him on are strong, he spends a lot of his days sleeping now."

"Lung cancer is a painful way to die," she answers, keeping a watchful eye on Ira. Despite the fact she's been forced to care for him, she still looks at him with eyes full of empathy. She back talks and pushes me, but Quincey is everything I'm not. *She's good.* "Unfortunately, it'll only get worse for him. It's for the best he sleeps through most of it."

"I just need to make sure you keep him comfortable." The slight edge to my tone isn't missed.

"I'm not happy to be here, Mr. Laurent," she says my name like a curse. "But I'm not going to take my anger out on Ira. *He* doesn't deserve it."

Will she still say that when she finds out she's only here because he requested it?

"Good."

"I'm not evil." Quincey glares up at me. "That's more your gig."

I could sit here and argue with her, but there is no need to prolong this exchange. With a stiff nod, I back out of the room. She doesn't bother watching me go but instead stuffs her nose back into the worn paperback. I would bet a lot of money she's not comprehending a single word she's reading right now. Based on her erratic heartbeat, she's bothered more by my presence than her cool and collected exterior shows.

She can pretend all she wants, but I know fear still fills her when I'm close.

I'm three feet away from the door, from ridding myself of her for the night when the unmistakable sound of a growling stomach fills my ears. My escape is so close and the option of pretending I didn't hear it is still very much an option, but instead of leaving like I want to, I pause.

Quincey doesn't return her attention to me, but I know she's still aware of my presence. The way she bites her bottom lip nervously and her heart stays racing in her chest tells me this.

Let it go, just walk away, the little voice in my head whispers but instead I say, "Miss Page?"

She releases a dramatic sigh as she turns the page of her book. "Are you going to hover all night, Mr. Laurent? You're already a kidnapper, might as well add stalker to your resume, I guess."

When people call me by that name, it's usually said with respect in their tone. The name means something to them. When Quincey says it, it's like she's rolling her eyes at me. Even though I'm the one who told her to call me that, and only that, I'm finding it doesn't please me as much as it usually does.

I'm somehow successful in forcing myself to ignore her comment. "Did you eat today?"

Quincey finally peeks up at me from behind her book, her brows pulled in confusion, but she doesn't answer me.

"I instructed someone to show you the kitchen today." That someone being Duke. I'd asked him to show her around the house a little. I made it clear to him the places I wanted to make sure she knew were off-limits. She isn't to go anywhere near the wing where my bedroom resides. "Did you eat today?" I hate repeating myself.

She looks at me like she's taking a test she knows she's going to fail. Instead of answering me truthfully, she lies. No surprise there. "I'm not hungry."

As if on cue, her stomach growls loudly again. Even without my heightened senses, the noise is audible. Any human standing within fifteen feet of her would have heard that hungry rumble.

"You're a stubborn woman," I comment. "Anyone ever tell you that?"

"Anyone ever tell you that you're an ass?" she quickly retorts.

"I'm sure of it." I nod, my lips pulling in a cocky smirk. "They don't usually live to say it again."

She stuffs a piece of scrap paper into her book, marking her page, before closing the book. "Well, I'll warn you, I'm going to say it again." Quincey puts her book down on her chair and moves around the bed to pull the thick blanket further up Ira's body. He's always cold now. The fire in his room burns most days. If my body was still capable of fluctuating temperatures, I'm sure I'd be miserable sitting in a room as warm as this one. I'm just now starting to understand why Quincey would opt to wear as few clothes as possible. "So, I guess you'll just have to add me to your growing list of victims."

Victim. Flashbacks to my dream play in my head as I relive what it was like to drain the life from Quincey. I brush the unpleasant thought of her dead body away from my head and focus once more on the problem at hand. "Let's go."

"Go where?" She looks at me cautiously.

"I'm leaving here shortly, but I will escort you to the kitchen so you can feed yourself since it's clear you haven't done so all day." I gesture with my hand for her to follow me.

"I told you I wasn't hungry."

"I don't like liars, Miss Page," I rumble unhappily. "I need you to take care of yourself so you can take care of Ira."

She pauses as she brings the forkful of pasta to her mouth. "Are you sure you don't want to eat?" Quincey asks for the second time since she sat down in one of the barstools with her bowl of food. "I feel weird eating when you're not."

"I already ate," I tell her as I lean against the counter with my arms crossed. I had three bags of blood tonight, that's one more than I usually ingest, but for some reason, my hunger was a lot stronger than usual. I blame my dream. Even now, I feel the slight burn in my gums as my fangs threaten to descend. I shouldn't still be craving blood after I got my fix.

"Okay," she drawls before sticking the bite of food into her mouth. Instantly, her eyes widen, and she makes a low moaning noise that makes my whole body freeze. "Oh my god, this is amazing. Who made this?" She quickly takes another bite.

I clear my throat as it's suddenly dry after hearing that noise come from her. "It's Della's recipe."

"I don't know who that is." Quincey shrugs.

"She works for me. Cooks for the employees who are here throughout the day and cleans the house." Della has been with me for years, just like Ira has. "She looked after Ira the best she could when he first started to deteriorate. When it got to be too much for her to handle, Ira and I decided it was time to consider finding a trained professional."

She pauses before concluding, "So she's your maid?"

My body bristles. "She's paid more yearly than you'll see in a decade. She's much more than a common maid," I snap at her, feeling defensive of Della.

Quincey's mouth sets into an angry flat line while she holds her hands up in surrender. "No need to bite my head off. I don't know anything about you or the people who work in this house. So, *pardon me* for trying to play catch-up and learn more about the epic shit show I've found myself in." She angrily drops her fork back into the ceramic bowl, the sound it makes fills the suddenly tense space. She hops off the barstool and grabs her still full bowl of food off the counter before moving toward the sink.

"What are you doing?" I question.

"I'm suddenly no longer hungry." She glares at me, her blue eyes look like thunderclouds. Before she reaches the sink, she pauses and whirls around to face me. "You know, you've made it clear you don't want me here and I've made it clear I don't want to be here. The difference is you had a choice in the matter. You *chose* to bring me here, you *chose* this." Quincey motions between us with her free hand. "So, I would suggest, Mr. Laurent, you learn to lie in the bed you've made because unfortunately, I'm here for the foreseeable future." With that, she turns back around and returns to her task.

She's just about to dump the contents of her bowl into the large sink, and without thinking, I'm across the room, grabbing her arm before she can dispose of her food. Quincey's breath hitches in surprise and she shifts away from me, attempting to pull her limb from my grasp, but I hold tight "Shit! How the hell do you move so fast?" She sounds more annoyed than scared over my inhuman speed. "Let go of me, your hand is freezing."

I don't answer her question and I refuse to let go of her. "You need to eat."

"Why do you care if I eat or not?" she questions. "You've made it clear you don't give a rat's ass about my personal safety or health. I'm tired, I haven't slept in thirty-six hours. Just let me go."

She hasn't slept or eaten since she's been here? Despite the circumstances of how she got here, I don't want to torture her. She hasn't displeased me to that point. *Yet*. "No one should go to bed hungry."

Quincey glances around the gourmet kitchen full of nothing

but high-end stainless-steel appliances and pristine white marble countertops. "Like you have any idea what it's like to go to bed hungry," she scoffs.

My fingers dig deeper into her sensitive flesh. "Don't pretend to know anything about me or my past, Miss Page," I warn. "You have no idea what kind of hardships I faced, or how many days I went with an empty belly before I became the man I am today." That is the only information she will ever learn of my history and the last time I will speak of it to her.

The thunderclouds in her eyes disperse and are replaced with a sympathetic expression I don't particularly enjoy. While that look is what makes her good at her job, it's also what makes her weak. Quincey needs to learn to harden herself before life rips her to shreds. You would think after the situation her dad had left her in, she would be more jaded.

Our eyes stay pinned on each other, one set like a summer's day, the other like the night sky. This close to her, I feel like I'm suffocating on the sweet scent of her. It washes over me and I already know when I leave this house for the night, I'll smell her on me.

"Let me go," she whispers after a minute.

I don't follow orders, but this one time I comply, taking a large step away from her. It's more for my sake than hers, I need to get away from her. "I have a meeting I have to attend to. Do yourself and your body a favor and eat something."

"You have a meeting?" she questions, ignoring my request for her to continue eating. "Isn't the workday over?"

Mine is just beginning.

"All of my business is done after sundown, Miss Page," I explain as I begin backing away to the exit.

"Of course, it is," she says dryly, her lips pulling into a smirk.

I freeze. "What does that mean?" Surely, she hasn't already started to piece what I am together? Even Della didn't figure it out this fast.

Quincey just shrugs a narrow shoulder. "Criminals don't typically do business in broad daylight," she says simply before taking a bite of food. "Have fun at your meeting, Mr. Laurent. Try not to kidnap anyone tonight. I don't know if my fragile ego could handle sharing the title of *captive* with anyone else." She turns away, her bowl of food in hand, before waving goodbye to me in a flippant manner.

CHAPTER 8

Silas

I can feel him looking at me in the rearview mirror, but I ignore him. Duke has been acting like he wants to ask me something since I got into the SUV. If he wants to say something, he should spit it the fuck out, I'm not going to beg to hear his thoughts and concerns. Part of me wishes he'll just keep whatever it is to himself because after spending time with Quincey tonight, I'm full of frustrated energy and it needs to come out somewhere. If Duke keeps this up, he's going to be the unlucky recipient.

"So…" Fucking finally. "Did you see her at all today?" Duke asks, but his tone tells me he knows something more than he's letting on.

I don't look up from the phone in my hand as I answer. "I ran into her when I went in to check on Ira. She was in there reading at his bedside." My finger hits the send button for the email I'd just typed out before I meet his eye in the mirror. "She was starving, said she hadn't eaten all day. I thought I instructed you to give her the tour of the house, to show her where she can and can't go."

Duke looked unfazed by my accusatory tone. Not shocking. "I thought you might like to show her around?"

"Why the fuck would you think that?"

"I don't know, just thought you'd like to be the one who told her she wasn't actually being held captive in Ira's room," Duke offers. "Thought you could use the brownie points."

"Why would I need—" A thought occurs to me. "*Wait*—are you telling me she believes she is to stay in Ira's room all day? That she can never leave unless she needs to sleep?"

Duke shrugs casually. "She's been treated like a prisoner since she woke up in that house, what would have given her the impression she's free to wander—*within reason*—around?" he quickly adds the last part knowing how I feel about having people in my wing of the house.

"*You* were supposed to give her that impression, when *you* gave her the tour, like I asked *you* to do," I grit out. She didn't think she could leave Ira to feed herself, that's why she was fucking starving.

"I thought it'd be better coming from you. She'll be less… *hostile* toward you if you're the one who gives her back some freedom since you're the one who originally took it."

My jaw grinds as I think this over. "Why on earth would I give a shit if Quincey was less hostile toward me? We're not friends. She's just another one of my employees. I don't *need* her to like me, I just need her to do her job."

"I just thought if she liked you more, she'd be less of a royal pain in your ass and that pinched, '*someone just shit in my Cheerios'*, look you've been wearing since she showed up would go away." Duke chuckles to himself, obviously finding his commentary humorous.

"I do not look like someone—" I can't even force myself to finish such an absurd comment. "I don't look like that."

"Yeah okay, *sure*, if you say so, boss."

"Just shut up and drive, Duke," I growl as I return to my emails.

I'm going to kill someone.

Liquid rage spreads through my body the more Louis speaks to me about the events that took place on one of my docks tonight.

We stand in front of the shipping container, the lock on it is partially cut off. The blow torch that was being used to cut through the locking mechanism still lies on the ground from where it was abruptly dropped. The two men who had attempted to rob me also lie on the ground with bullet wounds in their foreheads.

I spend mass amounts of money a year to ensure my docks are secure. Louis is in charge of the security company that watches this specific dock. Tonight is a great reminder that money that goes to him and his team is worth every penny. There are millions of dollars' worth of merchandise in this container. I'll make double if not triple that once the guns and ammo are sold to their designated buyers.

"Who would be stupid enough to steal from you?" Duke asks the question I've been asking myself since we received the phone call from Louis. I'd been at a meeting with a manager of one of my properties when I got the news.

I should have known after having that dream my night was going to turn to shit.

"We tried askin' them, but dumb fuckers pulled knives on my men," Louis explains after releasing a plume of cigarette smoke. "We had no choice but to shoot them straight through their skulls after that."

"I really wish you hadn't," my voice is a low growl.

"Was I supposed to let them hurt my men?" Louis dares to question me.

"At the end of the day, your men are replaceable. That information, however, was vital to me." Most of Louis's men are highly trained mercenaries, they could have handled a simple knife. "Have someone come deal with this, Duke," I order, taking one last look at the mess in front of me before walking away. "If anyone touches that container, you'll be the next one to be replaced, Louis," I warn over my shoulder.

Duke talks quickly with Louis before following close behind me. Not until we are at the car again and out of earshot does he say, "The cameras were tampered with as well. They were down for less than sixty seconds before the backup software kicked on." I know what he's going to say before it even comes out of his mouth. "This is just like the other incidents. Do you think they're all related?"

Six months ago, someone started attempting to hack into my security systems at various properties. It's not just the ones here in New Orleans that have been hit. No, they even started targeting my international locations. I sent Duke out to the affected one in South America, but he didn't find jack shit. Whoever is doing this is highly skilled or at least has hired a talented individual. If they weren't trying to hack me, I may have been interested in bringing them on as an employee myself, but unfortunately for them, I just want them dead now.

From what we've gathered, they're trying to track the routes in which I ship my merchandise. We figured this all out quickly and have since adjusted shipping routes, but it's clear they aren't giving up without a fight.

Tonight is the first time they've tried to steal from me though. They're growing cocky. They've either gotten tired of trying to gather information and are going in blind, or they thought they knew enough to hit my cargo container tonight.

Either way, I'm bumping up my security on all accounts.

"Get the word out." I open the back door to the SUV. "I'm willing to pay for any information on this. If someone knows who this might be, I want to know about it."

I own this city and the people who reside in it, if anyone knows something, they'll talk. They know the consequences if they don't.

"On it," Duke tells me as he types away on his phone. Duke has people stationed all over the city that are his eyes and ears. "Are we going home now?"

"No." I need to work off this pent-up energy or I'll go home and snap. I don't feel like killing an employee tonight. Quincey's face comes to mind—the way she looked up at me in the kitchen with those soft eyes and her scent… fuck. No, I can't return to that house in this state with her there. If I do, my dream will become a reality. "Take me to Rowena's."

"Rowena's?" Duke repeats skeptically. "Are you sure?"

No.

"I didn't stutter, Duke."

CHAPTER 9

Quincey

He's not anywhere to be found the next morning when I walk into Ira's room.

Not… that I was looking for him and wanted to see him. No, I saw him in my dreams enough. That's right. After tossing and turning for hours in my new foreign bed, I fell into a fitful sleep, where I started dreaming of the fucker. He promised I wouldn't see him much, but it seems I can't escape him even while I sleep.

Now that I've seen him multiple times out of the dark shadows and know exactly what he looks like, it's like his face is ingrained in my mind. I was right in the alleyway when I observed his strong cheekbones. His face looks like it was carved out of marble by an artist. It's perfect. A strong bone structure people would pay thousands of dollars to achieve. His jawline is covered in neatly trimmed facial hair that is just a little bit more than a five o'clock shadow. His hair is as dark as his eyes, jet black, styled to perfection. He doesn't seem like someone who spends mass quantities of time styling his hair, so if I had to guess, it lies perfectly with little to no effort. That would seem fitting since everything about him is perfect. He doesn't have one fine line or wrinkle. You would think with all the scowling he does he'd have a deep line between his dark eyebrows, but nope. The man's face is void of any imperfection.

Even his clothes are flawless. The suits are tailored specifically for his six-foot-four frame. There's no way Silas Laurent buys off the rack.

"Are you settling in okay, Quincey?" Ira asks once he's settled back in bed after we finished getting him washed up and changed for the day.

He wears clean maroon pajamas today. If it weren't for the fancy lift that helps move him from his bed to his wheelchair, I never would be able to get him out of bed by myself. The bathroom connected to his room is also modified to his needs. It won't be much longer until we are unable to move him at all. Soon we will be resorting to sponge baths in bed, but I will do this for him as long as possible.

"Oh yeah, Ira, I'm living the dream here," I muse sarcastically as I work on reattaching all the tubes and wires to his body. "It's like being on vacation, but better."

Ira wheezes as he laughs. "I bet Silas loves your attitude."

"You would lose money on that bet." I shake my head, smiling. "He is not a fan of me, nor am I of him."

"Be patient with him," Ira advises. "He's not as bad as he makes himself out to be."

I scoff, "He killed someone in front of me and then kidnapped me. I'm pretty sure that makes him a bad person."

"I never said he was a saint," he clarifies, smiling fondly as he talks about his boss. "He has some redeeming qualities."

"I'll have to take your word for it, Ira." I plop down into the chair I'd moved closer to his bed yesterday. If I wasn't sitting in it, reading the book I'd brought with me from Lucy's, I was pacing in front of the windows like a caged animal. No one has instructed me on whether or not I can leave this room during the day, and I haven't been brave enough to risk it yet.

"If he was truly the monster you think he is, would he be going through all this trouble for me?" he presses.

I already figured out on my own that Silas has a soft spot for Ira, but I don't say that, instead I deflect. "I just figured you have some really good dirt on him, and he needs to keep you happy so you don't spill the goods."

That knowing look flashes in his eyes again. "I've worked for Silas for a long time, honey. I know more about that man than most."

I want to ask him questions—so many questions, but I find the strength to stay quiet. It's too soon to press him for answers, I'm going to gain his trust and then get him to spill the beans.

I'm about to change the subject when there's a knock on the door. My body whirls around in my seat, expecting to find my tall, dark and brooding kidnapper, but instead, I find an elegant woman wearing a navy shift dress and blazer. She's on the plumper side and short like me. Her gray hair is tied back into a fancy chignon that I will never be able to do. I can barely braid my hair. Her eyes, that sit behind a pair of black-rimmed cat-eye glasses, are cynical as she stares me down.

Awkwardly, I raise from my chair and give her a wave. "Hi, I'm Quin—"

"I know who you are, girl," she cuts me off. "I've been briefed on the situation."

"Uh—" *Damn*, looks like there's another person in this house who doesn't like me. *Great*.

"Della," Ira rasps. "Don't be so rude to Quincey. She's a nice young lady."

Oh, this is the infamous Della.

"I've heard she's got a mouth on her." Della walks into the room, her low high heels clicking on the hardwood.

"So do you, but we still find a way to like you," Ira jokes.

"Oh, *joy*! Someone woke up with jokes this morning." Della purses her red-painted lips at him, but despite her hard exterior, I can tell by the way her eyes soften that she likes Ira. She steps closer to his bed and adjusts the blankets I'd just fixed. When she's done, she looks me over once again. "Silas didn't inform you of the dress code of this house?"

I glance down at my black leggings and tank top. Once again, I don't have shoes on. At least I brushed my hair today and put it into a ponytail. That's a win, right? "Nope." I rock back on my feet. "Not yet, anyway."

"Hmm," Della mumbles.

Ira meets my eye and smiles reassuringly. "Leave her be, Della," he scolds. "She's watching over me, she doesn't have to dress all fancy like you."

"Silas won't approve." Della clicks her tongue critically.

"He doesn't approve of anything I do, so why change it up now?" I give her a great big smile just to rub it in.

"I can see why he wouldn't approve," she sounds thoroughly unimpressed with me. With a dismissive look, she returns her attention to Ira. "Are you hungry this morning? Can I bring you anything?"

"Maybe just some hot tea, if it's not a problem," Ira requests.

"It's never a problem." Della's hand wraps around Ira's frail, boney one. "Now—" she says, turning back to me. *Oh no.* "—*You*. Follow me."

"Why?"

"I'm to get you some breakfast," she explains, sounding totally put out by it. "Also, Silas asked that I give this to you."

From the pocket of her blazer, she pulls out a sealed envelope. Hesitantly, I take it from her. Across the front, my name is scrolled in perfect, precise cursive.

"What is this?" I ask.

Della rolls her eyes. "How the hell should I know? I usually try to refrain from reading someone's private letters."

"*Okay*, lady," I drawl. "I was just wondering if he gave you any other information when he gave the note to you. That's all. There's no need to be a snippy bitch about it." If she insists on being rude, well so can I. I'm a patient person, but I'll only be talked down to so much before I snap.

Instead of looking at me with more anger, Della almost looks pleased with my response. The corners of her mouth even tip up a little.

"What?" I can't help but snap at her.

"Nothing." She shrugs. "I just appreciate someone who stands up for themselves. Come on, let's go get you fed."

Where I stumble through a kitchen like a colt learning to walk, Della moves around it like the chef of a five-star restaurant. It's almost like a dance as she floats between the stove and the oven, not once does she get overwhelmed or frazzled. She's nothing but calm—completely at ease in this environment. I always end up forgetting about something and burning the crap out of it.

She didn't ask what I wanted to eat, not that I thought I got a say in the first place, instead she just started whisking eggs and frying bacon. She put something in the oven in a skillet, but I was so distracted by the letter in my hand, I didn't see what.

I don't know what I was expecting him to write me, but a note telling me I'm not metaphorically handcuffed to Ira's bedside wasn't it.

Miss Page,

It's come to my attention you've been under the impression you are not permitted to leave Ira's room. While I appreciate and respect such dedication, it was never expected of you. Though Della will surely disagree with this, please help yourself to anything in the kitchen. The library and downstairs sitting room are also places you may explore. Don't mistake this as me giving you free rein of the house. I will be personally showing you what is off-limits. -Laurent

Seriously who still writes like this? If I didn't know better, I would have thought this note came by carrier pigeon. His handwriting is beautiful, looks like something straight out of the Victorian era. My finger absentmindedly traces the way he loops the L in his name as I reread it.

I can't help but roll my eyes at his parting remark. In one breath he gives me some liberty, but just as quick, the leash he's got me on tightens on my neck painfully.

"What did he say?" Della's question finally pulls my attention away from the letter. She refuses to read someone's mail, but it would seem she has no qualms about being nosy and asking about the contents once it's opened.

Deciding to mess with her a little, I say nonchalantly, "He asked me on a date." Bringing the coffee cup up to my face, I hide my smile.

As if someone had electrocuted her. Della gasps and spins so fast in my direction, the egg she's been holding in her hand falls to the black-and-white checkered tile below.

"He—" She pauses, grimacing at the mess at her feet. "—he did… *what*? There's no way he did such a thing."

Feigning hurt, my hand clutches my chest. "I'm wounded, Della. You don't think Mr. Laurent would go for me?" Calling him by his last name is so stupid. I hold one of the metal spoons up so I can look at my distorted appearance. "I mean, I know I'm not a *supermodel*, but I'm not a total goblin or something."

"What?" Della stammers. "Don't be ridiculous. It has nothing to do with what you look like, Quincey." She waves me off. "Silas doesn't—" She pauses again, realizing she's said too much.

I'll give Silas credit where credit is due. He has some very loyal employees. Which once again, makes me think I'm missing something about him. Surely all these people aren't loyal to him because he threatens their lives on a daily basis. Not a single one of them talk about him with contempt in their eyes like I do. They seem more than happy to be here. Hell, Ira is going to die under Silas's roof.

"He doesn't?" I press as I take a sip of coffee.

"Silas doesn't date," Della finally explains before turning away from me to grab whatever is cooking in the oven.

Silas doesn't date? "That doesn't make any sense," I argue. "How on earth doesn't that man have women flocking to him everywhere he goes? He's an asshole and an expert in blackmail, but he's attractive." No, he's not just attractive. He's hot, like turn your panties into a pile of ash, *hot*.

"I never said there weren't women," she corrects herself. "I just said he doesn't date."

"Oh." Silas Laurent is a manwhore. *Shocker*. "He doesn't seem like the type of guy who wants to settle down and pop out a couple kids." The thought of Silas in a minivan makes me fight a smile.

Della frowns a little, her eyes going distant like she's remembering something. It's a quick change in attitude, but in a brief second, she's back. "No, those things aren't in the cards for Silas anymore." She pushes the one loose strand of hair on her head behind her ear. "Silas is very content with the life he lives."

"I'm sure he is," I muse. "Who wouldn't like to instill fear in everyone they encounter?"

"He prefers respect, but if he can't get that he'll settle for fear."

I'm not dumb, I know that comment was directed toward me. When he does something that earns my respect, I may be more inclined to give him some. Until that happens, he's going to be stuck with my rage and yes, fear.

"Noted," I say dryly. "And I was joking, he didn't ask me on a date. He's just showing me where I can and can't go in this prison—*oops, sorry*. I mean, house."

A *hmph*-like noise is her response, but I can tell she wants to say more on the matter.

Della is quiet as she finishes cooking everything. When she pulls the skillet from the oven, I realize she's made a Dutch baby pancake. This is so gourmet to me, I usually just settle for the frozen waffles you pop into the toaster.

"Wow," I whisper, leaning forward on my barstool to get a better look at it. I wouldn't know the first steps in making something like this. "I ate the pasta you made last night, so I already knew you were talented, but this is so fancy. I could have just had a bowl of cereal."

"It's not just for you. Duke will be by shortly. I like to make him a nice breakfast when he's in town." Della's tone is softer when she talks about Duke, almost like a mother talking about her favorite son. "And what pasta? The one in the fridge? I didn't make that."

"Really?" I frown. "Laurent said it was your recipe."

"It is," she confirms as she plates up some food. "But I didn't make it."

"Then who did?"

"Silas probably."

I was not expecting that answer. "He cooks?"

Della smiles fondly at this. "He's actually quite good at it. May be better than me, but I won't ever tell him that." She hands me a plate piled with food and I happily take it, mouthing thank you as I do. "Nothing about Silas's life is peaceful and calm. He needed an outlet that wasn't destructive to himself or others. Cooking became his."

"I would have guessed his outlet was torturing people in the basement." This house is old, there very well could be a dark, dingy cellar down there for all I know.

Della chuckles but makes no move to tell me I'm being ridiculous. Probably in an attempt to maintain plausible deniability. *Smart.*

The kettle on the stove starts whistling and Della quickly pours the water into a teacup before adding it to a wooden tray. "I'm going to bring Ira his tea. I'll look after him for a little while so you can enjoy your breakfast in peace."

Okay, maybe she's not that bad.

"Thank you, Della." I gesture at my plate of food with my fork. "And thank you for making me breakfast."

"Just doing my job, Quincey." Everyone but Silas calls me by my first name. Della pauses by the door. "May I offer you some unsolicited advice?"

My spine goes rigid as I brace myself, thinking she's resorting back to her original bitchy ways. "Sure."

"You're looking at this situation the wrong way," she starts. "You keep saying Silas blackmailed you into being here, but you haven't considered the alternative if he hadn't stepped in. If you hadn't been able to repay those other men, where would you be right now? From what I've heard, there wouldn't be anyone making you breakfast."

Silas's comment comes back to me. *Nothing but a warm cunt for them to abuse.* That pit of dread returns to my stomach. Based on what Gallo's man said the other night, he was done waiting for the money. If I'd been taken by Gallo, I'm positive my situation would be a lot worse than what it is right now.

But… "He still kidnapped me."

"I never said I agreed with how you got here."

"He keeps threatening to send me back to Gallo." My voice isn't as strong as I'd like it to be. The thought of being taken by Gallo making me feel even more helpless. "Do you really think he'd do that? Send me back?"

Della simply nods. "If you push him too far or cause more problems and headaches? He'd do it in a heartbeat."

CHAPTER 10

Quincey

The best part of being abducted by a wealthy sociopath is hands down the spa-like en suite bathroom in my room. After getting Ira settled for the night, I ran myself a bubble bath. I sat in there until the water grew cold, thinking over what my life has become.

I can't believe I'm working with a patient after I swore to myself I never would again.

Each time I touch Ira, I cringe a little inside. The slurred warning from my mother all those years ago plays on repeat in my head like a song I can't forget.

For most of my life, I've never put any stock into the readings my mom did. I was a woman of science. I need to see actual evidence before I believe in something like fortune-telling or curses, but my mother is the complete opposite. She always believed. She would tell me tales when I was younger of all the things that go bump in the night. At three years old, I fully believed things like witches and werewolves walked among us. When I was five, I finally started to piece together that her stories were just induced by the alcohol she consumed. It was then I stopped believing in the fairy tales she told. It's when I stopped believing *her*.

That is until all my patients started to die.

Even if she was wrong, all those people died on my watch, it's clear I'm no longer good at what I do and have no business trying to save lives anymore.

Wrapped in one of the fluffy black towels, I pad out of the bathroom in search of some clothes to sleep in. My fingers work their way through my long hair, detangling the knots in the wet strands. I used to wear my hair at my shoulders, but after leaving town years ago, I let it grow out. It's now inches below the center of my back.

Distracted by my hair, I'm not paying attention to my surroundings. Not until I've flipped on the light next to the bed do I see the figure leaning against the far wall. And when I do, I'm almost positive my heart stills in my chest. My hand flies to my mouth to cover the scream building in my throat.

"You're always screaming," Silas comments, stepping out of the shadows. "I thought you were braver than that?"

I am.

As he walks closer, I instinctually take steps back to maintain the distance between us. Scowling at him, my hand grips my towel tighter to my chest. "You're the one who keeps putting me in situations that scare me," I accuse him. "As you said, you crave my fear, so this must be a grand ol' time for you."

"I was going to announce my presence when you were in the bathroom, but I assumed you wouldn't appreciate me walking in on you naked in the tub." Silas holds his hands behind his back as he continues to move slowly around the room. His midnight eyes scan the room looking for I don't know what.

"I don't appreciate or enjoy you seeing me in nothing but a towel either." I hate how uneasy he makes me feel. I also hate how he's taken all my control. I despise him for it.

He doesn't even bother looking at me when he coldly says, "Don't worry, Miss Page. I don't enjoy seeing you in nothing but a towel either." His insult cuts deeper than I want it to. "Then again, I haven't much cared for anything you've worn since you've been here."

A sudden, unexplainable boldness surges through me. He's done nothing but make me feel uncomfortable since I've been here. He enjoys making me squirm. Maybe it's time he got a taste of his own medicine. The warning that Della gave me comes to mind, but I push it aside before I lose my nerve.

With one last steadying breath, I loosen the knot in the towel and unapologetically let it pool around my feet. "Problem solved." I shrug my bare shoulders,

I don't get the impression someone like Silas Laurent is easily shocked. Duke has already informed me that Silas doesn't enter a situation if he doesn't know every angle of it. Meaning he's never in a position to be surprised. So, this moment has become priceless to me.

He masks his shock well, the only tell that he's rattled is the way his lips part ever so slightly in a silent gasp and his eyebrows raise just a hair.

With my head held high and my shoulders back, I kick the towel out of the way and strut confidently across the room. I stop less than two feet in front of him and boldly meet his eyes. The desire to cover myself up is strong, but I find the willpower to stand still.

He's tried to strip me of my power, but I'm demanding some of it back right now.

"Now, what can I do for you, Mr. Laurent." I smirk cockily up at him.

He stares down at me, his nose flaring, but doesn't say anything.

One second I'm standing in the middle of the room, the next I'm whirled around, and my bare back is connecting harshly with the plaster of the wall. Silas's large hand presses into my collarbones, keeping me pinned against the wall. My head is spinning from how fast we just moved, it takes me a second to catch up. I blink repeatedly until I can clearly see Silas's pissed-off face. He's leaning down so we are face to face, the height difference between us now nonexistent.

Even though I know he won't let me move an inch, I still attempt to push free of him. Silas's response is to just shift his hand from my chest up to my neck. He doesn't press hard enough to cut off my oxygen, but his grip is just tight enough to tell me who's really in charge. Who's been in charge the whole time.

"Was that fun for you? Did you enjoy that little show?" His voice is low, raspy. I don't know if it's his voice or the way his thumb brushes over my pulse point over and over again, but my skin breaks out in chills. "What's your plan now? How did you see this going, Quincey?"

The way my name sounds coming out of his mouth has me freezing in place—I even stop breathing. The way my body responds to hearing him say my name is not something I'm proud of. Tendrils of unwanted and unexpected desire ghost through my veins, making my skin grow hot.

"I didn't have a plan," I tell him honestly.

His eyes flick from my mouth to where his hand holds my neck. I watch as the strong column of his throat moves as he swallows hard. When his eyes drop from my neck and move toward my bare breasts, he stops himself. Looking in my eyes once more, he snarls, "Clearly." His breath whispers across my lips. "You keep testing me. I've been as patient as I can with you thus far, but even I am only so strong. My *control* is only so strong. It would be wise of you to remember that in the future, because the next time you parade around me naked, I will have you on your knees choking on my cock before those sweet little lips of yours can whisper *please*."

I'm ashamed my pussy quivers at the thought of having my lips wrapped around Silas's dick. The fear I have for him is only making the twinges of arousal grow within me.

My tongue sneaks out to wet my bottom lip, his eyes watch the movement with almost a predatory look. "You told me I wouldn't have to repay the debt with my body."

"Who said it had anything to do with the debt?" His thumb swipes gently over my pulse once more before he pushes away from me. "Get dressed, Miss Page. We still have a tour to go on."

I much prefer when he calls me Quincey.

CHAPTER 11

Silas

I thought the scent of her blood was intoxicating, but it doesn't even come close to the scent of Quincey's arousal. It took every ounce of strength I had in me to not sink my fangs into the pulse I caressed with my thumb. She had no idea how much danger she was in with my hand on her throat. If she knew, her pupils would have been wide with fear, not heavy with arousal.

From what I've already learned of Quincey, I should have seen her act of defiance coming. I should have predicted she would attempt to loosen the hold I have on her. While she's dragged her feet and complained every step of the way, she's been as compliant as possible for someone like her. But I'll admit, she's thrown me off.

The last person that rattled me in the way Quincey does is long gone now, but her memory still haunts my head like a ghost. The longer I spend around Quincey, the more she reminds me of the woman I lost all those years ago. Their fiery spirits and boldness are almost identical.

With the hacking and now the attempted break-in at the docks,

I can't afford to be rattled. The kingdom I've created wasn't built on distraction. No, my kingdom was built from the blood I spilled and my unwavering devotion to it.

And Quincey is nothing but a distraction to me right now.

My skin feels too tight for my body as I lead her down the long hallway. She'd done what I'd asked and gotten dressed. Granted, she wears nothing but a pair of cotton shorts and a tank top, but at least her pussy isn't on display to me anymore. Though the hungry monster inside of me isn't as thankful about it as I am.

Like the other outfits I've seen her in, the material of her tank top is threadbare and well worn. While I waited for her to finish her bath, I looked around her room and found she barely brought anything with her when she moved in. Where are all her belongings? She had an entire life back in Boston. From the research I had done on her from a private investigator that's on my payroll, she had an apartment. It was dated and old, but it was hers. Surely, she has more belongings than the few bits of clothing I saw hanging in the closet.

Quincey's been quiet since we left her room, the fire that burned in her eyes having dimmed since my remark about her going on her knees for me. Her heart rate picked up at the thought of sucking me off, but if I had to guess she isn't upset I said it. Rather she's upset with herself that the idea isn't as unappealing as it should be.

I'm equally if not more upset that for a brief second as I stared down at those pouty lips of hers, I thought about throwing her onto the bed behind her and devouring her body and then her blood.

Despite the fact I visited Rowena's last night, my hunger is always strong when I'm around Quincey. Which is just another reason I need to stay away.

I stop under the archway of carved stained wood and finally turn to look at her for the first time since we left the room. She stands there, looking innocent with her bare face and damp hair hanging down her back. Her thumb is pressed between her lips as she anxiously nibbles on her fingernail. "This hallway leads to the east wing of the house. Also known as my wing," I begin to explain. "Nothing beyond this point concerns you."

Quincey leans around me so she can look down the dark hallway. "Your office is down there," she remembers from when I brought her there the other night.

"It is." I nod curtly. "I don't allow people in there—even Duke hardly goes in there. You being permitted access was a one-time thing."

"Roger that." She brings two fingers to her temple in a mock salute.

I give her a stern look. "I'm being very serious. If you venture down there, I will know and you will be reprimanded for ignoring my rules."

"Let me guess?" She quirks a brow. "You'll send Della to put me in my place?"

"No, Miss Page, the only person that is allowed to punish you is me. I've paid quite a large sum to have such a right."

It's multiple hours later, when I'm walking past her closed bedroom door that I hear the noise. It's faint, but my sensitive ears pick it up with no problem. I'm not supposed to be in this hallway, but I thought I'd check in on Ira before I retire to my own bedroom for the day. If I hadn't thought to do so, I would have missed the noise completely.

The little voice in my head tells me to keep walking, but my body feels like it's made of lead and I couldn't move if I really wanted to. One little noise has rendered me immobile.

A moan. The softest, most delicate sound I've ever heard comes from behind her door once more. The sweet scent of her need once more fills my nose as I stand there listening to her.

For the briefest second, I'm filled with an unreasonable rage thinking she isn't in there alone. That someone else is causing those soft sounds of need to come from her, but as I listen, I only hear one heart.

Hers.

She's alone, touching herself.

The realization makes me swallow hard, fighting against the burn in my throat as my hunger for her rears its ugly head once more. But it's not my thirst for her that's painful, it's my painful need for her.

She moans and pants as she chases her release, go straight to my cock, making it press painfully against the confines of my slacks.

Fuck!

My hand reaches for the door handle without thinking, my fingers just brush the cool glass of the knob before I realize what I was about to do. Gritting my teeth, I force myself to stay put. If I was truly strong, I would walk away right now, but the need to hear her come has me staying in place.

In my head, I picture the way she touches herself. What gets her off? Does she like is slow and gentle? Or hard and rough? I lean my head against the cool panel of the door, squeezing my eyes shut as I imagine the way her fingers play with that sweet pussy of hers. They delve inside of her, thrusting into her slick walls. The heel of her palm rests on her sensitive clit and she grinds herself against it.

Silently, my own hand moves to the belt of my slacks. In seconds, my dick is free and I'm fisting it, swiping the pearl of precum around the crown with my thumb. I should feel filthy doing such a thing, where anyone could see me, but I can't stop myself. A need like I haven't felt in centuries is soaring through me.

I set my tempo to how I think she would do it as I continue to picture how she's touching herself. I imagine as one hand works between her thighs, the other plays with her pebbled nipples. They pinch and pull at them until they hurt. When that's not enough, she trails her fingers up to her throat, and wraps her hand right where my hand rested just hours ago. In her mind, she remembers the way I looked at her and the way my thumb pressed into her pulse point. She squeezes her own throat, but I imagine it's my own hand slowing the blood flow, just like I imagine it's her hand around my cock.

Her breathing and heart rate become more erratic, the moans becoming more intense. She's close. I work my cock faster to catch up with her. We may have gone into this alone, but we are coming together.

As she comes, she cries out my name, "*Silas*." The sound is muffled, like she covered her mouth as she did it. But it's still the sweetest sound. It sends me right over the edge. In a flash, I've pulled the pocket square from my suit jacket. As I come inside it, I picture it's her hot cunt I'm filling.

I can't move, I stay leaning my head against the door panting softly as I come back down. It's been months since I've come that hard. Nothing and no one has kept my attention or filled me with such need until Quincey. It wasn't really her that did this, so what would the real thing be like?

She said my name as she came, she was thinking about me as she touched herself. Suddenly the idea of her calling me by my first name doesn't sound as unpleasant as it did. In fact, if she said my name the same way she said it just now, I may insist she call me nothing else moving forward.

The creaking of the floorboards on the other side of the door drags my mind away from my illicit thoughts and the reality of what just happened crashes down on me like a bucket of ice water. *Shit*.

Quincey moves across the room, her footsteps getting louder the closer she moves toward the door. I silently curse myself for being so weak as I quietly stuff my cock back into my pants. *How could I be so stupid?*

In a blink of an eye, I've moved from her door to a dark shadowy corner down the hallway. There isn't even the slightest possibility she can see me with her poor human eyes, but still, when her door creaks open, I freeze. She steps out barefoot into the hallway, her head swinging from side to side as if looking for something. *Me. She must have heard me at some point*. Even in the dark, I can see the faint flush to her cheeks. Her hair is mussed in the back as if she'd been thrashing her head.

Not finding anything, she slips back into the room, once more putting a door between us. We are going to need more than a door to keep us separated if I keep losing my control.

CHAPTER 12

Quincey

I can count on one hand the number of times I've been in the same room as Silas in the past two weeks. He's avoiding me and honestly, I'm avoiding him. It seemed like a good idea at the time, but the act of boldness has since filled me with nothing but shame and embarrassment.

It's not because I pranced around butt naked in front of him either. It's because of what happened later that night.

The way he touched me and looked at me with such a hunger in his eyes, awoke something in me. It awoke a need I was too weak to ignore. That night as the rest of the house slept, I touched myself as I thought of him. I thought of all the dirty wicked things he'd do to me as I made myself come with my fingers.

Of course, I wasn't thinking about the real him—the jerk who scares me. I was thinking about the version I saw just for a moment while I stood in front of him naked. The man who looked at me like I was a delectable treat for him to feast on. That's the man I want—*or wanted.*

As the lust-induced fog lifted and I lay there in bed panting, the crushing humiliation that I've felt since filled me. How could I masturbate thinking of someone who'd kidnapped me? Who scares me?

Stockholm syndrome. That's the excuse I've settled on and the only one I'm willing to accept. Even if deep down I know it's not true, but like I've said, I'm not good at facing my realities.

"Della?" Ira's eyes peel open, looking dazed from his pain med-induced sleep. He's been having a rough couple of days and I've upped his dosage to keep him comfortable. Due to this, he's been pretty out of it, rambling on about things that don't quite make sense, but I still just sit and listen, responding when I can.

I put down the romance novel Duke picked up for me when he was in town. He laughed at the sexy man on the cover as he handed it to me, claiming that romance books are nothing but porn for women. I'd just rolled my eyes and slapped him in the arm with the hardback while telling him to shove it.

Reading has become my only escape since being here, all the silence is starting to drive me mad. I'm not even allowed to go for jogs around the property to clear my head. The restlessness is starting, and I know I'm this close to going completely stir crazy.

Della's attitude toward me has softened some, but I wouldn't go as far as to say she likes me. She's been great about sitting with Ira while I take a break. Sometimes I go read in the library Silas showed me during his tour, other times I just wander the large house.

Each time I stop right in front of the hallway I know leads to Silas's office and his bedroom. I've been good thus far and haven't passed the imaginary line he drew, but each day, as the boredom sets in, the more curious I get.

His work hours are weird, I know this, but I only ever see him at night. No one has said where he goes all day, and I haven't been brave enough to ask. I don't want Della or Duke to get the wrong idea if I go around asking about their boss—shit. *Our boss.*

"No, Ira, it's me." I lean forward, placing my hand over his. "It's Quincey."

"Sorry, dear." Ira blinks multiple times, trying to clear his vision. On the bedside table sit his wireframe glasses that I had slipped off his face while he slept. I hand them to him silently and wait for him to put them on. "Your hair. I thought you were Della for a second. She used to be blonde too, you know? I used to joke with her that working for Laurent all these years has turned her hair gray." His voice is labored like he's fighting for each word, because well, he is.

"I already feel like I've aged ten years and I've been here for just two weeks," I joke with a playful smile even though it's the truth. The stress of this situation is going to also make my hair turn gray. "Mr. Laurent has that effect on people I think."

"Indeed," Ira wheezes on his next breath. "I've spent so many years working in this house. My blood and sweat built this house—or at least I like to think I helped in some way. Laurent will probably disagree with me and take all the credit." He chuckles. "I wouldn't change any of it. Sixty years I've worked for Mr. Laurent—in this house—but I wouldn't change it for anything. I will die content with my choices."

I listen to him ramble incoherent words about his time here, none of it really making sense as the pain meds pull him back under. While I listen, I can't help but fixate on one thing. *Sixty years?* Ira said he's worked for Mr. Laurent for sixty years, meaning he's been here since he was just slightly younger than fourteen. Silas doesn't look a day over thirty, which makes Ira's math completely impossible. Unless Silas's father was Ira's original employer?

It's just the ramblings of a man on copious amounts of pain medication, Quincey, let it go, I silently order myself. The boredom is making my imagination go haywire.

"Roses," Ira suddenly mutters before his eyes close once more and he falls into a drug-induced sleep. "I really miss my roses."

"You're not eating," Della observes even though her back is to me as she's busy cleaning up her mess from making dinner.

I glance down at my untouched plate of food and find it's still *staring* back at me. I mean, *literally* staring back at me. On my plate is a whole cooked fish. The skin, little fins, and *eyeballs* are still attached.

I'm not a squeamish person, by trade I can't afford to be—I don't even bat an eye at blood—but the one thing I refuse to eat is seafood. I loathe it. Have since I was a child. Della's made some other seafood dishes since I've been here and I've been able to force down a couple of bites of them thus far, masking the actual fish by taking large bites of the sides, followed by drinking copious amounts of water to flush it down. But tonight, I can't do it. Tonight, my food is *looking* at me and there is no way in hell I'm putting any of that in my mouth. My throat tightens just at the thought.

"I'm not hungry," I lie as I make plans to sneak back down to the kitchen when she's left for the night so I can grab a bowl of cereal or something. I know the logical thing to do would be to just admit to her that I don't like seafood, but Della's been nicer, and I don't want to mess with it. Plus, I can't muster the courage to return food at a restaurant when my order is wrong, there's no way I can look Della in the eye and tell her I don't like her food. "I had a snack this afternoon, remember?"

"Yes, I remember that handful of almonds you squirreled away in your pocket." She cuts me a look from behind her glasses.

"My hands were full," I defend my actions. "Where else was I supposed to put them?" I'd been eating them in the kitchen when the new medical supply order came. I had shoved them into my hoodie pocket while I carried the boxes upstairs. "It's not like I walk around with nuts in my pockets frequently, Della. Don't make it sound weird."

"Thank God for small miracles, I suppose." Della reaches across the counter and scoops up my plate. "I'll give this to Duke, that boy will eat anything."

Feeling relieved the food isn't going to waste, I relax into my seat. "Can I ask you a question?"

"If I say no, will you still ask me anyway?"

I shrug. "Yes, probably."

"Fine," she sighs, sounding less than pleased about it. "What's your question?"

"Ira said earlier today that he missed his roses. Do you know what that means?"

Della pauses in what she's doing and finally really looks at me for the first time tonight. She's a busy woman—hardly ever stops moving. "Amongst his other jobs he did for Silas, Ira was also the groundskeeper for the property. He took great pride in keeping the property well-groomed and beautiful. He has quite the green thumb, I swear that man can make anything grow." She smiles as she talks, like she's reliving a fond memory. "But the roses he grew in the courtyard out back? Those were his pride and joy. He spent so much time tending to them."

I peer out the large picture windows that have a view of the courtyard, in the waning light of the sun, I search for the roses, but come up empty. "Where are they?"

"When Ira got sick a year ago, he was too weak to tend to them. The gardener that Silas hired tried his best, but the poor things died without Ira," Della explains sadly. This is the most emotion I've ever seen her show. Much like her boss, she comes off pretty cold and standoffish. "Ira was devastated."

My heart hurts for Ira. He's gotten a really bad deal in life lately. Despite all the good years he claims he had. I don't want him to leave this earth thinking of all the bad. I want to add a little joy back into his life. An idea comes to me. It won't ease his pain, but it will make him happy and that's what's important.

"How willing do you think Mr. Laurent will be to do me a favor?" I ask Della. She knows him better than me—arguably better than anyone in this house. “It won’t actually be for me, it’s for Ira,” I add quickly.

Della hesitates, pursing her lips as she thinks something over. “My gut says he’ll say no, but then again, what do I know? I never thought he’d put up with someone like you, but hey, it’s been two weeks and you’re still breathing. Maybe he’ll surprise me again and say yes.”

I elect to ignore the comment about me still breathing as if I don’t already worry about the fragility of life on a daily basis. “Will you ask him for me?” I plead, giving her my best puppy dog eyes.

“Nice try, but that crap doesn’t work on me, girl. You best go bark up another tree or buck up and ask him yourself.”

Ugh. So much for avoiding him.

“Fine,” I sniff. “I’ll ask him. Is he home? I’ll go ask him now.”

Della looks out the windows once more and shakes her head. “No, he won’t be around for at least another hour or so.”

Confused, I glance between the windows and her. “Did you just use the sun to tell the time? What? He doesn’t appear till after sunset or something?”

“Don’t be ridiculous.” Della waves me off with a flick of her wrinkled hand before quickly changing the subject. “Go check on Ira and ask him if he’d like some hot tea before bed.”

The people who work in this house are so weird and cagey. Despite knowing I have no right to be let in on the secrets that fill this house like silent ghosts, I’m starting to grow tired of being in the dark.

CHAPTER 13

Silas

I couldn't check on Ira when I woke for the night because as I made my way to his room, she was in there and it was not safe for me to be in the same room with her. My hunger has been steadily building since Quincey came into my life. I was ravenous when I woke up.

Instead of going to the meeting with the landowners of a new property I'm looking to purchase as planned, I'd instructed Duke to drive me to Rowena's. A year ago, I made her underground club off-limits to myself, it'd become more trouble than it was worth. In the past two weeks since Quincey arrived, I've visited there three times. Each time I know it's a mistake, but the bags of blood just aren't satisfying my hunger like drinking from the vein does—*or usually does*. Despite feeding off a live source, when I leave the twinge of hunger is still alive.

In the back of one of the dark secluded rooms, the woman whimpers and moans as I pull mouthful after mouthful of her blood from her veins. The venom that coats my fangs makes the whole experience pleasurable

Rowena is able to keep girls employed. Like a drug dealer, she gets her girls hooked on the high of being fed on.

Valerie's hands slip from where they'd been clutching my shoulders as her body starts to go limp. It's my sign I need to stop soon.

This isn't the first time I've fed off her, she's been one of Rowena's girls for years. Val's loyal and smart enough to keep her mouth shut about what happens within the walls of this establishment. She understands the repercussions if she doesn't. Just like me, Rowena has little spies stationed all over town, if one of her girls starts talking about the existence of vampires like Rowena and myself, they're taken care of without hesitation. There's a reason that Rowena has been able to keep this club running for so many years, she's ruthless. If there's the slightest suspicion one of her girls is thinking about talking, Rowena will silence them permanently.

Yes, the morality of this place is lacking. It's nothing more than a whorehouse serving the upper-class vampires of New Orleans. Instead of selling sex, Rowena is selling blood. Though I suspect sex isn't completely off the table for many of the vampires who visit here. It would be easy to take advantage of the women, the euphoric high that they experience after being fed on makes them compliant. Easy.

I'm not a good man, I've done things I'm not proud of and I've taken more lives than I've saved, but what happens in this club is something that fills my black heart with guilt. That's one of the reasons I stopped coming, I couldn't stand the lingering shame I felt each time I left.

But the overwhelming hunger I've had as of late is overpowering any guilt I may have.

Before Quincey, the way Val fills the room with breathy whimpers and moans would have gotten me hard. I've never touched one of Rowena's girls, but that doesn't mean my body didn't react to the way they enjoyed being fed on. But now, Val's sounds of pleasure do nothing to me, my cock has never been less interested in someone before. I can kid myself and say I don't know why it's different now, but I know the answer. It's because none of the noises she makes compare to the ones that Quincey makes. They definitely don't compare to the way she cried out my name as she came.

As thoughts of Quincey fill my head again, I push Val off of me with a frustrated growl and stand to my feet. Coming here was supposed to relieve the desire I had for my newest employee, not make my mind run rampant with more thoughts of her. "Fuck!" I hiss as I pull the pocket square from my suit so I can remove any blood from my mouth.

Val, with her eyes closed, curls into the red velvet chaise lounge we'd been sitting on. She looks completely content; a smile even grows on her lips as she falls into a peaceful slumber.

I'm glad someone found some peace during this transaction.

I leave the room and attempt to make a clean exit through the club without being seen. With the lingering hunger itching at the back of my throat, I feel irritable and not in the mood to engage in small talk.

I should have known I wouldn't be that lucky. Ten feet from the exit, a hand snakes out of the shadows and caresses my chest, halting me in my steps.

"Leaving so soon?" She purrs like a cat as she slinks out of the dark corner she'd been hiding in, presumably waiting for me.

"Rowena." My tone tells her exactly what I want her to do. I'm being courteous by giving her the opportunity to do it herself, because if I remove her hand from my body, I'm going to break her bones in the process. I might even smile while I do it.

Slowly she pulls her hand from my chest but makes a point to drag her fingernails seductively against the fabric of my shirt. "Did you enjoy your time tonight? We've missed you coming here." Her blood-painted lips pout dramatically. "I've missed you."

"I'm sorry I can't return the sentiment," I tell her dryly as I take a step away from her in case she gets any ideas to put her hands on me again. We've played this game before, in the past I may have been reckless in indulging it, but I realized my mistake last year. Rowena is a power-hungry snake, and she knows the one way to cement her authority is by taking me as her mate. I vowed to myself and the woman I lost so many years ago that I would never take a mate.

"So cold," Rowena murmurs. "You didn't use to be this way toward me, what happened to you, Silas?"

"You know what happened." I couldn't control the growl in my voice if I wanted to. "You know what you did—what you almost did."

Her dark green eyes roll in her head as she scoffs, "Come now, Silas. You can't still be upset over *that*. I told you it was a simple misunderstanding. I got caught up in the heat of the moment."

In one fast, fluid movement, I'm standing directly in front of her. I invade her space but make a point to not touch her. "Almost forcing an irreversible mating bond isn't a *simple* misunderstanding." I keep my voice low, but even. "You attempted to take something from me that I'm not willing to give you. Or anyone, for that matter. Nothing has changed since that night. I don't want you, Rowena. You were simply an easy fuck—you'll never be more than that to me. Certainly not my mate."

Her face contorts with anger and hurt as she shoves away from me. "You're wrong, Silas. One day you'll see what I've been trying to tell you. We would be good together."

I chuckle coldly. "You're delusional, Rowena." With that, I stride out of the dark club, ignoring Rowena's attempts to call me back.

She should be asleep, the hour is too ungodly for any human to be awake, but when I walk into the kitchen after returning from Rowena's, I find Quincey sitting on the counter, legs crossed under her. A bowl of cereal sits in her lap as she types away on her phone with her fingers. She hadn't bothered turning on any lights, the only light in the entire room comes from the moon beaming through the French doors and the blue light of her phone.

The dim light highlights the soft angles of her heart-shaped face, not that I would need any light to make out the features of her body. I can see her perfectly.

The smart thing would be to turn around before she spots me, but instead my hand flips the light switch on the wall. I half expect her to jump out of her skin like she usually does, but she doesn't flinch a single muscle. Instead, she simply tilts her chin in my direction. Pastel blue eyes scan over me slowly before returning to the screen in her hand.

"Hello honey, did you have a good day at work?" Quincey asks, in a fake upbeat way.

I frown, taken aback by her question. "Wha—" I begin to ask but stop when I figure it out. "You're joking with me."

She laughs quietly, the sound almost musical. It's in this moment I realize I've never heard her laugh. She's cried and begged, but never laughed at me. I'm disappointed in myself that I enjoy the noise and the smile on her lips. I like even more that even though it wasn't intentional, I made her do it. What is this girl doing to me?

"Gold star for Mr. Laurent." She gives me a small mocking applause. "So, did you?" When I give her another confused, blank stare, she shakes her head. "Did you have a good day at work? Or should I say night?"

Della, who's known me for decades, doesn't even ask me about my day but Quincey does. Feeling suspicious of her sudden interest in small talk, I raise a brow. "Are you asking because you're being meddlesome or because you truly want to know?" Even before we were both blatantly avoiding each other, she didn't seem overly interested in having such mundane conversations with me. For the most part, I myself don't enjoy having conversations in general.

"Well, I originally asked because I was genuinely curious about your day, but based on that *lovely* tone of yours." The smile slips from her face, and the guarded look she wears slips back into place. So does her frown. "It's clear you don't want to talk about it, so just forget I asked."

Quincey picks up the bowl and takes a bite of the colorful cereal. Della always buys that shit for Duke because he still, at the age of twenty-eight, has the palate of a toddler. He'll eat anything put in front of him, but if left to his own devices, he'd live off fast-food burgers and sugary cereal. Della knows this and that's why she insists on always making him meals.

Sighing, I walk farther into the room and closer to her. Instantly I'm drowning in her scent and against my better judgment, I take a greedy lungful of it and savor it on my tongue.

Leaning against the counter next to her, I hesitate before I answer, this kind of small talk relatively foreign to me. "My day was the same as usual. Nothing exciting or of import to tell you about. I missed a meeting because I had a last-minute appointment I had to attend."

Quincey can't hide the shock from her face at my answer, her jaw drops before she promptly clamps her mouth shut.

"What?"

"I just didn't expect you to answer," she explains. "I thought you'd tell me it was none of my damn business and then threaten me with something new and exciting. Are you feeling okay? Was the appointment with a doctor? Did they finally give you something to fix your chronic grumpy mood?" Her hand reaches for my forehead like she's going to pretend to take my temperature, but she catches herself just as her fingers brush against my forehead. Yanking her hand away from me, she sheepishly looks down at her food. "Sorry," she mumbles.

When Rowena touches me, it fills me with an uncontrollable rage. However, Quincey's touch, albeit brief, has the opposite effect on me. It's like it settles all the nerves in my body, a calming balm of sorts.

Bypassing her question about whether or not I'm feeling well, I find myself asking, "How was your day? Ira? Was he better today?" I know he's been having a rough couple of days. Sadly, those last few good days are running out. Soon it will be nothing but bad days moving forward.

"He slept for most of it, I upped his pain meds. The last dosage just wasn't cutting it anymore," she tells me as she scoops up a bite of soggy cereal. Her nose wrinkles in distaste when she looks at it, before letting it slowly drip back into the bowl. Giving up entirely on it, she places the bowl back on the counter. "His breathing is becoming more labored by the day. If it were an option, I would say he's quickly deteriorating to the point that a ventilator will be necessary to breathe but—"

I cut her off before she can finish. "He doesn't wish to be put on a vent," I snap, feeling protective of Ira's wishes.

Quincey motions with her hands for me to calm down. "I'm aware of Ira's DNR order, Mr. Laurent. I was simply saying that's where he's headed—he won't be able to breathe on his own for much longer. Without the vent, he'll die, but those are his wishes and I'll respect them." Her voice remains calm, and I imagine she's using the same tone with me as she does when dealing with her patient's family members. "Terminal patients should be able to die with whatever dignity they have left, not connected to machines keeping them alive if that's not what they want."

"I didn't agree with Ira when he signed that DNR, but I see now that I was just being selfish," I find myself admitting to her. "Would you have chosen the same thing for yourself?"

Quincey nods her head softly. "If the only thing keeping me alive are machines and tubes, I don't want to be kept alive like that. And if my heart stops for longer than four minutes, I don't want to be brought back. The risk of brain damage is too severe."

"And Ira wishes the same thing," I confirm.

"Yes." Her mouth pulls into a sullen, but comforting smile. After everything she's been put through—what I've put her through—she wants to comfort me, once again proving to me that she's too pure for my world. "But I assure you, I'll make sure he's in the least amount of pain as possible and I'm not just saying that because I know you'll make my head into a trophy if I don't. Ira's a good man—a flat-out saint for putting up with you for so many years."

She has no idea just how many years Ira's been with me. "That he is."

Quincey opens her mouth like she wants to say something else, but she quickly changes her mind and returns to looking at her hands in her lap. If Della saw her sitting on the counter like she is now, I'm sure she'd be scolding her for being so impolite. I find I don't mind as much as I should.

"Say what you wanted to say, Miss Page."

It doesn't go unnoticed the way her face wrinkles at the sound of her formal name. She bites her bottom lip nervously before finally saying what's on her mind. "I learned today about Ira's roses and how they all died when he got sick. I was thinking that maybe…" She trails off.

"Maybe what? Please do spit it out, I'm growing old waiting for you." My comment is funny only to me because I know the truth. I'll never actually grow old physically, but mentally, I feel every single one of those years.

"I was wondering if you could replant some rose bushes for him. Obviously not from seeds—we don't have time for that—but maybe you could find some mature ones that could be planted back into the courtyard?"

I'd forgotten about Ira's roses, hadn't really paid attention to them when they were planted there for decades, but when they all shriveled up and died, I finally took notice. Centuries of being alive has made me numb to the truly beautiful things in life. Like the roses. "Yes, I believe I can arrange that."

The smile that splits her face catches me by surprise. The small smile she'd worn earlier doesn't remotely compare to the one she has now. I haven't felt the sun in a long time, but warmth like the sun radiates off Quincey when she's truly happy. I want to bask in it—suck up all the warmth I've been deprived of all this time.

"Thank you, Silas." Her eyes widen when she realizes her mistake, quickly her face drops. "Shit, sorry, *Mr. Laurent*," she corrects herself. Emphasizing my last name for effect.

A simple nod is my only response. The relief that comes off of her is almost palpable. In her defense, I haven't given her any reason to believe I won't fly off the handle each time she steps out of line.

Sliding off the counter, she grabs her bowl and rinses it in the sink. "I guess I should probably go to bed now. It's pretty late."

The clock on the oven tells me it's almost two in the morning. "Is there a reason you're up so late eating soggy cereal?"

Quincey chuckles softly like she's exchanging an inside joke with herself. "Let's just say I'm afraid to hurt Della's feelings."

She must not know Della that well yet, because nothing hurts that woman's feelings. I swear she's stronger than me at times. "I'm not following."

Looking sheepish, Quincey tucks a strand of long blonde hair behind her ear. "She made fish for dinner and I'm not exactly a fan of seafood. So, instead of telling Della I don't like her food, I snuck down here for some cereal."

"You've gone toe to toe with me, but you cower to Della?"

"I'm not afraid to hurt your feelings, mostly because I'm not convinced you have any." She gives me a pointed look. "Although Della hasn't been entirely welcoming, she's not *that* horrible, and I don't want to hurt hers."

Where I will hurt whoever it takes to get what I want, Quincey wants to save people, not hurt them. She's a nurturer, and I'm a destroyer. We couldn't be more different.

"While that's very considerate of you, it's foolish. Della will not be bothered by you not liking her food. She will, however, be bothered you lied to her." Knowing Della, she already knows how Quincey feels about seafood, but she's waiting her out to see how long it'll take Quincey to speak up.

"Well, I'm still hoping that she never finds out. So, let's agree to keep this to ourselves for the foreseeable future." She smiles sweetly. "I'm choosing to think of it as a challenge for myself. This job is quite boring, and I need all the entertainment I can get. My goal is to hide my dislike from Della for my entire stay here."

I knew this job would be boring, but it gives me peace of mind that someone is here twenty-four hours to attend to Ira. Even if most of the time he's sleeping. Part of me sympathizes with Quincey. I wouldn't do well cooped up in this house for days—no, weeks—on end. It's just dawning on me that she hasn't even gone outside since she's been here.

"That seems childish," I criticize. "Surely there's a better game you could be playing."

"Ira tried to play chess with me, I'm sorry to report I'm not good at it." She leans her hip against the marble countertop in front of me, mirroring my stance. This is the closest I've been to her since I had her pinned to the wall, naked. "He's got a couple years of experience on me. I think it makes him happy to beat me, so I'll keep playing with him."

"He's a competitive man." I've always been too busy to play with him as much as I'd like. "Much like me, he likes to win."

"Hmm," she murmurs. "I don't get the impression you ever lose." Her head tilts up, allowing me to look into those soft blue eyes of hers.

"You'd be correct," I answer, my voice low. "I always get exactly what I want, and I'm not afraid to kill or steal to get it."

"Oh, *I know*." The corner of her mouth tips in a smirk. "I'm a prime example of how far you'll go to get something."

"What I did to acquire you was child's play in the grand scheme of my life. The lengths I'll go to protect or obtain something that's mine are unimaginable. There aren't any lines I won't cross." I inch closer to her, our chests only centimeters apart. My neck cranes down some too so we are eye level. My eyes can't help but flick to those lips I've been dreaming about. "This is my kingdom, and no one could stop me from burning the whole fucking thing down if I wanted to."

Her heart beats loudly in her chest. We stand so close, I can almost feel it through my button-down. "Are you trying to scare me again?" Quincey whispers softly. Her breath brushes against my face as she speaks.

I don't answer her question, but instead ask her a question of my own. "Are you scared, Quincey?" Her name rolls off my tongue before I can stop it.

A gleam, one I haven't seen in her eyes before, appears. It's almost wicked. The look intrigues me, making me wish I could hear what she's thinking in this very moment. "No." She smirks. "I'm not scared. I wasn't oblivious to how powerful you are, that was never a mystery to me." Those eyes of hers flick to my lips as her hand comes up and her fingers trace across my white button-down. "You have red lipstick on your shirt, Mr. Laurent."

Her warm palm lies flat on my chest, the heat that radiates off her almost sears into my skin as she pushes away from me. Without another word, she walks out of the room, not once looking back at me.

On my shirt, I find an unmistakable red smear. I'd gone multiple hours without noticing the blemish.

Rowena is marking her territory now? She's sadly mistaken in thinking I'll ever be hers.

CHAPTER 14

Quincey

The only explanation for the sudden surge of jealousy that coursed through me like a poison when I spotted the lipstick stain is that I truly do have Stockholm syndrome. Or after being stuck in this fucking prison for weeks on end, I'm starting to go crazy. The lack of social interaction with anyone but him and his employees is making me lose my mind.

I'm fixating on him as a distraction. *That has to be it.*

The alternative is I actually am jealous of the woman he was with last night and that's just not acceptable to me.

I need to get out of here—just a small reprieve from this house to clear my head.

Another day spent sitting with Ira and wandering the halls of the house. Still, I stay within the guidelines Silas gave me when he gave me his tour, but each day I stand at the mouth of the hallway that leads to his room, and each day I grow more and more curious. It's my unfortunate and unhealthy obsession with him that is driving me to go searching.

His room is sure to hold some answers.

I told him I wouldn't go rifling through his underwear drawer, but I'm so bored and feeling nosy, I'm seriously considering doing just that.

With gloved hands, I carry the bag of hazardous material downstairs after changing the IV in Ira's arm. Yet another one of his veins had blown, and blood was leaking out of it. I'm worried if this keeps up, a doctor will need to come and put a port in his chest so I can administer his fluids and meds.

It's almost sundown, yet another day of my life has passed being stuck here. It's odd, time is moving fast, but so slow at the same time. It's only been a little over two weeks since I was blackmailed into this, but in the same breath, I feel like I've been here for months. It's a wonder to me how Della and Ira could dedicate years of their lives here.

The hazardous material bin is kept in what could be considered a mudroom in the back of the house. Unlike a normal home, there aren't any shoes or jackets kept in here. For the most part, it's empty, only a simple black bench and the bright red bin sits in the corner. There's a glass-paned door that leads to the backyard, but it's always kept locked. Just like every door and window in this whole mansion.

Of course, I've checked every exit before, but each door has a fancy keypad on it that keeps it escape-proof. What kind of house locks from the inside? Silas Laurent's, that's whose. He's not trying to keep people out, he's trying to keep people in. *People being me.*

Opening the lid to the bin, I pause when I see them on top. Empty blood bags. Why are there empty blood bags? Ira isn't getting any transfusions and nowhere in his records have I seen that he was ever given blood. Confused, I place my bag on top of them and toss my gloves inside as well.

Is someone else getting blood transfusions? Maybe someone else is sick and they haven't told me. They're all very skilled at secret-keeping, and Silas is shady as hell. There could be another sick person in this house and I'd never know.

With my mind wandering wildly with thoughts of blood, I almost miss it, but the soft breeze that blows across my skin has me halting in my tracks. Turning back around, I find that the door has been accidentally left open today. Moving toward it slowly, afraid someone is going to pop out and scold me at any second, I open it wider and peek my head outside. The warm night air rushes over me and I sigh in relief. I haven't felt fresh air in weeks, and I want to bathe in it right now.

Feeling daring, I check behind me before stepping fully outside. The sound of the bugs in the grass and the slight rustle of the wind moving through the trees fills my ears. Closing my eyes, I savor the feeling of false freedom.

Fuck it.

Della is sitting with Ira right now. When I left them, she was playing a card game with him while he's conscious. *He's in good hands*, I tell myself before walking farther away from the house. It's not like I'm going to go far, if something happens, I can be back in no time.

The dread of the repercussions of this are overpowered by my need to walk away for a little while. I know I'll be in trouble, but I don't care.

I just need a second to myself.

The farther I get away from the house, the more I feel like I can breathe and think clearly. In Boston, I used to go on runs when I started to get too much in my own head. I would run as far and for as long as I could until I felt like I had clarity again. Since I've been here, the voices in my head have grown louder and the constant state of confusion and worry is weighing heavy on my body.

Not to mention I'm slowly losing the ability to think of anything but him. He's found a way to crawl into my head. Even as I sleep, I don't get a reprieve from him. His presence is just *everywhere*.

CHAPTER 15

Silas

The second I open my eyes, I start putting a plan into motion for the night. I send off a couple messages to people telling them I need to push my meetings with them to later in the night and I get a hold of Duke to have him start arranging my plans.

Looking at my watch on my wrist, I know she'll be in Ira's room now. She always is. She never sticks around when I show up. Quincey usually excuses herself and disappears into her room while I visit with Ira for a little while. When I'm far enough down the hallway, I hear her door open and her bare feet pad across the hall back into his room.

I'll give her credit, she's good at avoiding me.

I'm halfway down the hallway to his room and I know immediately something isn't right. The delectable scent of her isn't as strong as it should be and her heartbeat, one I'm quickly finding myself in tune with, isn't present. The warm energy that fills the space wherever she

When I broaden my senses, I can't sense her anywhere in the house. Not bothering to contain my inhuman speed, I sprint into Ira's bedroom. The wooden door slams into the wall as I thunder inside, making both Della and Ira jump in fright.

"What on earth, Silas?" Della scolds like a mother would as she stands to her feet.

"Where is she?" I bite out, ignoring her question completely.

"Who?" Ira questions, wheezing as he speaks. "Quin?"

"*Quin*?" I repeat. "I didn't realize we were giving nicknames now."

Ira laughs. "She has one for you too, but I don't think you'll like it."

I'm sure not. "Where the fuck is she? She's not in the house."

Della's eyes widen behind her glasses and she drops the cards she holds in one hand back on the tray attached to Ira's hospital bed. "What do you mean she's not in the house? She just went to throw away something." Looking out the windows and the now set sun, Della looks at me with worry crossing her features. "I hadn't noticed she'd been gone so long."

"Goddammit." Anger bubbles up in my chest as I stalk out of the room.

The sound of Della's heels clicking on the floor follows behind me as I trace the faint scent of Quincey through the house. I knew she was brave, but I didn't think she'd be stupid enough to try to escape. She knew the consequences if she did such a thing.

In the back room that holds the hazardous material bin, I discover the back door has been left ajar. "Who didn't lock this?" I seethe, spinning around to face Della.

The look on my face makes the color on Della's face drain and she takes a step back. She's never afraid of me, but my unstable emotions regarding Quincey have me acting unlike myself. "It was an accident, Silas. I must have left it open when I brought in the new groceries." She attempts to push past me as she says shakily, "I'll go find her."

"No." I stop her in her tracks. "I'll deal with this. Go back to Ira."

Della nervously rubs her arm while she pleads, "Silas, don't kill her."

That depends solely on how far Quincey feels like pushing me tonight.

It doesn't take me long to find her. The sweet scent of her blowing through the wind might as well have been a ship's beacon in the night. Part of me that I don't want to acknowledge knows that even without my powerful senses, I would still be able to find her. Her blood calls to me so intensely, I'm sure I could find her while blind.

The anger I felt when I first discovered she was gone hasn't lessened. No one disobeys me or my orders. She was told to stay in the house and at the first opportunity, she slipped away. This is my fault. I've been too soft toward her, making her believe that she's more than just another possession of mine. She's forgetting her place.

Under a moss-covered tree, she sits with her legs bent to her chest, her chin resting on her knees. She stares out at the pond that sits on the back side of the property. The moonlight reflects off it, casting a glow on her. When the wind picks up, gusting around her, she lifts her chin and closes her eyes, almost as if she's savoring the moment.

Quincey hasn't heard me approach, none of my victims ever do. If I wanted to, I could have her in my grasp and my fangs in her slender throat before she took her next breath. Despite my anger at her for disobeying me, I don't want her dead.

Watching her from the shadows for a moment longer, I wonder how someone built of sunshine and warmth can look so at peace in the moonlight. She's not meant for this world, but she looks beautiful in it.

Finally, I step into the light and announce my presence by *tsking* lowly. "You had me fooled, Miss Page. I thought you had found a way to follow my rules, but here you are, blatantly breaking them."

Quincey is on her feet in a movement shockingly fast for a weak human. Panicked eyes collide with mine as she hastily pushes the long strands of hair that had blown into her face away. I can almost smell her fear. *That's right, sweetheart, you fucked up.*

Her lips part, I'm sure a justification or worse, an apology sits on the tip of her tongue, but I silence her by holding up my hand and cutting her a stern look. "I don't want to hear it. I don't much care for excuses and while I'm sure you believe you have a good one, I simply do not care. I instructed—*ordered*—you to stay within the walls of that house and yet here you sit," I seethe as I slowly stalk closer to her. "I don't know what has given you this misguided belief that you are able to do or say as you please."

Once I'm close enough to her, my hand snaps out and my fingers wrap painfully tight around her forearm. A small gasp comes from her when I yank her harshly to me. "Was there some kind of miscommunication that I'm forgetting about that made you believe you could go on nightly strolls?" I ask, but don't really want an answer. Without remorse, I pull her with me as I stalk briskly back to the house. Thoughts of locking her in chains filling my head as I go. "It was a kindness when I allowed you to leave Ira's bedroom during the day. It was a kindness when I allowed you to venture through parts of the house. You think this has been your prison? You just wait."

With an angry growl, she shoves at my torso as she attempts to break free of my hold. She only causes my fingers to dig deeper into her flesh. It's not until she cries out my name that I stop dragging her behind me. "Silas! Let go! Just stop and listen to me!" she pleads. "Silas! *Stop*."

I stop but I don't let go of her. "Don't call—"

Quincey releases an exasperated groan. "*Yeah, I know*! I'm not allowed to call you by your first name. I get it and I get why. When I call you by your first name, it humanizes you and we can't have that because you need to remain the big scary monster in my eyes to keep control over me." She has the audacity to roll her eyes at me. "You can stop trying to prove to me just how scary and powerful you are. *I get it.* I know what you're capable of, I know you're more than capable of hurting me and that you're more than willing to get your hands dirty. What you don't get is that you don't have to be *Mr. Laurent*—the terrifying man who feeds off my fear—for me to do as I'm told. I'm more than willing to listen to Silas. And yes, I'm aware that's hard to believe since I'm currently breaking a rule, but you have to understand..." Her hand points at the house in the distance. "I'm going insane in there. Being cooped up is making me feel crazy. I wanted to come out here for a little while and just breathe, I thought it'd help me feel more like myself again. I'm sorry I broke your rule, I won't do it again. I promise." I can't be sure if her voice is shaking with adrenaline or fear. "Della once told me you prefer respect over fear. I can't say I respect you yet, but I can tell you I'm done giving you my fear. So, if you're going to kill me or hand me over to Gallo, do it. Just fucking do it, I'm tired of your threats hanging over my head." Her chin lifts, and she bravely meets my eyes once more. "You're the king on this chessboard of yours. I know I'm nothing but a pawn, so just make your move already. I'm tired of waiting, Mr. Laurent." She spits my name at me like it's venom.

I knew she was cooped up in the house, I just hadn't realized how much it was affecting her. This discovery eases the burning rage inside of me until it's a bearable simmer. I can't quite remember the last time someone yelled at me the way she just did. Duke, Ira, or Della haven't once been brave enough to do something like this. She's made of something else, an iron resolve masked in a sunny disposition.

"Did it help?" My hand releases her arm, but she makes no move to step away from me. Her hand however does rub the spot where I'd grabbed. I'm sure I've left bruises. The primal side of me finds that I quite enjoy knowing I've left my mark on her.

"Did *what* help?"

"Did coming out here help you feel more like yourself? Did it help you feel better?" I clarify for her.

"For a minute there it did, but then you showed up and ruined it."

"Then I'm glad it was worth it to you in some way to disobey me." Taking hold of her arm in a less punishing grip this time, I pull her toward the house. "Let's go, Quincey."

A look I can't quite understand crosses her face before her chin dips in defeat.

She keeps her head down as I lead her back inside. She doesn't say anything to me again or even acknowledge Della who'd been waiting in the kitchen for our return. The unmistakable look of relief fills Della's eyes when she sees that Quincey is unharmed. Silently, Quincey disappears back up to her quarters when I let her go at the base of the stairs.

I stand and watch her go until I can't see her anymore. Sighing heavily, I roll my neck and shoulders, trying to work out the stiffness I feel in my muscles after dealing with her.

"You've got to give her some props—going toe to toe with you like she does isn't for the faint of heart." Duke appears from around the corner, a half-eaten apple in his hand. "Hell, I've seen big scary criminal types almost shit their pants when you go at them like you do her."

"She's too bold for her own good," I mutter, rubbing my face.

"Nah." Duke makes a dismissive sound before taking another bite of fruit. "I think she's exactly the right amount of brave. If you'd brought in anyone else in the manner that you brought her in, they'd be so afraid and timid they wouldn't be able to do their job. They'd be focusing on their own life instead of Ira's. She's exactly what you needed, and you know it."

"She's disobedient and she's got a mouth on her."

Duke's face splits into a shit-eating grin. "Are you upset she's like that, or are you upset that you're starting to enjoy it?"

My muscles stiffen and a low growl emanates from my throat. "You're out of line, Duke."

The bastard just shrugs. "That may be true, but she wasn't. She just went for a walk, Silas. I just checked the video feeds around the property. Quincey could have tried to make a run for it, she had the golden opportunity to do so, but instead, she just wandered around for a while before sitting down by the tree. She didn't even attempt to look for the side roads or paths that could have led her away from here." Duke shuffles closer. "I know you don't want my opinion but I'm going to give it to you anyway. Tightening the leash on her throat isn't going to make her fall in line, if anything it's going to make her fight you more."

"I had planned on giving her a taste of freedom tonight," I remind him. The plans I'd had Duke put in motion had been for her benefit, not mine.

"I'm assuming that's off, right?" He rubs the back of his neck with his free hand. "I need to make some calls if it is."

I pause, pondering the events that unfolded tonight.

Quincey was right when she said I prefer to hold people's respect instead of their fear. In my world, fear is a powerful tool, and it's often the best way to obtain the things that I want. People don't tend to push back or debate with you when they know you hold their lives in your hands. The business connections I have with people where there's mutual respect are the ones that I favor. It's not very often I'm able to have such relationships. I find I don't hold many people in high regard.

When she first got here, I didn't care if she respected me or not. I wanted her compliance, and I didn't care how I got it. Maybe I was wrong in that thinking.

"No, don't cancel it," I finally instruct. "We leave in five minutes, go get the car ready. I'll go collect her."

I don't bother knocking when I reach her door, I just allow myself entry. It's my house, I don't need permission to go where I please.

When I find her half dressed in the doorway of her closet, I second-guess my decision. In pure Quincey form, she simply passes me an annoyed look as she finishes pulling on a pair of faded jeans with holes in the knees.

“What can I do for you tonight, *my lord*?” She even goes as far as to give me a mocking bow. “Here to shackle me to the posts of my bed?” Quincey holds up her arms, crossing them at her wrists as if she’s waiting for me to place handcuffs on her.

“While the thought has occurred to me.” My admission makes her face fall and her eyes widen. She thinks I’m referring to keeping her chained in here like a princess in a tower, but really, I’m referring to the impure dreams and thoughts I’ve had of her over the past few weeks. “That is not what I’m here for… *now*. Finish getting dressed, we will be leaving here shortly.”

Quincey’s whole body jerks before she freezes in place. The grip she has on the black shirt she holds in her hands tightens to the point that her knuckles turn white. “*Oh*. I see,” she whispers. “Guess I should have seen it coming.”

Confused by her odd comment, I shake my head. “Hurry along, they’re waiting for us.”

Her powder blue eyes drop sorrowfully before she slowly turns to the closet and grabs her checkered slip-on shoes. She moves slowly as she pulls them on and then walks toward me. Just like when I walked her inside, she keeps her head down, refusing to look at me as we leave.

CHAPTER 16

Quincey

I don't know what I expected would happen when I gave him my little speech outside. It was foolish of me to believe that the man with the inky black heart would take pity on me. After basically daring him to make his move, it shouldn't be surprising that Silas would take the bait and actually do something. He's not a man who enjoys being challenged; it only makes sense he would be showing me exactly what I get in return for my taunting.

In the back of his luxury SUV, I can't help but nibble on what remains of my thumbnail. A disgusting habit I only indulge in stressful situations. Like this one. If there were ever a situation where I get a free pass for chewing on my nails, it would be now as I'm undoubtedly being driven to my death.

Or worse, to Gallo.

I never thought there would be a time that I would pray for death, but I'm sitting here now praying for a swift, painless end.

I told him to make his move and I guess he's made up his mind

Duke has tried to meet my eye multiple times in the rearview mirror, but I can't look at him knowing what we both know. I need to find a way to tell him to make sure Lucy knows I'm gone, that I didn't just disappear. If she knew there was a chance I was still out there somewhere, she'd never stop looking for me. I don't want that on her conscience.

Silas has sat across the bench seat from me like a piece of stone the entire drive, not once has he moved. I'm not even sure I've seen his chest move as he breathed. He's so calm, it's disturbing, but then again, this is a normal Thursday night for him. I doubt he'll even lose any sleep over this.

It feels like we've been driving for an hour before Duke pulls up to a large white building. A man I don't recognize stands out front. When he sees us pulling up, he hits a button, and a garage door opens that Duke drives through. The inside of the building is almost blinding due to the many fluorescent lights up above. Silas finally moves, but it's with a silent wince as he shields his eyes.

Attempting to see what impending doom waits for me, I peek out the windows but don't see anything but a couple other cars parked inside. There's a door that looks comically small compared to the two-story ceilings on the far wall.

"Come along." Silas's voice pulls my attention away from the window. Turning in my seat, I find him waiting with the door open for me. *He's going to kill me, but at least chivalry isn't dead, am I right?*

When I climb out, I try to keep some space between us, but just like earlier tonight, Silas's large hand wraps around my arm and he pulls me to the door I saw.

I thought I could do this with some grace and not have an outburst, but as we get closer to the white door, the panic I've felt since he told me we were leaving bubbles over. Grinding my heels into the ground, I frantically shake my head as I try to pull away from him. "No, no, please wait. I—I need to…" *God, what do I need? Time? It appears mine is running out.* "Just promise me you'll make it fast, and you'll tell Lucy and my mom that it was some tragic accident, so they don't mourn too long."

Silas recoils from me, letting me go. "Quincey—"

I don't let him finish.

"If at all possible, can you please somehow get my body to Lucy? I don't want to be buried in some shallow grave on the side of the road or fed to the alligators. Actually, I don't want to be buried at all. Cremated would be ideal. I know I'm not in any position to make requests, but I don't want to rot away in an ugly dress in a coffin—"

Cold hands placed on both of my shoulders and a not so gentle shake silences my pleading.

"*Quincey*," Silas says louder this time, his smooth voice bouncing off the empty space we're in. "What the fuck are you talking about?"

Blinking away the sudden wetness that has appeared in my eyes, I meet his eye for the first time in over an hour. "When you kill me, please just have some mercy and don't make me suffer," I croak, my throat suddenly tight.

"Wait, Quin—" I hear Duke mumble behind us, but Silas quickly quiets him with a shake of his head.

Eyes like midnight look into mine. "Quincey, we're not here to kill you." In a gesture that shocks me to my core, he brings one of his hands up and he catches a fallen tear on his thumb.

"Is Gallo here then?" I whisper hoarsely.

"Gallo knows better than to step foot into my city without my permission or touch things that no longer belong to him." Silas shocks me further by bringing his thumb to his mouth so he can suck my tear off of it. The gesture makes my already wild heartbeat even harder against my ribcage. "No one is going to hurt you here, I promise you."

I struggled to pull in a relieved breath, the panic I'd been experiencing making my chest and airways tight. "Then why are we here? Why did you let me leave the house?"

"This." His hand still on my shoulder moves to my lower back as he ushers me once more toward the door. "Was something I'd arranged to bring you to prior to your escape artist routine earlier." Duke holds the door open for us and I'm blasted with hot, humid air as we enter. "I could have hired someone to pick them out for me, but I thought since it was your idea to start with, you should have the honor."

Thousands of plants fill the large warehouse—no, *greenhouse*. Understanding hits me, and I gasp, "Ira's roses."

The entire ceiling of the building is made of glass, allowing the plants to receive sunlight and thrive in the space.

"Yes," Silas confirms. "You'll pick out the rose bushes you wish to have in the courtyard. They'll be delivered and planted in the next couple weeks."

I whirl around so I can look at him when I say, "Thank you, Silas." For the first time.

I've cursed him and his entire existence, but I've never had a reason to thank him.

His brows pull together. "This is for Ira," he says slowly as if I'm not following what's happening.

"I know, but bringing me here tonight wasn't for him."

"No," Silas concedes. "I suppose it wasn't." He pauses like he's unsure how to say the next words. "You're welcome, Quincey."

The roses I picked out are dark crimson red.

Originally, I had been looking at the pretty snow-white ones, but out of the corner of my eye, I saw Silas stop and admire the red ones. He even ran his fingers over the soft velvety petals of the flowers. In that moment, it became really important to me that not only did I get some Ira would enjoy, but ones Silas would like as well. I couldn't tell you in words why it mattered to me to do so. Maybe it's because I still don't know what he likes. His dislikes are more obvious to me and I've already got a running list of them, but the only definite thing I know he likes is cooking. And now I can add red roses to the list of things I know about him.

Even though I'm not totally free with Duke and Silas both watching my every move, the short break away from the house allows me to feel like I can breathe a little better. The weight that has been pressing into my chest is lifted just enough for me to fill my lungs easier. Sometimes, even though the relief is short, it's enough to make you feel like you can keep going.

I hadn't been paying attention to where we were actually heading when we left Silas's house, but now as I look out the window of the car, familiar buildings pass by me. We're in the city, just blocks away from the Quarter. Lucy is so close to me right now, but I know it'd be too much to ask for Silas to stop.

A small brick building with a red and white awning catches my eyes and I perk up in my seat and point at it through the heavily tinted windows. "That's where my dad used to take me for ice cream when he was in town."

I don't know why I just volunteered that information, but the sudden nostalgia that crept into my bones made it just pop out.

"The same father who made you collateral for a debt he knew he'd never be able to repay?" Silas offers dryly next to me.

"He wasn't always the bad guy in my eyes." The man that used to take me for ice cream cones is very different from the man who offered me to Gallo. "I didn't use to hate him like I do now. I used to idolize him. He wasn't around much when I was growing up since Mom and him were never actually married. He worked odd jobs all around the south and each time he came back into town, he'd take me to that ice cream parlor and tell me these wild stories from his time on the road." Ronald Page always had a story, his long stretch of bad luck meant he always found himself in strange or crazy situations. The car fills with awkward silence that makes me cringe a little on the inside. "Sorry,

I didn't mean to start rambling on like that," I mumble my apology quickly before slinking down in my seat once again.

Silas tucks the cell phone he'd been typing on since we left the warehouse into his suit jacket, before nodding his head at Duke. "Turn around."

"What? Why?" Duke turns his head quickly to pass his boss a confused look.

"It's a good night for ice cream."

CHAPTER 17

Quincey

Twenty minutes later, cup of ice cream in hand, we walk back to where Duke had parked the car. He'd offered to get the car and pick us up in front of the shop, but Silas had turned him down. The confused and somewhat shocked look on Duke's face told me that this wasn't Silas's usual practice. A king like him probably demands to be carted around in his luxury chariot, I guess.

Either way, I'm not complaining. For a night that started off so horribly, I feel more content than I have in weeks. Even though I should be more on edge like both Silas and Duke are. Both of them keep a vigilant eye on our surroundings like at any time they think someone is going to jump out at us. It hasn't gone unnoticed how close Silas stands to me as we walk, as if he's *protecting* me from whatever unknown threat is out here.

It makes sense to me that Silas would be wary of his environment at all times. I'm not completely sure what it is that he does, but based on what I know of him, he's bound to have enemies lurking in all kinds of shadows. *Hell*, with his shitty attitude, he probably develops a new enemy each time he goes to the grocery store and gets coffee. *Yeah right, like this man goes to the grocery store.*

Regardless of how many enemies he has, Silas is more than capable of taking care of himself, even if he didn't have an armed Duke with him. I hadn't noticed the gun in Duke's waistband until we were in the ice cream shop and he stretched, causing his shirt to ride up and the butt of his gun showed.

"I can't believe you turned down ice cream. Who says no to ice cream?" I chide Silas as we walk. "Are you sure you don't want some?" I lift the dessert in my hand to him.

His dark eyes glance at the ice cream briefly before he shakes his head. "I have… food allergies. Unfortunately, I have a pretty limited diet and ice cream isn't on the list of approved foods." Silas almost looks *uncomfortable* telling me this, like he's divulging a secret he shouldn't be.

"That's a shame, especially since you like to cook. You make all that food but can't eat it." I have no idea what ungodly hour he's in the kitchen, but there's been many mornings I've found new Tupperware in the fridge full of fresh food. It's so odd to me that he works all day and most nights, only to come home and cook food he can't eat in the hours he should be sleeping.

"How—" he begins to ask, but he figures it out himself fast. "*Della.*"

"Don't worry, she wasn't gossiping. I'm pretty sure that woman keeps secrets better than the CIA." You can bet I've tried to pull information out of her, but she's like a vault. "I complimented her on the pasta you gave me that one night and she informed me it was actually you who had made it."

"Della informed me many years ago that I needed a hobby," Silas explains after a brief pause. "I'd watched her cook many meals for the house staff throughout the years and she showed me a thing or two. I suppose I've just run with it since then."

"I've never had a hobby," I find myself telling him. "I was so focused on getting through nursing school and then with work, I never had time to pick something up. I tried knitting once, but it was so boring, I gave up within five minutes. The only outlet I have—or had—is running. I used to run five miles before I'd have a shift at the hospital. It helped clear my mind and center me."

He's quiet as he listens to me talk, but the way his brows furrow with concentration, I know he's truly paying attention to what I'm saying. "You read all the time. That's a hobby."

The knowledge that he's been watching me enough to know I'm an avid reader makes me grow warm and my heart sputters. Is he watching me when I don't notice him there? More importantly, why do I like the possibility of this? I should be upset that he's been watching me.

"My mom had a stash of romance novels on her nightstand when I was growing up. It wasn't very often that she actually made it to bed where she could read them. She usually just passed out on the couch." *Sometimes the kitchen floor.* "When I was a little older than twelve, I started reading them."

"You and those damn romance novels." Duke snickers. "My little sister used to read them too, but I never would have pegged you as a sappy hopeless romantic, Quin." Duke has a sister?

I glare at him around Silas's large frame. "Trust me, I'm well aware those books are nothing but a fantasy. Real men aren't like the ones in books. I like escaping to worlds where women find these men who will literally burn down the world to save her or make her happy. So, sue me for enjoying that fantasy."

Duke holds up his hands in surrender. "Damn. easy girl. I was just joking." He laughs easily. That's the one thing I like about Duke. You don't have to work hard for his smiles or laughs. He gives them effortlessly and freely. Whereas I think I may have to sell my soul to the devil again to get a simple smile out of Silas.

I shrug, taking a bite of my ice cream. "I'm just saying, I'll cut you if you keep coming for my romance novels." The grin I give him is radiating with an evil gleam.

Silas makes an unamused scoff in the back of his throat. If he was capable of showing any other emotion besides anger, I'm sure annoyance would be written across his face. Maybe he'd even roll his midnight eyes.

We enter the parking lot and Duke digs through the back pocket of his jeans for the car keys. Frowning when he doesn't find them in the first pocket, he moves on to the others before even checking his jacket pockets. "Fuck," he hisses. "I think I left the keys on the counter when I paid for the ice cream." Silas pays his people well, that much I know, but I don't think he pays them well enough for Duke to be carrying around a black card. Undoubtedly, the card belongs to Silas and he was in fact the one who paid for my treat.

"Are you fucking serious?" Silas murmurs, a heavy sigh coming from between his lips.

"I'll be right back." Duke stops five feet away from us, before looking back. "Unless you think we should all go back?" He's not asking me this, he's looking for confirmation from his boss who stands beside me.

"Quincey and I will be fine here for a couple minutes," Silas relents. "But Duke? *Run*. I don't like standing out here in the open."

I watch Duke disappear around the corner we'd just come from, just like Silas instructed, he's sprinting. Smiling and softly shaking my head, I lean against the back of the SUV. "I like him." I didn't want to after he helped kidnap me, but he's broken me down.

Silas turns to me, still scowling. "Who? Duke?"

"Yeah, he's a good guy. I like him." I wave my spoon in the direction he ran. "Now that I'm feeling less angry at him, I can see what Lucy saw in him."

Silas moves toward me, inch by inch, he slowly invades my space until my only option is to tilt my head back so I can see his face. "Just how much do you like him, Quincey?"

I freeze in place, unsure if he's being serious or if this is as close to joking as Silas can get. Deciding to play along, I smirk. "If I was going to go after anyone in the house, it wouldn't be Duke. *Ira* however is perfect, too bad he's just a little bit too old for me. It's a shame I didn't know him in his prime, I would have been all over that." I'm not being serious, but Silas doesn't need to know that.

"I'm sure he would have loved to have all your attention directed at him," Silas muses. "You have an energy that pulls people in. Like a siren."

"You think I enchant people and when they get close enough, I pull them down to their dark, watery deaths?" I'm not sure I'm enjoying this analogy.

"I haven't yet discovered what happens once you've lured them close." His thigh brushes against mine, he's so close. When he's this close to me, I swear my brain starts to short-circuit. He's not warm by any means, but somehow, he still melts me into a gooey puddle who can't function correctly. "Do you think your anger for me will ever lessen like it has for Duke?" he asks lowly as his eyes travel lazily over my face.

"Maybe," I whisper. "But you have to stop doing things that piss me off."

The corner of his mouth twitches, as if he's fighting a smile. The fact that I made him want to smile makes my spirit soar. "That may be difficult, seeing as all I do is anger you."

"Tonight was a step in the right direction if you don't want me angry at you anymore," I tell him softly. "I don't know if I can ever forgive you for what you did, but being angry at you all the time is becoming exhausting."

I know it takes more muscles and effort to frown than smile, but what about the energy used to stay angry? Letting go of the anger is the hard part, but once it's lifted from your shoulders, the relief will be worth it. Or so I think... I'm fairly skilled at keeping grudges. Just take my mother, for instance. For over a decade, I've held nothing but contempt and bitterness toward her. I know it will make me feel better to let go of the anger, but I guess deep down, I'm not the bigger person I always thought I was.

Even if I can't forgive my mother just yet, I'm just about ready to let go of the darkness I feel toward Silas. If I'm going to make it through the rest of this debt with my sanity intact, I have to find a way to see some of the light again or I'm going to let it consume me. I don't want this to turn me into someone I'm not.

"I know the feeling," Silas murmurs. "Anger was the thing that motivated me for a long time. It was the catalyst that allowed me to build the empire I have."

For some reason this makes me sad for him. What happened to him that made him so angry? "That anger is also what made you into the man you are today," I surmise without him having to say the actual words.

"Yes." He nods somberly. "Without the anger driving me, I never would have been able to accomplish all the things I have."

Scanning his face, I commit every angle to memory. I've never thought a man was beautiful, but Silas is. In a haunting, terrifying way, this man is beautiful. "Aren't you tired, Silas?"

I don't know the exact moment we started calling each other by our first names, but I hope we never go back. Each time my name comes from him, my body floods with warmth and a shiver runs down my spine. And each time I utter his name, I feel like I'm breaking down one of the stones he's built around himself. An impenetrable wall. If he built it to protect himself from others, or others from him, I'm not sure.

The wind picks up, cutting through the buildings all around us. Strands of hair cling to my lips, still sticky from the melting ice cream in my hand. Before I can reach to remove them myself, Silas's fingers pull the strands. The air catches in my throat as he gently tucks them behind my ear.

His fingers are so cool, cooler than they should be in the swampy Louisiana climate, but despite that, I find myself leaning into his touch when his palm caresses my cheek.

"A siren indeed." His smooth voice washes over me like liquid heat. The need for him to do something other than just touch my face growing stronger the longer I stare up at him. Flashbacks to the night I'd touched myself flood my memory, only making matters worse.

"Silas…" I breathe. "I want—"

The plea for him to touch me—to kiss—me dies on my tongue when Silas's entire body goes stiff and he's whirling away from me at a speed so fast I can barely keep up with it. In the blink of an eye, he's standing with his back to me. His defensive stance makes him look taller—*bigger*—than he is.

Confused, I try to look around him, but his body shifts to block me once more. I can't see what's happening, but the sound of high heels clicking against the pavement of the parking lot fills the night air. Whoever it is, they're not in a hurry. They move in a lazy, unhurried pace. The closer they get, the louder the noise becomes.

"*Well*, this looks… *cozy*," a feminine voice says. "I apologize. I didn't mean to interrupt this tender—*moment*—you were having."

"You weren't interrupting anything," Silas easily dismisses the woman.

The woman chuckles, but it's not a sound full of humor, it's almost mocking. "Now Silas, there's no need to lie. I know what you look like when you're interested in something. There was a time I was very familiar with such a look." The woman all but purrs at him, instantly making my hackles rise. Who the hell is this girl? "And clearly you are very interested in whatever conversation you were just having."

Growing frustrated that his much bigger frame is blocking my view, I try once more to step around him. Without having to see me, he counters my move and continues to conceal. "What are you doing here?"

She ignores his question, still fixated on me it would seem. "Oh Silas, stop that. Let me see who your new plaything is," she chastises him, her fake, lighthearted tone not once wavering.

A low, almost inhuman growl emanates from Silas's chest. I'm standing so close to him I can feel the rumble in my bones. "She's no concern of yours, Rowena."

Rowena. I have no idea who she is to Silas, but I've decided I do not like her. With a pissed-off noise of my own, I shove around him and this time he lets me. Though he doesn't let me get too far away from him. His hand finds my forearm and with a subtle yank, he pulls me to his side.

One of the most stunning women I've ever seen stands before us. The elegance and poise she has radiates off her in waves. She's tall—much taller than me—and willowy. Her hair, the color of red wine, is pulled into an elaborate braided crown—she truly looks like she should be wearing a tiara with such a fancy hairstyle. Tendrils of her hair frame her perfect face. The contrast of her dark hair and pure, porcelain skin, make her emerald eyes stand out even more.

Her lavish skintight lace blouse and dark red silk skirt make me feel incredibly underdressed in my torn jeans and *Vans*. She looks like she would fit perfectly in Silas's world, whereas I stand out like a frumpy sore thumb.

"*Ah*," Rowena hums when she finally can look at me. "Look at this sweet little treat. No wonder you were hiding her from me, Silas." With her fingers on her chin, she looks me over, as if she's appraising me for market. "She looks absolutely delectable."

Unease settles in my bones, but I refuse to let her see what effect she's having on me. That the way she's eying me reminds me of a hungry panther watching her prey. Keeping my chin held high and my shoulders back, I look her directly in the eye. "It was Rowena, right?" I confirm, cocking my head.

Her painted lips curl into a grin. "Yes, but I'm sorry, I haven't quite caught your name."

"It wasn't offered," Silas lashes out. Without thinking, I lay my free hand over the hand that is still holding on to my arm. As if I somehow hold the power to calm him, the faint growling ceases in his chest. An odd sound for someone to make, but I dismiss it for now.

When Rowena's eyes slice to where I'm touching him, her nostrils flare and her eyes narrow. In an attempt to defuse the situation, as quick as I can, I pull my hand away from Silas and take a small step away from him to create some space. Risking a look up at him, I find his dark eyes staring at me intently, an emotion I can't quite place on his handsome face.

"Interesting," Rowena murmurs softly, as if to herself. "Why come visit me on multiple occasions when you clearly had her, Silas?"

I'm not stupid, I recognize a taunt when I hear one. She wants a reaction from me, she wants me to lash out at her and get angry. Despite the rush of jealousy that surges through my veins, I force myself to remain outwardly calm. Besides, I have no claim on Silas. Not like he does on me. Silas is looking at me still, I know this without having to look at him because my body is buzzing, but somehow, I find the will to ignore him.

"Is it because she's not giving you what you need?" she continues to goad. "Regardless of what you may feel about me right now, you still know I can always give you *exactly* what you need."

Even if I wanted to, I can't stop myself from rolling my eyes and sighing dramatically. "Jeez lady, give it a rest. If he wanted you, he'd be with you. Don't you know there isn't anything Silas wouldn't do to get what he wants?" I may not know much, but I know that. "If he's not putting in the effort anymore, he's just not that interested."

If it were possible, it's as if the temperature in the air drops with Rowena's mood. Eyes burning with hatred, she praises darkly. "Look who's got a mouth on her." She takes a couple steps toward me.

It must be too close for Silas, because in a second he's moved forward multiple feet, putting himself between us once again. The speed with which he moves never ceases to amaze me. "If you want to leave this dirty parking lot alive, I recommend you leave now, Rowena. If I have to escort you out, I can assure you that you won't do it breathing."

She bares her teeth at him. "Never thought I'd see the day that the merciless Silas Laurent developed a soft spot. For a pathetic human nonetheless."

Pathetic human? I'm a lot of things, but up until recently, I never considered myself pathetic. Having that thrown in my face is a real blow.

"You're talking out of turn again, Rowena. That seems to be a reoccurring occurrence with you as of late." Silas towers over her, glaring daggers. "You also have no idea what you're talking about."

"You don't give me enough credit," she bites back. "I'm smarter than you think."

Silas chuckles. "I disagree, it's just another reason I never would have ended up with you. This is your last warning, leave. Or I promise the consequences will be detrimental."

"You can't keep threatening me, Silas."

Taking one last menacing step forward, he snarls, "Fucking watch me."

Holding her hands up, she backs away from him. "You're making a mistake. You'll realize that soon enough." Is her parting comment before she slinks off into the dark shadows. Silas doesn't move an inch until she's completely out of sight. For a second, I worry that he's going to go after her and make good on his threats, but eventually he slowly turns back around to face me.

"So…" Awkwardly, I rock on my heels as I stir my melted ice cream. "You're into redheads."

A sarcastic comment during an uncomfortable situation? Classic move.

"*No*," he snaps.

Confused by his one-word answer, I press, "No, you're not into redheads or no—"

"No, as in I'm not having this conversation with you," he finishes for me, effectively ending the conversation.

My distaste for Rowena grows even more the longer I stand in heavy silence with Silas. She ruined the night—our night. I was enjoying my time with Silas. He looked like he'd wanted to kiss me before she'd showed up and now, he's back to not looking at me at all. Whatever moment we'd almost had, has officially passed.

Duke comes jogging around the corner and comes to an abrupt halt when he sees the looks on our faces. "What happened here?"

Tossing my ice cream in the trash can nearby, I thrust my thumb toward Silas. "We met his ex-girlfriend."

"What?" Duke looks thoroughly confused. "Who?"

"Rowena," Silas offers unenthusiastically.

"Oh, shit." His eyes cut to me. "What'd you think of her?"

Planting a fake smile on my face, I cover my heart with my hand dramatically. "I *loved* her. I think we are going to be great friends. Right after she's done peeing her circle around Silas, we're going to go get our nails done together and everything."

Duke grimaces, finally unlocking the car doors. "It went that well, huh? I've never liked that bitch."

I nod in agreement. "Yeah, his taste in women sucks." I point at Silas again. "But there must be something about her that appeals to him since he keeps going back. Maybe it's the color of her lipstick. It's a lovely shade after all." It was the same color as the smear on Silas's shirt, confirming Rowena's comment about him visiting her. With that parting cheap shot directed toward the man of the hour, I climb into the car. I'm mature enough to admit that I slammed my door shut just a little bit too hard.

Turns out I’m a *smidge* more jealous than I originally thought.

CHAPTER 18

Silas

I knew Quincey would be in danger if I allowed myself to get too close, but I always thought that the danger was going to be me. With the way she makes my iron-tight control weak, the fear that I would sometime soon snap was an ever-present thought in the back of my head. Now I have to worry about outside forces being a threat to her too.

Even though Rowena doesn't blatantly cower to me, that does not mean she's not still afraid of me. She's been around long enough to know what happens to the vampires that step out of line and don't adhere to the rules I've set in place. That being said, she also allows her emotions to dictate her actions. If she feels as if she's been betrayed or if she's angered enough, it doesn't matter how much she fears me. There's no telling what she'll do.

This is what makes me worry about Quincey's safety. I slipped up tonight by allowing my ruthless façade to drop while in public, where any prying eye could see. The fact that it was Rowena of all people who witnessed it does not work in my favor. One of her favorite ways to gain power is by trading secrets. Her career has allowed her to obtain many over the years. Quincey thinks I'm skilled in blackmail? Rowena is a savant in the matter.

If Rowena starts spreading the news that I may or may not have a soft spot for the human, it will only be a matter of time before someone comes for Quincey in hopes of using her against me.

She doesn't wait for me to come around and open her car door for her once we're back at the estate. Duke barely has time to put the car into park before she's climbing out and walking briskly to the front door. Quincey also doesn't bother waiting for me or even looking back to see if I'm following before she disappears into the house.

From the front seat, Duke chuckles softly as he watches her go. "Are we leaving now, or are you going to go deal with that first?" I don't appreciate the knowing look he passes me in the mirror.

He didn't have to ask, Duke already knows my answer. "I'll be right back."

"That's what I thought."

I shouldn't be going after her, but I can't stop myself. Everything about her has me behaving in ways I haven't in a long time. Then again, no one has captured my attention like she has in a long time.

It's no surprise to me that I track her sweet scent to the kitchen. She sits on the counter, feet swinging back and forth with a cup of lemonade already in hand. She doesn't look up from her swaying legs when I enter, so I take the opportunity to move in front of her before she has the chance to protest.

Patiently, a skill that doesn't come easily for me, I wait for her to say something.

"Tonight didn't start well or end well, but the middle part?" Finally, her chin tilts up so I can see her pretty face. "The middle part I enjoyed. I would say I wouldn't mind doing that again sometime, but I have this sneaking suspicion that tonight was a one-time thing."

She waits for confirmation and when I give her a slow nod, her lips pull into a sad smile. Taking one last drink from her glass, Quincey jumps gracefully off the counter. Pausing in front of me, she asks softly, "Is it because of her?"

"Partially," I tell her honestly.

Quincey's face pinches, but she's quick to conceal whatever emotion she's feeling. "Figured as much," she whispers. "Regardless, thank you for tonight. Ira is going to love his roses, I'm sure of it." In a move that shocks me to my core and has my body turning to stone, Quincey leans up on her tippy-toes and places a chaste kiss on my jaw. My body is now a stranger to that kind of tender affection, but the simple touch awakens something in me. "Good night, Silas."

I'm stuck in place as she pulls away from me. The voice of reason that screams at me to let her go is drowned out. I can hardly hear it over the intense need to pull her back to me.

My body moves before my head can catch up. She doesn't get farther than three feet away from me before I'm dragging her to me once more.

"Silas—" My name is cut off by my lips colliding with hers.

It's hard to remember when something is a bad idea when it feels and tastes like her.

She's stiff, unyielding at first, as the shock of what I've just done consumes her, but it lasts only a second before, with a moan, she's melting into me.

Giving in to me.

My mouth owns hers, taking and claiming without permission or care. And by doing so, I'm breaking every single one of my rules, but in this moment, I can't find a fuck to give. Humans are off-limits, *Quincey* is off-limits, but I can't stop myself once I taste her on my tongue. Sweeter than sin, but somehow more tempting than a sin itself.

I haven't kissed anyone in centuries, the act itself always felt more intimate than sex, but with Quincey, it feels like something we've been doing for years. A well-orchestrated dance we could perform blindfolded. A dance we could go decades without practicing, but still would be perfect.

Her hands, slowly, almost timidly smooth over my chest, leaving a trail of heat behind them. A heat that is foreign to my cold body and soul, but as it spreads through my body, I revel in it.

My blunt teeth capture her bottom lip and pull it with a sharp nip. Her tongue swipes out to soothe the sting and I seize the moment to lick inside her hot mouth. A mouth so compliant and yielding to me now, her sharp tongue for the moment obedient to me.

If she's this submissive with just a kiss, I wonder how she'll behave with my mouth on her pussy. Wicked thoughts of Quincey eagerly doing everything I ask fills my head.

Oh, the things I could do to that body. I would make her call my name as she came, just as she did that night. This time it wouldn't be the thought of me bringing her to orgasm, it would be the real me, licking, biting, *taking* until she screamed.

With a growl, my hands snake down to her ass. Squeezing roughly, I lift her up and drop her onto the marble countertop behind us. Her thighs part to allow me to stand between them. My hardening cock presses into her jean-clad core, but despite the clothes between us, I can feel the heat radiating off of her. My cock aches to delve into that heat.

Quincey must be thinking the same thing because her hips roll, grinding herself softly against me. The warning rumble that builds in the back of my throat only makes her smile. She has no idea who she's playing with right now. One wrong move, one wrong flick of my wrist, I could fucking kill her. Even now, my gums burn and ache, my fangs threatening to descend at any second.

My hand tangles around her long hair. Yanking the strands harshly, I angle her head exactly how I want it. The hissing sound of approval that comes from her appeases the dominant monster lurking inside of me. He likes knowing she can take a little pain, that she approves of being manhandled like this.

And so do I.

I kiss her harder, taking everything I can from her and at the same time, leaving my brand on her. I want to sear this moment into her memory. Every time she looks at her lips, I want her to think about how I took her mouth. When she kisses another, I want her to compare it to how I kissed her. I want to ruin any other man for her.

I want to ruin her—corrupting her soul until it matches mine.

The thought of another man touching her—touching something that is mine—causes an unexplainable anger to build in me. The logical part of me knows Quincey won't always be mine, her debt will be paid in full when Ira dies. After that, she'll be free to kiss whomever she desires, and that knowledge fills me with rage.

The kiss turns to a desperate frenzy, as if both of us know that we must get our fill now as this will never happen again. Only when she winces and the most delectable taste rushes into my mouth do I realize my mistake. My fangs are out, and they've cut her lip.

It takes every ounce of power I have to pull myself from her. Needing to put space between us, I all but throw myself across the room, quickly putting multiple feet between our bodies. I keep my back to her, as I try to regain my control and force my fangs back, but the residual blood on my tongue and the aroma of blood in the air is making it difficult.

Behind me, she's panting hard as she attempts to catch her breath. "I don't think I've ever been kissed so hard that I bled," Quincey chuckles. If only she knew how much danger she was in, she wouldn't be laughing right now. She'd be running.

The sound of her shifting off the counter has me raising a hand and ordering harshly, "Stop. Stay where you are."

"Silas?" she says my name, sounding so confused. "What's wrong? I—"

I don't let her finish. "This was a mistake and never should have happened. It was a lapse in judgment." The stern tone returns to my voice, not allowing room for her to question what I'm saying. I cut her the briefest look over my shoulder to ensure she hasn't moved closer. "I apologize for creating any confusion, I don't know what I was thinking, but this—" *was the first thing that made me feel alive in a long time?* "— meant nothing to me. Please do not start getting any ideas."

"Silas…" she tries again, the hurt she feels evident in her voice.

"Enough," I snap, louder than necessary, but I need this to be over. I need her to leave before I make an irreversible mistake. "This was a misstep on my part and nothing more. It would be wise for you to return to your quarters now, Miss Page."

Miss Page. It no longer feels like her name when I say it.

There's a pause before, with a shuttering breath, she whispers, "Yes, sir." I can't help the wince that comes from hearing the formal title. "I have a lot of regrets myself, I'll be sure to file this—*moment*— with the rest."

I don't watch as she hurries from the kitchen because I fear I won't be able to stop myself from following after her.

CHAPTER 19

Quincey

It didn't matter how dark my life got or how bleak things started to look for me, I never lost my hopefulness that things would get better. In my mind, things could only be so bad before they took a turn for the better, all I had to do was keep my head up and ride out the storm. Sooner or later the sunshine was going to return, but the longer I'm here, the more of my sun he steals from me. The storm is slowly consuming me, and I fear if I'm here too long, I'll be overtaken by the darkness that has infected Silas.

The only thing keeping me going is that this isn't for forever. I'm clinging to that knowledge like it's a life raft keeping me from drifting into the bleakness.

Being here is different from the chaos I thrive in, this isn't chaos. It's emotional warfare and I'm losing the battle. The constant hot and cold with him is hard to keep up with. With each interaction I have with Silas, he chips away another piece of my optimism. Two weeks ago, when he told me our kiss meant nothing to him and subsequently

I meant nothing to him, he chipped away an even bigger piece of it. No, chipped isn't the right word—he *smashed* it and smiled while it shattered into a thousand pieces at his feet.

Okay, I know he didn't actually smile, but part of me almost wished he would have. It would have been easier to see that than the fleeting pained look on his face. A pained look that is the creation of his own doing. He was the one who declared it was a bad idea—*a mistake*—and despite knowing deep down he was right, it didn't feel that way in the moment. It felt perfect, like it was something I was always meant to do.

Feeling this way is what makes it hurt so much.

When he called me Miss Page instead of Quincey again, it felt like a bullet to the chest. A bullet may have hurt less.

The hurt is fueling the anger that had just started to subside that night. Now it's raging inside of me, and over the past two weeks it's grown into an uncontrollable wildfire. I've snapped not only at Duke, but also Della because of it. I apologized immediately after since they don't deserve my wrath. The only person I've been able to keep my calm with is Ira, and that is mainly due to the fact he's one of the sweetest souls I've ever met. His tender heart doesn't fit in Silas's world.

"Quincey, where'd that pretty mind of yours wander off to now?" He wheezes from his bed. Ira's having a good day, even sitting up in bed with his eyes more alert. Good. Today something special is happening.

From my spot next to the window, I pull my attention away from the commotion down below to smile softly at Ira. "Nowhere Ira, I'm here."

Ira places the crossword puzzle he's been working on for hours onto his lap and squints his eyes at me. "Whatever happened to that bright smile of yours, dear? It lit up rooms and lifted spirits."

Sighing heavily, I shove my hands through my hair, pushing it from my face. "Sadly Ira, I think it may have been stolen by a dark, brooding man. I don't think he plans on giving it back either, he enjoys toying with it too much, I fear."

"What has that man done to you now?" The remorse in Ira's voice is clear.

Dropping into my chair next to his bed, I cross my arms tight against my chest and focus on the ripped knees of my jeans. "He found a way under my skin and no matter how much I scrub myself clean, I can't rid myself of him."

"You're a strong girl. You can do *anything* you put your mind to. Why do you think you can't find a way to free yourself of Silas?"

Snapping my head up, I meet his insightful eyes. So much knowledge sits in them, the stories he could tell are endless. If only he had the energy and time to tell them. I wish there was a way I could buy him more time.

I shake my head in frustration. "I don't know," I croak. "I have so much anger and hurt toward him right now. *It* should be easy. I have every reason in the world to hate him. But…"

"But?" Ira presses.

"Despite the anger, I don't hate him and that only makes me angrier." It's a vicious circle I can't escape.

Ira's thin, wrinkled hand reaches for mine. "Do you want to know what I think?" When I nod, he continues, voice low and hoarse. "If you truly wanted to rid yourself of him, you would, Quin. You would do it easily and never look back. If you can't find the strength to do it now, it only means something is holding you back from doing just so."

"I don't know what could be holding me back," I whimper, feeling the exhaustion of the whole situation in my bones. "Do you?"

Ira's chuckles turn into raspy pants. "I can't tell you that, dear. That's something you need to find out for yourself."

"They'll be done in the next hour," Della assures me as she finished squeezing yet another lemon. She's making another batch of lemonade because the universe likes to find little ways to remind me of that night.

"Or so they tell me."

Popping the last bite of food in my mouth, I rise from the table. "Okay, I just want them to finish sooner while Ira is still having a good day. He won't want to come down here and see if he starts to feel horrible again." The nurse in me knows it's only a matter of time before he's back to spending his day sleeping the pain away.

"I'll keep going out there to keep the pressure on them. If it helps, I'll keep looking at my watch and sigh dramatically, so they'll hurry," Della promises me, a true smile on her face. Those are rare, but today's an exciting day. She has a good reason to smile.

Ira's roses are here, and they're being planted as we speak.

"Sounds like a plan." I laugh, tossing my plate into the dishwasher. "Holler when they're done, I'll go sit with Ira while we wait."

Walking the halls back to the stairs, I take in the beautiful features of the house. Even after over a month of being here, the design of the house never ceases to amaze me. The original features mix perfectly with the modern updates and touches. No doubt whoever Silas paid to make the renovations was a talented individual.

Taking the curved staircase back upstairs, I pause at the top. The internal debate I have with myself each time I stand here starts up again. One direction will take me to the wing where Ira's and my bedrooms are, the other will take me to Silas's forbidden wing.

Biting my lip, I battle with myself as I stare down the hallway that is always so quiet. Devoid of any life or movement. I'm not convinced Silas even lives here, it's so still down there. He's gone till the wee hours of the morning doing hell knows what, and during the day, I have no idea where he is. Come to think of it, I've never seen him during the daytime hours. So that begs the question, is he even here during the day?

The need to find out drives me forward.

Halfway down the hallway, I expect an alarm system to start blaring and red lights to start flashing, but they never come. The only sound is the pounding of my blood rushing in my ears as my adrenaline spikes.

This is a bad idea. I *know* this, but I don't stop until I reach the doors that I know lead to Silas's office.

My time in there my first night here is a total blur, I just remember it distinctly smelling of his cologne.

Creeping silently to the door, I press my ear to the wood and wait. Just like I expected, there is no movement, not even the slightest rustle of papers moving across a desk. I wouldn't go as far as to say that it's safe for me to go in there now, this house is never safe, but if I'm actually going to follow through with this, now is my chance.

Holding my breath, I turn the door handle and slip inside before I lose my nerve. Slowly, I close the door behind me as softly as I can so no one hears it. I can't imagine Della would be any happier with me than Silas would if she found me in here snooping.

Yes, snooping. I'm a big enough person to admit that's exactly what I'm doing.

Three out of the four walls are made of dark—almost black—bookcases. Each shelf is lined with books and other random knickknacks, but knowing the kind of man Silas is, I highly doubt they are pointless or useless objects. I'm sure each of the items is worth more than any car I could ever afford. In the middle of the room is the desk he sat at when he told me I was going to be a permanent prisoner here, it had felt like a death sentence at the time.

Starting on the right side of the room, I begin tiptoeing around the space. Occasionally, the hardwoods under my feet creak and each time they do, I pause, thinking someone has heard and they're going to barge in at any time, but they never do.

His books vary from first editions of the classics that my fingers at my sides itch to touch, to historical biographies by significant historical figures. Some of those books look just as old as the classics, their spines worn and colors faded with time.

I'm not totally sure what I'm searching for in here other than just some insight on the man that's stolen me and captivated my every thought.

What's clear right off the bat is Silas is a neat freak. Not a completely shocking revelation, considering nothing on his person is ever out of place. Not a single hair on his head is ever wild. His black suits he wears daily never have a speck of lint or fuzz on them. Meanwhile, a lint roller is my best friend and ten minutes outside makes my hair frizzy. I'm a mess compared to Silas.

Running my finger along one of the shelves, there's not even a hint of dust in sight. Does that mean he allows Della to come in here and clean? I can't exactly see Silas on his hands and knees scrubbing these floors.

I was right. The little knickknacks all look to be artifacts from all over the world. Unlike the gift shop souvenirs most would bring back, it looks like Silas collects only the real stuff. Metal coins that look to be from France from many, many years ago sit in a shadow box. Not far from those is another small display case that ancient-looking skeleton keys are kept in. I wonder what they once opened? Surely Silas isn't keeping them because they open something insignificant. A sword, the metal has long ago lost its sheen, sits in a case on one of the taller shelves, worn books anchoring each side of the glass case.

The items are everywhere, and each time I turn around, I find new ones. It would take more time than I have now to look at everything. Peeking through the dark curtains covering the windows, I find his office sits over the courtyard. The men hired to plant the flowers look like they're nearly done, I'm running out of time.

Scanning the room, something catches my eye.

Tucked between a wall and the last bookcase is a narrow door. It's made from the same wood as the shelves, making it almost blend in. It's clear to me that this was done purposefully. Silas doesn't want to bring attention to this door, which only intrigues me further.

I half expect the door to be locked, but I find the ornate metal doorknob turns easily. At first, I figure that whatever is in here can't be that important if he doesn't lock the door, but then I remember he has no reason to need a lock. No one would dare be stupid enough to snoop through his office.

No one but me.

I was always daring, never backed down from anything, but I never sought out danger. Not until I met Silas. Now, here I am, literally in the heart of the wolf's den knowing that if I get caught my ass is as good as dead. Even knowing that, it doesn't stop me from entering through the narrow door.

The room is pitch black and freezing. My hand blindly reaches for the light switch. Fumbling around for a minute, my fingers finally brush against the cool plastic of the switch.

I don't know what I was expecting to find. In all honesty, given what I know about Silas, there could have been a tiny torture chamber in here and I wouldn't have been surprised in the least. However, I am shocked to find there's nothing in here but a set of stairs made of stone. They don't lead up to the attic. They lead down, because *of course* the mystery staircase would lead down into dark nothingness.

I would expect *nothing* less at this point.

CHAPTER 20

Quincey

Anxiously, my fingers tap on the sides of my bare legs. The cool air coming from the stairs makes goose bumps break out across my legs. Looking back into the office, I contemplate my next move. How far am I willing to go today? Ira is waiting for me to come back and Della could come looking for me at any second. *Worse*. Silas could show up and those threats of punishment could become a reality.

Scoffing, I brush off any concern over seeing Silas today. He's been avoiding me like the plague. I haven't seen his devastatingly handsome face since the night he kissed me with such urgency it was as if, in that very moment, he needed me to breathe. I could lie and say it didn't feel that way for me too, but what's the point? That kiss made me feel more alive than I have in years. The kiss stole my breath but gave me life at the same time. It's devastating to feel that way when I know he doesn't feel the same way. He only reinforced his opinion on the matter by completely disappearing for the past two weeks.

"Fuck," I mutter before steeling myself before taking the first step down.

The stairwell is tight, just barely wide enough for one person to descend. I imagine it's a tight fit for someone like Silas, I'm half his size and I have just inches of spare room on either side of me. I thank my lucky stars I'm not claustrophobic because this would *not* be a fun time. There are more steps than a normal staircase. They lead to the basement or cellar of the house. I knew there had to be one here, but it wasn't on my approved list of places I could go.

Neither was Silas's office, but here you are, dumbass.

I expect the cellar to be just as dark as the stairs, but instead I find a short hallway with lanterns hanging from hooks on the walls, their soft light leading the way. The musty smell of the damp earth is strong down here and the faint sound of water dripping somewhere echoes through the stone walls.

Suddenly feeling like I've found myself on the set of a bad horror movie where the dumb heroine puts herself in a dangerous situation, I begin to turn back. The warning bells in my head are going off like crazy and being down here just feels *wrong*. And not just because Silas told me not to, there's something about the energy down here that makes chills run down my spine.

The soft light coming from the room just a ways farther is what makes me halt my retreat and cautiously continue on.

I've come this far. I might as well know what he's hiding down here. As long as it's not a living person being held hostage like I originally theorized weeks ago, I can handle it.

Holding the air in my lungs, I walk through the stone archway into the room. Immediately, I come to a screeching halt as confusion sets in my bones.

"What the hell..." I breathe as my eyes slowly work over what's before me.

Built into the walls are glass cases, just like the items in his office, the items are on display, but this is different. The items down here aren't being shown off like they are upstairs, no they're being *preserved.* Like a museum, the items are in cases that are climate and temperature regulated. The control panels on the walls are evidence of this and so is the faint humming coming from each of them. Soft blue light illuminates each one of them, bathing the rest of the room in a blue hue.

The items are old. Centuries older than I am.

In one case, there are a couple dresses. One is beige, but if I had to guess, it was once white. Over the years, the linens and silks have changed colors. Parts of it even yellowish, but despite this, I know once upon a time, it was a stunning piece of clothing. Next to it is a blue and gold masterpiece that probably took hundreds of hours to create.

Why the hell would Silas preserve dresses? With a quick scan of the rest of the case, I find it's not just dresses and shoes. It's all kinds of women's belongings. An ornate metal comb sits next to a pretty glass bottle I assume once held perfume. On the glass shelf below, is a change purse of sorts. A simple gold ring sits lonely on its own shelf, whatever stone that once sat in the empty setting is long gone.

Completely engrossed, I slowly move around the room. In some of the other cases, are men's clothes and accessories. Unlike the women's attire, the men's look like there are pieces from various centuries and times. There're even a few weapons, also ranging in their time periods. The daggers are ornate, medieval-looking, but the revolver looks like one on display at the World War II exhibit we took a field trip to in high school.

Coming to the conclusion that Silas is just a weird, closeted, history buff, I begin to relax. It looks like cooking in the middle of the night isn't his only hobby, collecting artifacts from dead people is also one of his pastimes.

"So, he's just a big fucking *nerd.*" How disappointing. I thought I would find something about him that would help me better understand him, but all I've found is he's got a boring fascination with the past. "You couldn't have been interested in serial killers like the rest of us?

That would have been more… *interesting*…" The words slowly die on my tongue as I come to the next case. "What the *actual* fuck?"

It's not as clear and obvious as it's not a digital picture like I'm used to, but there is still no denying what I'm seeing. I wish there was a way I could rebuff it or brush it off as coincidence, but I simply can't, because part of Silas engraving himself into my soul is that I will never forget his face. For the rest of my life, I will be able to find him in crowds of thousands, his dark soul calls to me like a beacon in the night. Even if I couldn't see his whole face, I could recognize him by those midnight eyes of his.

Gasping, I back away from the case, my shaking hands covering my mouth. My brain searches for a plausible explanation for what I'm looking at, but I can't come up with a single one. The idea that the man in the painting is just a distant relative is an idea, but even as I think it, it doesn't feel right.

He doesn't look exactly like he does now. The clothes are wrong, the hair is wrong, hell even the facial hair is wrong, but it's Silas. It's *impossible* for it to be him, but nonetheless, the man in the painting in front of me is *my* Silas.

The man in the painting looks content—a look foreign to the man I know.

The darkness and anger that swirls around Silas like a gloomy shadow are absent from this painting. While the eyes are the same color, the heaviness and burden that are constant features in Silas's aren't there. Silas has never seemed to enjoy another's company, but it appears that he did *hers*.

The woman he stands proudly behind with his hand on her shoulder is unknown to me, but she wears a gentle smile on her face. Her dark hair is pulled up, the perfectly curled tendrils hang on either side of her face. Even with the inability to truly capture someone's expression during that time, she looks happy.

They look happy together.

She means something to him. Something about her is special to him.

Only when I'm about to pull my eyes away from the painting, do I make the startling revelation. Turning to the case I'd just left minutes before; I confirm what my brain is trying to tell me. The pretty woman in the painting is wearing the blue dress that sits preserved in the case behind me.

No, that doesn't make sense.

The confusion only builds the longer I'm in here. There's only one case left and against my better judgment, my feet carry me there slowly. This one holds more pictures, the longer I stare at them the more my body trembles.

"It's not possible," I whisper to myself over and over again.

The paintings turn into photographs as the years go by. Each year the technology progresses, growing and changing with time, but the subject of them never changes. Never grows older. His style changes and his wardrobe adapts, but in each picture, he's exactly the same.

In the span of centuries, the man—*Silas*—never changes. It's as if he's frozen in time, forever stuck the way he is.

"But it's not possible," because if it were, that would mean he's… "*Immortal*."

And there is no such thing as immortality. People have been chasing it since the dawn of time to no avail. If it were out there, we *would know* about it. In the age of science and technology, if there were immortals, the world *would know*.

But how can I argue with physical evidence in front of me? *I can't and that's the problem.*

He acts as if he's untouchable—*indestructible*. He doesn't write like he's from this time and sometimes, he doesn't speak like he's from this time. If what's before me is true, this would make him centuries old.

"It's not possible."

Sixty years I've worked for Mr. Laurent… Ira's earlier comment floats through my mind. I shrugged it off as just being the byproduct of pain medication and senility, but now I'm not so sure.

Shaking my head, I slowly back away from the wall of perfectly preserved history. I feel like I'm going to be sick. The chills I had when I first came down here are long gone. The adrenaline has made me hot and sweat coats my skin.

When my back connects with something, the surprised yelp that escapes me bounces off the walls. I spin around so fast my head spins. The relief I feel when I don't find anyone standing there is short-lived because sitting before me is a small black mini fridge. It reminds me of the ones that would be in a college dorm, but what is it doing down here?

Don't open it. You're not going to like what you see.

It seems to be a theme of the day to ignore my inner voice, so why stop now? With a long sigh, I kneel in front of the door and with shaky fingers, I slowly open it. Part of me expects for something to jump out at me. It would be par for the course at this point, but to my relief, nothing happens.

I'd hoped it was just a refrigerator Silas used to store his booze. That may have been a selfish hope stemming from me feeling like I need to drown my thoughts in vodka right now. Utterly disappointed, the only things I find inside are bags of fresh blood.

Blood.

Just like the empty bags I saw in the waste bin weeks ago.

Finally, my knees give out and I drop to my ass on the stone floor as the most insane thought crosses my mind. I can't help but laugh at it, but the sound is anything but humorous. It's almost pained.

Was she fucking right this whole time?

My mom tried to convince me it was all real when I was younger, that the monsters in the night were truly out there and I did have something to be afraid of. As a child I believed her tales, but eventually I wised up, and concluded she was nothing but an alcoholic, spinning fairy tales for money. That has been my *truth* for over a decade, and the possibility that she's been right this whole time is too much for me to handle.

He doesn't age. I've only seen him during the day. He's incredibly strong and fast. *The blood…*

If Mom's been right, that means I've been living in a world full of monsters.

That means I've been living under the same roof as one.

It means I kissed a…

"*Vampire.*"

CHAPTER 21

Quincey

Ever had a world-shattering, life-changing, revelation that literally knocks you on your ass? I thought my world had been rocked enough in the last month, but it turns out the universe has decided to throw me one last curveball just as a little *fuck you.*

Vampires.

This is just the cherry on top of my downward spiral. There was a time I didn't think I was going to make it out of this house alive, now I'm not sure I'm going to make it out of here with my sanity intact. I'm pretty sure I've been booked a non-refundable ticket to the funny farm and at this point, I may go willingly. Straitjacket and padded mittens no longer needed.

By some miracle, I got out of the creepy basement *shrine* and Silas's office without being caught. So maybe the universe hasn't decided to totally fuck me in the ass just yet and someone is still out there looking out for me. I checked in on Ira and when I found him peacefully working

I've been hiding in here ever since, but the sound of my bedroom door opening and high heels clicking against the hardwood of my bedroom tells me my time is up.

The footsteps come to an abrupt stop in the doorway. "What's wrong with you now?" Della's irritated voice fills the small room.

Slowly, almost lazily, I drag my eyes away from the tiny scuff mark I've been fixating on for however long I've been in here. She stands with her hands on her hips, staring down her nose at me. "Della, I don't even have enough time to begin to explain to you why I don't have enough time to explain that to you."

"What are you yapping on about now, girl?" Her eyes roll behind her cat-glasses. "Why are you hiding in your closet?"

That's a valid question and I'm not quite sure why I'm lying flat on my back on the floor of my walk-in closet. It felt right when I walked into my room after leaving the mystery room behind. "Can't you tell? I'm having a nervous breakdown. Felt like I was owed one, you know? And what better place to have one than in the solitude of my closet where no one can witness my existential crisis."

"Well can you hurry it along? They're all done," Della says impatiently. "We can show Ira now."

Right... the roses.

With a dramatic sigh, I slowly pull myself up so I'm leaning back on my elbows. "Sure, Della, anything for you."

"*Mmm hmm*," she mumbles, clearly not convinced.

In her defense, that's fair.

I begin to pull myself up the rest of the way, but pause. "Will he be there?" Not knowing who I mean, Della just gives me a bored, blank stare. "Will Silas be there?" I all but choke on his name when I say it.

Della shakes her head. "No, he's still staying at his apartment in the city. He'll see the flowers when he comes back."

Apartment in the city? "That's where he's been the past two weeks? He hasn't been home at all?"

"No," she confirms. "He said he had some business to attend to. Which is odd for him, but what do I know?"

"*Business*," I repeat like a fucking parrot. "Sure, okay."

She gives me an incredulous look. "Is there another reason you know about as to why Silas wouldn't want to come home?"

Tapping my chin a few times for effect, I pretend to really think her question over. "You know, now that you mention it, there may have been a *little* incident. Totally not a big deal or anything to write home about." *Liar, liar, panties on fire.* "I'm pretty sure he's avoiding me because of it."

It's for the best, especially after today. I don't have any desire to be around him and honestly, the need to get as far away from this house as possible is strong. If I didn't already know that all exits have been locked down tight, I would be running for the hills right now. I have nowhere to run, which is why I'm hiding in my closet.

"What did you do to him now that he's avoiding you?"

I gape at her, appalled she's pinning this on me. "I resent that statement, Della. Why do you always think that *I* did something?"

"Because you're always doing something to anger that man."

My shoulder lifts apathetically. "What can I say? I'm only human." Feeling bold, but also desperate, I lock eyes with her. "But can we say the same for him?"

I'm playing with fire, but I want to see her reaction—I want her to confirm my theory. Theory isn't the right word. I have all the evidence I'll ever need, but I still need the validation that this isn't all the doing of my over-imaginative brain.

She hides it well, but the soft inhale and slight widening of her eyes tells me all I want to know. Della covers it fast, her surprise is quickly replaced with a stern, impatient look. "Ira's roses are waiting."

Pursing my lips, I nod once. "Of course, we don't want to wait too long. As you know, nothing good happens after sundown."

She doesn't hide her nerves as well the second time around.

Ira's eyes light up more than I've ever seen them as we roll his wheelchair into the courtyard. The look of pure happiness on his face is something I'll never forget. I'll look back on my time here and always remember this minute. The bad memories of this place will take up most of the space, but this will always be a prevalent highlight.

I couldn't take away his pain or cancer, but I could put a smile back on his face and sometimes that just has to be enough. The little things are sometimes the biggest.

Della stands behind his chair, beaming at the newly planted flowers. They're stunning now, but I know they'll be even prettier when they all bloom.

"You did this for me?" Ira chokes out. His green eyes look at me briefly before returning to the flowers.

Smiling back, I tell him, "Well, I wouldn't say *I* did it. Silas made it happen, it was just my idea."

Tears fall down his face. Pulling out one of the tissues I'd stuck in my pocket just in case, I gently wipe them from his face, all while being careful of the oxygen cannula.

"Just the fact that you got Silas to do something like this…" He trails off, his head shaking in disbelief. "It just means you truly are a miracle worker."

Della nods her head in agreement, but when she notices me looking at her, she's quick to turn her head. She's avoided any form of eye contact since we left my closet. Even as she helped me prep Ira to bring him down here, she never once met my eye. I know she thinks by acting like this she's keeping his secret, but she's only further confirming it.

"The real test is going to be if I'm able to keep them alive." I chuckle, though it feels forced now. "You're going to have to talk me through it because I won't lie, I've killed many plants in my time." I'm not sure why I tell him this, because if given the opportunity, I'm getting the hell out of here. This is my first time outside since that night, if it were possible, I would take off right now, but Silas's property sits far out by itself, there's nowhere for me to go. I could try, but I have a sneaking suspicion I'd only get lost in my attempt.

Ira gives me a crooked smile. "I'll tell you everything you need to know."

"I'm counting on it." *Tell me about your roses, but more importantly, tell me about your boss.*

CHAPTER 22

Silas

The building that once stood in front of me used to hold millions of dollars worth of equipment and now it's nothing but a smoking pile of debris and ash. They couldn't get to my guns and drugs, so they've started coming after my legitimate businesses. This building held machinery for a construction company I own under a pseudonym, it's not common knowledge that it's one of mine, yet somehow these bastards knew.

The flashing lights of the fire trucks bounce off the rubble in front of me, the scent of wet earth and smoke fill my nose as I watch the firefighters attempt to put out the last of the flames.

Duke stands silently at my side, his own anger mixing with mine in the air around us. He's a loyal man and these attacks are wearing on him just as much as they are me. His sense of duty and his inability to find the people responsible adding to his frustration. Duke has many skills, but his ability to track and find people is unparalleled. A skill that was once esteemed during his time in a special ops unit, but it's a skill that is invaluable to me now. It's the original reason I brought him on as an employee, his loyalty and the strong work ethic of his coming secondary. I have big things planned for him that I'm slowly putting into motion.

"It took a lot of time and resources for them to learn of your involvement in this company," Duke finally mutters lowly, but he knows I can hear him just fine. "Whoever's behind this is highly motivated and money isn't an object to them. They're also not concerned about who gets hurt in the process."

The coroner is loading up the two bodies of the employees who we presume were accidentally trapped inside. Innocent bystanders who did not deserve that kind of death. Unfortunate.

"Who did you piss off this much that they'd go to these kinds of extremes to ruin you?" Duke asks.

"I left a trail of angry people behind me to get to where I am. It could be any one of them." The climb to the top was a bloody one. There was not a single person I wouldn't have cut down to reach my goal. "They have been at this for months, they're clearly getting frustrated and lashing out at the easier targets." My dealings in the underworld are better protected, as they discovered when they went after my shipping container. "This tells me they're driven by their emotions rather than money. If they were doing this for money, they would have stolen the equipment inside, not burned it."

"The attack on the firewall at Blackwood last week was almost successful. If Rory hadn't been there and stopped it, it would have been detrimental to you and that company." Blackwood is a tech company that has been a pioneer in advancing technology through the decades. One of the positive parts of living as long as I have is being able to be present for the creations that have made the world the thing it is now.

Being around as long as I have also means I have been able to invest money in many different industries. Some legal, many not. This just means I have multiple businesses these fuckers can go after to get to me.

"Lock it all down, Duke," I finally order. "Bring in more people, I don't care where you pull them from as long as they're briefed and standing guard over my assets in the next twenty-four hours."

"I'm on it."

"Let's go." I turn, leaving the burning remains behind me. All those items are easily replaceable, but that's not the point. By executing such a blatant—*obvious*—attack on me, they're giving others the idea that I can be trifled with. *That* is something I will not stand for.

"Are we headed back to the house yet?" Duke asks. I've been around him long enough to know that's not the real question he's asking. He wants to know when I'll return to Quincey. I haven't opened up to him about the events that took place, but he's not blind. He's annoyingly observant. "It's been two weeks."

A low growl cuts through the air between us. "You do not have to tell me how long it's been since I've been there." Or how long it's been since I laid eyes on her. Time is irrelevant to me—it means nothing. A year for me passes quicker than a month does for a human. I don't give the idea of time much thought, but I've all but been counting down the minutes since I was last with Quincey. I feel every single second apart from her in my soul.

The past two weeks have been the longest I've experienced in decades. Two weeks feels like months and it's taken everything in me to not return home to her. The only thing stopping me is knowing that I'm a danger to her.

When I brought Quincey in, I didn't think her safety would end up being such a concern of mine. Besides a few obvious exceptions, the well-being of my staff isn't something that weighs heavy on me. Mainly that's due to me knowing that in the long run, humans are expendable. They grow old—sick. I can't depend on them to be around for a long time.

She was supposed to be a means to an end, not something that consumes my every blood cell. She was not supposed to be something that has enthralled me to no return. And because of this, I cannot be the one who puts her in harm's way.

She is a safe haven for many, and I am a threat to all.

"They put the flowers in today. I'm sure Ira would like to see you and thank you for them." Duke presses on when we climb into the car. "Della sent a text; said he was the happiest he's been since his diagnosis after seeing what you did for him."

"It was not just me," I correct him stiffly. "I'm pleased to hear he enjoyed them, Miss Page should be proud of herself for putting the plan into motion."

"*Miss Page*," Duke mocks, rolling his eyes. "You need to get over yourself with that one. You just use that name to keep her in the safe little box you've placed her in, but I hate to tell you, that ship has sailed. The box has been blown to bits and there's no taping it back together."

"Duke..." I warn.

Not surprising, he elects to ignore me. "You're very old and you've lived a long time, but have you truly lived? You have the opportunity to experience the best things in life for… *eternity*… and you're wasting it on being bitter and angry. I'm not saying she has to be your forever, but I'm saying she could be a bright spot in your very dark life if you'd stop being a dumbass and pushing her away."

"Even if I wanted it, she could never be my forever." She will eventually grow old, and I'll remain the same. I'll have to watch yet another woman in my life die. "You know this."

Duke shrugs apathetically. "A rule that only exists because of you."

"It's in place for a reason," I snap irritably at him. "Or should I remind you of what happens when it's not strictly enforced?" Duke and his family know firsthand the devastating events that occur when the rule is broken.

He swallows hard, his Adam's apple moving in his neck. "No, I'm more than aware of what could happen, but Silas, it's not a guaranteed outcome."

"It's not worth the risk."

Duke is silent for a moment before he softly says, "The best things in life are worth every risk, even if they scare the shit out of you."

In the pitch black of the bedroom in my condo, I watch the screen in front of me. The video feed is from today from the exterior cameras placed on the house.

I could have been there today. Della offered to wait till after sundown to have the reveal for Ira, but I repeatedly turned her down. Now I'm not sure I should have.

I haven't experienced the emotion of regret for a long time but having to watch the way Quincey's face lights up as she shows Ira his gift through the screen in front of me instead of in person fills me with remorse. I gave up the opportunity to revel in that smile, to feel the warmth on my skin as it radiated off of her.

Two weeks apart from her should have been easier than it's been. Instead of focusing on the work I have before me, I find myself thinking of her. The threat that is somehow evading me and my team should be my main focus—*my priority*—but she's taking up my every thought.

It's been two weeks since our kiss, and yet, her sweet taste still remains on my tongue. No matter how many times I've showered, her scent lingers on my body. My sleep is fitful. I wake up frequently because I swear I hear her whispering my name softly in my ear.

The dreams of her lying limply on my bed, blood pouring from her delicate neck haven't stopped. If anything, they've only become more vivid and intense since I tasted her blood in real life. Part of me believes that they are no longer dreams, but instead premonitions of what will happen if I don't keep my distance.

The distance isn't supposed to be painful, and yet I ache for her.

I should be sleeping right now. The sun has long ago risen, but I can't turn my attention away from the video feed. After watching the feed from yesterday when they showed Ira his new roses, I pull up the live feed because it appears I've become a glutton for punishment when it comes to her.

Ira sits in his wheelchair in the courtyard. His eyes are closed, but his lips turn up as he listens to Quincey. On a plaid blanket on the ground, in a white sundress, Quincey reads to Ira from the book in her lap.

The morning sun shines down on them, her long golden hair all but glows around her shoulders and back. Ira mumbles something that makes her face split in two, her white teeth shine as she laughs at him.

The sense of longing hits me like a train. Even if I were to give in to temptation, we will never be able to sit in the sun, enjoying the warmth of it on our skin together. Our time together will be limited to the night—to darkness. That isn't fair to her.

It's something I can't take from her. This is a life, if given the choice, I never would have made for myself.

I miss the sun.

Quincey is my own personal sun now. Her warmth and heat burn me to my soul, but the pain is welcome. I can only hope I don't become the reason she loses her light.

CHAPTER 23

Quincey

"I'm not following," I repeat as Della rambles instructions to me over the phone. She's barely taken a breath since I answered her call, and the longer she talks the more confused I get. "Just back up a second. Where have you been all day? Are you coming in at all today?"

I elect to ignore her aggravated sigh. "No, I will be, but I had a personal thing to take care of and won't be there until later," Della explains, sounding flustered, an odd tone for her. She's usually calm—totally in control. I'm not sure why she's so bent out of shape about not being here today.

"Okay…" I drawl in the phone that is tucked between my ear and shoulder as I clean up the used medical supplies on my tray. "You're very important and a lovely person to be around Della but I think Ira and I have managed to feed and clean up after ourselves just fine." Ira nods in agreement when I glance up at him. We've spent the past two days out in the courtyard, enjoying the sun and roses. Today he's beat after exerting the extra energy, knowing this, he'll end up sleeping on and off most of the day.

"Contrary to popular belief, my job isn't always just cooking and cleaning, Quincey," she huffs. "I run different errands for Silas and today I was supposed to go pick something up for him, but it would appear I will not be able to make it in time to do so today. I had a… *family* emergency."

"So? Can't you just go tomorrow?"

"No, this is a… *delicate*… matter and fairly time-sensitive. It has to be done today and at the time originally agreed upon," she insists.

"Once again, I'm not following. Why are you telling me this? This sounds like something you need to work out with Silas." With one last look at Ira, I quietly leave his room to continue this conversation in the hall.

"No, that's the thing, I don't want Silas to find out about this little mix-up." There's a long pause before she continues, sounding completely put out by what she says, "I'm asking for a favor here, Quincey. I wouldn't ask this of you unless I really needed help, but I'm in a bind right now."

I never thought I'd see the day that Della wanted my help. She won't even let me help chop vegetables in the kitchen because she's such a control freak. Whatever this errand is, it's a big deal.

"I don't know how I'm supposed to help you from the house, Della." I pace up and down the hallway as I listen.

"In twenty minutes, a car service is coming to pick you up from the house, don't worry, I've already taken care of giving the driver the address you're going to. You'll wait under the green sign and someone will come by with a package. You'll take it and get back into the car that will be waiting for you down the street. You'll be home just in time for dinner tonight."

My pacing comes to an abrupt halt. "Della, this sounds like some sketchy drug deal. Absolutely not, I'm not doing this."

My job here is to take care of Ira, not partake in whatever illegal activities Silas is entangled with. *I'm too cute for jail, thank you very much.*

"No, no, Quincey, I swear on my mama's life that it's not drugs," Della assures me, but it does little to ease my concerns.

"Then what is it?"

"I can't tell you that."

"Of course, you can't," I snap. "I swear to God, this house runs on hostility and secrets. Every single one of you is exhausting to be around. I don't know how you keep all your lies straight, Della."

"It's taken many years of practice, I'll give you that." I want to ask just how many years. If Ira has been here over sixty, how long has Della worked for Silas? I would bet money it's longer than I've been alive. "Just in case you're tempted and knowing your obscenely high level of curiosity, you will, you should know the package will be locked. I have the only key to unlock it, so don't even try it."

Well crap.

This confirms it. Della might be a mind reader.

"This whole thing seems wildly suspicious." I catch myself before I can bring my hand up to my mouth to chew nervously on my nail. It's a habit I've been working on breaking. "What am I supposed to do with Ira? I can't leave him here alone."

"Constance is coming to sit with him, he hates her but with any luck, she'll only be with him for an hour or so until I get there."

Ira filled me in on who Constance was within my first week of being here. She's a night nurse Silas hired to watch over Ira when things got really bad. Ira never meshed with her, which is why they started looking for other options. *Enter me stage left.*

"He's going to be pissed." Between the gap in his open door, I watch Ira as he naps soundly. Maybe he'll sleep through her being here. "But fine, I'll do it."

I can almost feel Della's relief through the phone. "Thank you. I'll have my phone, call me if you run into any problems." Just as I'm about to end the call, she stops me by uttering a warning. "I don't have to tell you what will happen if you think you can use this as an opportunity to run away from him. You and I both know you're starting to grasp just who he is and what he's capable of."

My hand tightens on the phone. "Are we going to keep skirting around that discussion or are we finally going to discuss it?"

Her response is to hang up on me.

Real polite, Della. Your mama would be proud of those manners of yours.

For a city I lived in for most of my life, I feel like a stranger in it now. The streets I know like the back of my hand feel foreign to me after only a month of being away from them. I should have known this meet-up would take place back in the Quarter. Della swears up and down that this isn't illegal, but like anything that involves Silas, it's all very cloak and dagger. What better place to have a secret exchange than the busy streets of the French Quarter where everyone is too busy or too drunk to notice it's happening.

The driver dropped me off in front of the location. It's an empty storefront with plywood in the windows, the green sign that once held the business's name sways from its hooks above me.

Della told me someone would come with the package, but she never told me how long I'd have to wait here for them to show up. In the time I've spent leaning against this brick building, I've thought about running away no less than fifteen times. St. Sin is just blocks away—*Lucy* is just blocks away.

I've never needed my friend more than I do now. Even if I can't really tell her anything, just seeing her again would make me feel better. The impulse to run to her and proclaim my sudden belief in vampires is a hard one to fight. Della's parting comment about knowing who I'm dealing with stops me from doing it. Without a doubt, Silas has no limits to how far he'll go to protect his secrets.

You haven't even confirmed it, Q. This is all just a crazy theory in your head, the rational part of my brain scolds me.

Groaning, I lean my head back on the hard brick behind me and let the last bits of sunlight warm my skin. Now is the opportunity I've been waiting for to get away from it all, but the overbearing curiosity over this package has me sticking around. I'll see what it is and *then* I'll go.

Della said it was locked, but just how locked could it possibly be?

My question is answered when a surprisingly young guy appears out of nowhere in front of me. In his hands is a high-tech looking metal briefcase. Cautiously, I stand up straighter and eye the man warily.

He lifts his chin at me in greeting. "Della said some blonde chick in a ratty T-shirt would be meetin' me. That you?"

Self-consciously, I glance at my old, oversized, concert T-shirt. I'd tucked the front part into my torn-up shorts to make it look less big. It's a little disturbing that without even seeing me, Della knew what I'd be wearing. My limited clothing options have been on constant rotation and she's clearly been keeping track. "That's me."

His dark eyes flick over me quickly before he shrugs. "Cool, this is for you." He holds the case up for me to take, and when I don't immediately reach out to take it from him, he shakes it at me with a huff. "I don't got all day, lady."

Reluctantly, I take the case from him. It's heavier than I thought it'd be and nothing in it rattles or makes any noise.

With a two-finger salute, the man disappears into the crowd without looking back at me.

Case in hand, I think over my next moves. The lock on it doesn't look as complicated as I thought at first glance. Honestly, with a bobby pin or piece of wire, I could have this open in minutes. I didn't learn a lot from my mom or dad, but picking a lock is something that came in handy. Especially when the landlord would change the locks of our trailer when my mom didn't have the cash to pay the rent. When my mom was too drunk to do it herself, I'd pick the lock to let us back in. Eventually she'd con enough money to pay the guy, but it was a vicious circle that never ended.

I don't want to open the case right here on the street or in some alley. St. Sin comes to mind. I can sneak in really quick and use their bathroom or break room to open the case. Risky, but my mind is made up.

With my head down, I head in the opposite direction of the car that Della sent me. Intoxicated people run into me, slurring their apologies to me as I go. On the clock and quickly running out of time, I pick up my pace, not giving a shit when dirty looks are passed in my direction.

One of the promoters trying to get people to come drink at the bar he works in gets in my way. As he gets in my personal space, trying to smooth talk and bribe me into entering the bar, I try my best to politely tell him no and get around him. But he's annoyingly persistent.

The hair on the back of my neck rises as my anxiety increases. Feeling slightly paranoid, I glance over my shoulder at the crowd behind me, I don't expect to find a man with a hood over his head already looking at me.

Thinking it's just a fluke, I stare back at him, but he doesn't flinch or make any move to turn away. Instead, his eyes trail down my body until they lock onto the case in my hand.

Oh shit.

Call it intuition, but instantly I know what's about to happen. Without a second thought or glance back at him, I take off like a bullet through the crowd. Déjà vu to the night that Gallo's men chased me hits me, but this time, I don't think Duke or Silas will be able to come to my rescue. The only person who knows I'm here is Della and she's an hour away.

Thankfully, I'm wearing my slip-on tennis shoes this time instead of my pumps, I move faster and easier. I can't believe that this is happening to me again. The constant fearing for my life bullshit is getting old.

On pure instinct, I continue on the path to St. Sin, but I quickly decide that isn't a good plan. Who knows what kind of weapons this man has on him. The last thing I want to do is lead an armed man into the bar my best friend works at.

On a desperate whim, I dash into the souvenir shop as I pass it. I have no idea if he saw me slip in here and I'm not about to lose my momentum and check behind me.

I've been in this shop before, I know there's a back exit I can leave through. The woman working the register yells at me for running through her store. Without looking at her, I offer an apology over my shoulder as I slam through the back metal door.

I don't stop when I make it to the back alley. My legs keep pushing me faster and faster through the narrow space. I'm not sure what direction I'm headed now, but I don't stop moving.

Clumsily, I reach for my phone in my back pocket. I don't care that this call is about to land me in an ass-load of trouble, I need help and he's the best chance I've got.

The sound of the line ringing is barely audible over the rushing of adrenaline in my ears. My ragged breathing also makes it hard to hear when he finally picks up the line. "Quincey? What's going on?"

"Duke!" I shout. "I don't have time to answer questions. I just need you to listen to me."

"Are you running? What's all that noise?" He can clearly hear the bustling sound of streets around me.

"No questions!" I bark at him. "Della sent me instead of her to pick up whatever it is that Silas asked her to get. The metal case, Duke, I have the metal case and I'm being chased because of it."

There's a loud bang on his side of the phone, followed by a harsh curse. "What the fuck! Where are you now?"

"I'm running up St. Louis now, but I don't know where I should go, Duke." Panic bubbles up in my chest and my world starts to become hazy, my brain no longer able to focus on anything but keeping me moving forward.

"Shit, he's going to lose his fucking mind," I barely hear Duke mumble. "Q, listen to me, keep moving, don't stop. I'm coming for you, make it to the—"

I didn't see the group of drunk tourists until it was too late. I slam into them like a freight train, sending a group of us to the ground. My knee and hands burn in pain as I skid across the concrete on my stomach. People yell and shout, but I don't really hear what they say. My focus is getting to the case that has flown a few feet in front of me. My phone is nowhere to be seen in the fray of bodies and feet around me.

As fast as possible, I scramble to my feet. My fingers just circle around the handle of the metal case when I spot him, and this time he's not alone.

"*Shit.*"

The two men nod to each other, silently communicating with each other as they plan their attack. Like predators coming for their prey. In a desperate attempt to slow them down, I scream, "Help! They're trying to hurt me! Someone stop them!"

People passing by slow down and stare at the men I point at. They whisper amongst themselves, a few of them shift to look in the men's direction. While their attention is on the diversion I created, I make a break for it. Not sure how long my head start will last, I don't waste a single second.

I had no choice but to leave my phone behind. Duke was cut off, I have no idea where he was telling me to go. My only hope is that I can find a place to hide. Duke is resourceful and smart; he'll be able to find me.

I hope.

CHAPTER 24

Quincey

It's been decided, this is the last and only time I'm doing a favor for Della. If I make it out of this, she is *so* getting an earful from me. *Hell,* I might even beat her with this metal briefcase just to get my point across.

The only reason I haven't dropped it and let the men after me have it is because whatever's inside of it is important to Silas. And despite my best efforts and countless reasons not to—the biggest one being the possibility he's a fucking *vampire*—I have a crush on the man, and I don't want to fail him.

Yeah, I admitted it. I have a silly crush on the big scary, king of New Orleans. Just add it to the list of reasons I'm going to hell. Turns out I'm more morally gray than I originally thought.

Horns blare at me as I sprint across the main road. The drivers here are notoriously bad, but with some luck I make it across without being run over. More honking echoes behind me, alerting me that my there's a loud bang that sounds like they slammed their fist into the hood of a car. I don't turn around to confirm this.

The cemetery is in front of me. I could either run around it or run through it. The choice is made up for me when I see the wrought-iron gates are wide open, as if beckoning me inside. The concrete tombs that sit above ground shield out what's left of the setting sun, making my path dim, but I still don't slow down as I weave through the narrow walkways.

I've always hated these aboveground cemeteries in here. The stone is stained from all the storms and hurricanes. Moss grows on them, so much so that the names are no longer visible. Some have fresh flowers left on them, but many of them are so old, any of the loved ones that may have visited here are also long gone. Death, in general, doesn't scare me, but there's something so eerie about being in here.

Footsteps follow behind me in the distance. They're in the cemetery with me, but they're not as close behind as before. My legs burn with exhaustion and the panic makes me tire faster. I don't know how much longer I can run, and my knee is screaming in pain. With each erratic beat of my heart, more blood pours from the cut and down my shin.

A horrible idea comes to mind and my skin crawls with disgust just thinking about following through with it, but this may be my last chance if I have any hope of hiding from them.

A tomb that is meant to hold two coffins is empty. Whoever was laid to rest here originally has been moved, the narrow compartments are just big enough for me to climb into and hide. God knows what else could be hiding in there, all sorts of insects I'm sure.

Thinking fast on my feet, I pick up one of the rocks on the ground and hurl it toward the metal fencing that circles the graveyard. The loud *clank* of it hitting the metal draws their attention in that direction.

With a shutter, I climb into the dark tunnel, moving as far back into it as I can so I'm out of sight. If this doesn't work, I've just gone and single-handedly trapped myself.

"She's not over here!" one of the men calls out. "Did you see what direction she went?"

"I heard something over here," the other replies in a gruff voice.

"She wasn't supposed to be here." Their voices get louder as they wander close to where I'm hiding. My hand covers my mouth to muffle the sound of my breathing. My heart beats so fast in my chest I worry they'll be able to pick up the noise. "Where's the old broad? He said she'd be here. This was supposed to be an easy grab."

"I've never seen the new girl before. I'm not sure where Laurent found her."

"Are you sure we have to kill her? She was hot, hate to see a sweet ass go to waste like that. Do you think he'll mind if we play with her a little before we deliver her body to him?"

"Who says it'll be a waste if she's dead? The way I look at it, she can still be put to use." The other man snickers. "At least that way she won't put up a fight."

Bile builds in my throat and fear slides down my spine like a cold caress.

"I like it when they fight."

"Fine, you take a run at her when she's breathing."

I have to force myself to swallow the vomit that fills my mouth. My eyes water and my hands shake uncontrollably as I listen to their cruel words.

When their shadows come into view, I freeze in place and hold my breath. They're just mere feet away from me.

"She must have made it through the gate on the other side," one mumbles. "Let's go, I don't want to report to him that we lost his target."

I don't breathe until I hear the metal gate slam closed behind them.

The fear that the second I move from this spot they will show back up keeps me in place. For all I know, they've got someone watching the cemetery, and when I exit, someone will be waiting to snatch me up.

So, I stay in the tomb as the day grows darker and darker and only the faintest bit of sun remains in the sky.

I'm dirty, bleeding, and scared. I just want to go home.

Home?

Where even is home to me anymore? Lucy's apartment was never home. I would rather eat rocks than return to my mother's trailer. Silas's house… that's not home either. My apartment in Boston isn't mine anymore. Nothing is mine, hell my life isn't even mine anymore.

First my own father sold me off as collateral to Gallo and then Silas purchased me from him. I've been traded and bartered like I'm nothing more than a piece of livestock. The right to make any decision regarding my own life has been taken away by these men.

My life wasn't sunshine and rainbows before all this happened. I'm not completely sure what I'd be doing now if Silas hadn't stepped in, but I know for a fact I wouldn't be hiding—fearing for my life *again*—in a dark graveyard.

When they've been gone long enough and the only sounds are from the cars driving on the surrounding roads, I ease forward some. It's too dark way back here to see what I'm doing.

I pull out the bobby pin I used this morning to pin back the front pieces of my hair. Now loose, the strands fall forward, sticking to my sweaty skin. After bending it just right, I hold it between my teeth before turning the case so the locking mechanism is visible.

Once again, I'm a little flabbergasted at Silas's lack of security. It's a simple lock—easily pickable. When you're as big and scary as Silas, I guess you start believing that alone will act as enough security. Or he truly thought no one was watching this reoccurring exchange that Della participates in. Either way, the man needs to reconsider some of his safety precautions. I'm a nobody, and after less than three minutes of twiddling with the lock, a satisfying *click* fills my ears.

I pause before opening the case, realizing I didn't think this through. Della swore on her life there weren't drugs in here, but what about something else dangerous? The possibility of there being a bomb floats through my head for all of a second before I decide Silas would never have Della be in charge of explosives. In whatever way that is possible to him, he cares about her and wouldn't put her in that kind of danger. Whatever is in here, he's deemed safe enough for his beloved housekeeper to handle.

Despite knowing this, I hold my breath as I slowly pry the case open.

There's a hissing sound and a *whoosh* of cold air escapes the case when it's first opened, almost like I'd just opened a miniature freezer of sorts.

A dozen or so bags of blood sit inside the insulated case, a couple ice packs sit between the bags to ensure they're kept at the right temperature. They have the same kind of label on them as the ones I found in the mini fridge in the cellar.

This confirms what I already know, Della knows *everything* about Silas. His darkest secrets are trusted with her. Does this mean Duke also knows? I'd bet everything I own that he does.

I'm the only one left in the dark.

This wasn't a drug deal, or an illegal exchange, it was simply a—*food?*—run.

CHAPTER 25

Silas

The urgent heavy footfalls outside of my bedroom tell me something is wrong before the loud banging at the door echoes through the darkness of the room.

Just like my bedroom at the house, my room here at the apartment is also completely UV protected. The windows have a protective layer on them, and the heavy blackout curtains ensure no remaining sunlight may enter the room. I don't sleep the full twelve hours a day the sun is up, for many of those hours I work in the confines of the bedroom. Bedroom isn't exactly the right term for this space, it's more of a small apartment. There's a sitting room with a television that is hardly ever turned on and a spare room that is an additional office space for me.

I've been awake, working in here for hours on things that are still in my control. The attacks that have been taking place against me are out of my control until I can discover who the bastards are behind them. Duke has been out searching and talking to his connections throughout

He's not supposed to be back until sundown and based on the countdown timer on my desk, the sun won't be down for another thirty minutes. The persistent knocking combined with his erratic heartbeat instantly sets me on edge. I know without a doubt I'm really not going to like what he says.

With my unnatural speed, I'm at the door within seconds. The stench of his overwhelming anxiety comes through the door. Duke is one of the most levelheaded people I have ever met. He's been in war zones and some of the situations I've put him in would have made weaker men dissolve into a puddle of tears. *Nothing* rattles Duke, but he's afraid now.

"What the hell happened, Duke?" I demand through the door.

I can hear him swallow hard as he tries to find his words. "Had I known, I never would have let her go." He's stalling.

For fuck's sake. "Tell me what's happened!" I roar at him, my hand slamming against the door.

"It's Quincey, Silas." Anger builds in me, instantly thinking that she's made an escape attempt. I should have known this would happen after being away for two weeks and leaving her upset like I did. The lack of my constant presence must have made her feel daring. I'm going to hunt her down and make her beg me for forgiveness. "Della couldn't make it to the weekly drop today, she sent Quincey instead and something's happened."

The anger drains from my body just as quick as it appeared, it's replaced with an emotion I didn't know I was still capable of. Given the world I live in, I should experience a healthy dose of it frequently, but I've become the man I am today by inflicting fear on others, not feeling it myself.

But now, as I stand here, listening to Duke tell me that Della sent Quincey to the Quarter without any protection to pick up this week's delivery of blood, dread creeps into my being. The cold hand of fear slithers around my heart and squeezes until there is physical pain.

"We knew they were watching your movements, we never thought they'd be watching your employees. I think they planned on jumping Della and Q just happened to be there instead," Duke rambles on, but my care for why this is happening is borderline nonexistent. I'll care when Quincey is safely back with me.

"Where did she say she was going?" I ask between clenched teeth as I begin to pace in front of the shut door. This conversation would be better done in person, but the door can't be opened until the sun sets. I can't leave until the sun sets.

"She didn't," Duke tells me yet another thing I don't want to hear. "There was a loud crash, and the line went out. I've been calling her nonstop, but she hasn't answered. It's been five minutes since I heard from her, she could be anywhere now."

She's out there alone and in danger.

An angry roar comes from my chest as my hand sweeps across the shelf full of various décor and books. The glass pieces crash to the ground, shattering around my feet. Some of the items were irreplaceable, but I can't muster a fuck to give about it right now. Breathing hard, I return to the door. "Get out there now, Duke. I don't care what you need to do, fucking find her." With a glance at the timer once more, I growl in frustration. "I'll join you when I can."

"I'm leaving now," Duke assures me.

Before he can leave, I stop him. I barely recognize my voice when I speak, "If anything happens to her, there is no saying what I'll do." This isn't a thinly veiled threat directed at him, it's a silent order that if I become out of control, Duke will have to put a stop to the destruction I'll cause.

"She's smart, Silas. Knowing her, she got away and is with Lucy as we speak." Duke's attempt to put me at ease fails.

With each step he takes away from the door, the darkness and anger consume me. The anger isn't directed at her, this time, it's not her fault. The anger stems from the overpowering sense of helplessness that has started to eat me alive.

It's been centuries since I've felt this level of powerlessness. In each situation I find myself in I'm calm because I know that I have *complete* control of it. There is nothing that I can't handle and no one that can deter me from the steadfast path I've found myself on.

But then along came a little blonde woman with eyes like a summer day. My very being is rocked to its core because I can't help her right now. The fact she's only in danger because of me and my world only adds to the frustration.

Even with my attempts to ensure something like this never happens, Quincey is still being hunted by my enemies as we speak.

My hands rake through my hair, pulling harshly on the strands as I pace the room like a caged animal

I am one of the strongest individuals on this earth, and yet I'm stuck here because what little remains of the sun could take me out. What is the point of wielding so much power if you can't protect the people you care about?

My pacing comes to a screeching halt as the startling realization slams into me so hard I stagger back a step.

I care about Quincey.

She's no longer someone I'm using until they have nothing else to offer me like I had planned. She's no longer just my obsession because I'm fixated on her blood. No, she's more than that.

What she means to me exactly is not clear, but I know in my black soul that I truly care about her.

The knowledge that she could be out there bleeding or dead makes my distress multiply tenfold.

Feeling too confined, I rip at the suit jacket I wear, the seams make a tearing sound as I claw it roughly from my body.

Twenty minutes.

Time means nothing to me, but I'm feeling every single one of these seconds as they tick by painfully slow. *She* makes me feel the weight of time.

The relief from the jacket being gone is short-lived. It's not enough, I still feel trapped. I rip out my black diamond cufflinks and let them clatter to the floor before I roll up the sleeves of the black button-down. The buttons at the collar are the next to go.

Wandering aimlessly through the room, I make it to the fireplace. With my hands on the mantel, I drop my head and count in my head. I count out sixty seconds, once, twice, three times, to distract myself. As I count, I see her looking up at me. The fear that was in her eyes that first night was something I was delighted to see then, but the thought she could be looking at another with the same fear is unbearable.

Fifteen minutes.

My head lifts and I meet my own gaze in the mirror on the wall. I'm unrecognizable even to myself right now. My hair disheveled, the collar of my shirt is torn from my rough treatment of it, and my jaw muscle tics from how hard I grind my teeth together. Those aren't what catch me off guard, it's the wild look in my eyes that has me stopping and staring. The slightly unhinged look I've only seen once before in my life.

It was after *she* died, and I thought my world was ending. No, my world did end when she died in my arms. The things that I did following her death were catastrophic. I made a vow after it was over, covered in blood and surrounded by the bodies of my victims, I'd never lose control like that, but as the seconds go by, the surer I become, I'm about to break my vow.

The people of my city think I'm a monster now. Just wait. They won't like what they see after I devastate it if something happens to Quincey.

The phone in my pocket barely rings once before I'm bringing it to my ear and barking into the receiver. "Did you find her?"

"She's not at the club like I thought she'd be," Duke speaks loudly over the bustle of the bar. "I'm going to retrace her steps from the meeting place, I'll call if I find anything."

Of course, she isn't at the club. Like Duke said, Quincey is smart, she'd never knowingly bring danger to her best friend's doorstep. She would go the opposite direction, leading them far away, even if it meant putting herself in more danger.

Quincey's strength is her selflessness, but it's also her weakness. Her self-preservation is lacking at times. Her boldness is what draws me to her, but also what I despise most about her.

Ten minutes.

My fist connects with the glass of the mirror before I know what I'm doing. The glass sprays all around me, landing on my shirt and hair, but that doesn't stop me from grabbing the gold statue of a woman and hurling it across the room into a bookshelf.

I don't stop there—*can't* stop there.

The antique chair splinters into pieces as I smash it into the ground. The coffee table makes a satisfying crashing sound as I flip it over with a pained roar. Feathers from the pillows on my bed float through the air when I'm done tearing the bed apart. One of the four posts of the canopy bed is now broken in half.

Five minutes.

The bed groans under my weight when I sit on the end of it and drop my head into my hands. Reviewing what I know of Quincey, I attempt to come up with a theory of where she could be on the off chance she got away from her assailants. She's a runner, said she'd run for miles before work, but I know the panic she felt being chased would have slowed her down.

If only I knew who was coming after me—and now my people—I could better prepare and strategize. I've had enemies in my past, but none of them have been able to conceal themselves from me this well. This fact makes me believe they've had time—lots of it—to plan for this. The kind of time only someone like me could have.

Could it be another vampire?

The phone rings again across the room where I left it. I'm across the room and picking it up before the second ring. This time Duke doesn't wait for me to talk first. "She ran into a group of people on St. Louis street, one of the street artists cleaning up her booth saw the whole thing. Quincey screamed for help before she took off again. Silas, I think she's hurt. The artist said she took a pretty nasty fall."

As the timer on my desk clicks down to zero, a wicked smirk grows on my lips. "If she is bleeding, I will have no trouble tracking her."

Her blood calls to mine, like they are fated to find each other.

Hold on, love. I'm coming for you.

CHAPTER 26

Quincey

I can't stay here all night.

If Duke is out there looking for me like I hope he is, the last place he's going to look is the inside of a tomb in the graveyard blocks away from where I originally called him. The idea of spending the night with a bunch of ancient dead people is also incredibly unappealing. The lingering fear in my bones is making my imagination run wild and I'm starting to hear things I know aren't truly there.

Or shit, this place could be infested with ghosts for all I know. If vampires are real, that opens up the possibility that all kinds of other scary creatures exist. So, the faint knocking sounds and the random whispering very well might be coming from the dead laid to rest here.

Either way, my body is screaming for me to leave.

Deciding I don't want lugging it around to slow me down if I need to make another escape, I push the metal case into the back of the tomb. I'll make it to St. Sin and use Lucy's phone to call Duke. Or maybe I shouldn't call him at all. This is the perfect time to get away from them.

I wanted to run away from all of this just two days ago when I found the cellar, nothing has changed since then, so why isn't the need to run as strong as it was before?

Mind made up that I'm going to get to Lucy, I slowly ease out of the tomb. As quiet as I can manage, I jump down to the cracked stone pathway below. Even though I move softly through the walkways, each footstep I make seems as loud as a siren. This may be due to the sudden onset of extreme paranoia.

The exit to the cemetery is just yards in front of me, the safety of the bustling crowds just one street over from me. The warm lights from the storefront call to me. I just need to make it over there and I can blend into the mobs of people.

The sigh of relief that comes from my lips is premature.

Just as my fingers brush against the rough material of the wrought-iron gate, a hand threads through the long strands of my hair and I'm pulled back so harshly I can't help but cry out in pain.

"I told you she was hiding in here." Hot breath snakes across my cheek as I'm pulled back into his chest. "We just had to wait her out, and she'd come creeping out of wherever she was hiding."

The bald man who first started chasing me steps out from the shadows in front of me, a cruel gleam in his eyes as he looks me over. "You're quite the little troublemaker," he coos at me.

"So I've been told," I spit at him, trying my best to keep up my brave face.

His thick finger runs down the side of my face. When I attempt to turn my head away, the man holding me in place by my hair tightens his grip, making my scalp burn in pain. "I like trouble. You gonna put up a fight for us?"

Their vile conversation from before comes back to me. So, he's the one who wants his turn while I'm still kicking. The nausea that had somewhat subsided returns at full force.

Breathing slowly through my nose, I try to keep the bile down.

"You think I won't fight you? That I'll just lie back and let it happen?"

The man behind me chuckles in my ear. "Oh, on the contrary. We're counting on it, little one."

I jerk against his hold, throwing my elbows back into his chest and abdomen. My feet kick and thrash around, but all this does is make them laugh at me.

A flash of silver has my eyes widening and freezing in place.

The bald man holds a knife in his hand. The silver reflects in the soft moonlight as he moves closer to me with it.

I hold back a whimper as he drags it down my chest softly, not yet cutting my skin. "This shirt is so unflattering, let's see what you're hiding underneath it."

His beefy hand grips the fabric roughly, pulling it away from my body as he drags the sharp blade through it. Within seconds, the entire front of my shirt is ripped down the middle and just barely hanging off my shoulders.

He stares at my exposed torso like a man gone mad with hunger. The evil gleam in his eyes—eyes that tell me that he fully intends to follow through with this—makes my skin crawl.

"You missed the bra, we wouldn't want you hiding those from us too," the sick fuck holding me in place chimes in. Even though I can't see his cocky smirk, I can hear it in the way he speaks.

"Patience, brother," the man with the knife chastises mockingly as he brings the knife back to my chest. This time when he slices the material of my plain white cotton bra, the blade knicks my skin. The sting of pain and mortification of what's happening makes a single tear fall from my eye.

Out of desperation, my shaking fingers scramble to cover my breasts with the shredded fabric of my shirt. The man *tsks* and shakes his head at me slowly before the knife is pressed against my neck. "Now, that's just not going to work."

One wrong move and my throat will be cut open. If they hit the artery, I'll bleed out in ten seconds or less. *At least it will be quick.*

"I'll scream," I threaten, my voice thick with emotion.

"Do it," he whispers into my ear. "Scream so loud you wake the dead."

The hand that's knotted into my hair trails down my collarbone and moves slowly down. He takes my nipple between his fingers and squeezes hard, this time I can't keep the whimper at bay. The man in front of me breaks into a smile when he hears the sound of my defeat.

His fingers leave my nipple and swipe through the blood that dribbles from the cut on my chest. Lazily, he smears the blood across each breast. "I'm going to paint you red and leave you here on display like my own personal masterpiece."

My throat is so tight as vomit threatens to escape and the tears now fall freely. Who will find me after they dump my used and discarded body here? Silas comes to mind, will he even care that I'm gone? He's so hard to read, I never know what he's thinking, let alone what he thinks about me. Poor Duke, I don't want him to find me in that state either.

"Before we have our fun with you," the bald man starts, his eyes looking around our surroundings. "We need to know where you stashed the briefcase. You see, our boss won't be thrilled with us if we show up empty-handed."

If I could laugh, I would right now. Defiantly, I lift my chin and glare at him. "Even if I wanted to, I couldn't tell you. I don't know where it is. I got scared and dropped it."

"Don't worry about the damn case." The man behind me waves off the other. "We know it's in here, she probably just stashed it somewhere. Isn't that right, little one?"

I don't give him the satisfaction of getting an answer out of me, instead I stare blankly in front of me. Only when his calloused hand drifts further down my torso until his fingers play with the hem of my jean shorts do I begin fighting him again. The driving need to get away from him outweighs the risk of the knife at my throat. Weak, hopeless pleas escape me as I try to fight him and push his hands off of me.

When I feel the knife bite into my neck and warm blood drip down my chest, I don't stop. "Let me go!" my shrill cry echoes through the cemetery and goes unanswered by anyone. "Please don't, *please*."

I never went to my mother with skinned knees or bellyaches because I knew she couldn't do anything to help me. More so, I knew she *wouldn't* want to help me. This is still true today, but as I'm abruptly whirled around, my front pressed to the mossy wall of a tomb, I've never wanted my mother more.

"Hold her hands," one of them orders the other. They're twice my size. When my wrists are grabbed and held up above my head, any attempt to pull myself free is in vain. "You look so good right now, all hopeless with those pretty tears running down your face."

A choked sob bubbles in my throat as his hands pull my hips back to rub his erection against my ass. The breathy noise he makes causes my stomach to roll.

Fingers fumble with the button of my shorts. I try moving my hips away from him, but my movements only spur him on further. "That's right, make me work for it."

The angle that my wrists are being pushed against the concrete wall is painful and each time I try to pull my hands free, the stone rubs against my skin until abrasions start to form.

"Stop playing with her and get on with it," the one holding my hands orders impatiently. "We don't have all night."

The button of my shorts is now undone, he moves onto the zipper. Just to taunt me and drag out the rampant terror I'm experiencing, he drags it slowly down. Each centimeter he moves it down, my heart beats faster in my chest.

Unable and unwilling to watch what happens next, I squeeze my eyes shut. I want to block it out. If this is how I'm going to spend the last few moments of my life, I want to pretend I'm not in an eerie cemetery being assaulted.

My brain begins to conjure up something better. The image of the courtyard at the house fills my head. Ira's roses have all bloomed beautifully, their fresh scent fills the warm summer air. The breeze flows through the garden, blowing my hair all around my face. Smiling, I tilt my head toward the sun and soak up all the heat it can give me. Behind me, he laughs softly at me while his hands gather up my hair, so my neck is exposed to him. I'm not afraid because I know Silas would never hurt me. When he leans down and his lips press softly into my neck, I sigh contentedly. This is perfect. This is somewhere I can die.

The idealistic scene is ripped away from me when the body that's pressed against me is abruptly pulled from my back. The sound of something slamming into a nearby concrete grave is so loud it's like an explosion. The pieces of the grave break and skid across the ground.

The hands that hold my wrists against the wall are the next to go. "What the—" My attacker's question is cut off as he gasps in pain.

My world moves in slow motion and sound is barely audible as I whirl around to watch the events unfold. The man who'd been groping me lies in the rubble of a now demolished grave. It takes me a second, as he rolls from his side to his back, to put together that his head is gone—*torn* from its body. It lies feet away from the rest of him, eyes staring blankly over my shoulder.

If I hadn't turned when I did, I would have missed it. I would have missed the moment that confirmed what I've known for days. I would have missed how the villain of the story became my hero.

He came for me.

Silas holds the other man by his neck multiple feet in the air with one hand. With little to no effort, he dangles the man in front of him as a rumbling growl comes from him. Not a normal human sound whatsoever, but the elongated fangs that he bares up at my attacker are also not human.

Whatever denial that remained in me is dissolved in a second. I must have been holding on to it harder than I thought because the truth hits me like a bomb, shattering any of my doubt with it.

He's a vampire.

The bald man claws at Silas's hand, but Silas isn't deterred or bothered by the scratches covering his perfect skin. The man's face grows redder by the second as his oxygen is cut off.

Just when I think Silas is going to drop him, he brings the man close to him and with an animalistic snarl, he buries those sharp fangs into his neck. The man screams in pain for a second, before his eyes grow wide and his body jerks when Silas rips his head away from his jugular.

Harshly, Silas spits the contents onto the cemetery floor.

Oh my god, he ripped the guy's throat out... with his teeth.

I stand frozen in shock as I watch Silas roughly release the man. With a deafening thud, he falls to the ground and the gaping wound on his neck creates a puddle of blood around his body.

Silas stares down at him, a vicious smile on his face as he waits for him to bleed out. His shoulders heave as he breathes harshly, the fabric of his rumpled button-down has become untucked from his slacks. His hair that is usually perfect is unruly and wild looking. I've never seen him look so disheveled. So unkempt.

Black eyes that look like a piece of onyx in this light clash into mine when he finally lifts his head toward me. Blood covers his mouth, dripping down his chin. Fangs peek out from his parted lips. The lines of his handsome face are harsh, the skin around his eyes seems darker than usual. Dropping my eyes, I find blood dripping from his fingertips, no doubt from when he took off the man's head. *With his bare hands.*

The monster that headlines in so many horror films and stories stands before me. The monster that occupies nightmares is real. The monster that, despite what I just witnessed, I'm not terrified of. I should be afraid. I should be screaming for help, but I don't.

Instead, all I can do is whisper, "I knew it."

The words just barely leave my lips before I'm doubling over, and the vomit I've been fighting finally makes its ghastly escape.

CHAPTER 27

Silas

"I knew it."

She doesn't scream or run from me when she finally lays eyes on who I truly am. *What* I truly am. All she does is stare at me with a look of uncertainty on her face as she whispers those words.

Quincey Page has yet again found a way to completely astonish me. Even Della—levelheaded, strong-willed Della—ran when she first learned of what I am, but not Quincey.

She stands steadfast before me, using the back of her hand to wipe the vomit from her chin as her calculating eyes watch me. While the relief she's standing before me *breathing* is like a balm to the fiery rage that burns in my veins, I don't want to get too close and spook her.

I don't want to scare her away, I want to go to her and gather her battered body in my arms. She's wounded, but she's alive and right now that's all that matters to me. I don't care that she just stood witness to my monstrous side, I would have torn apart dozens right in front of her if it meant protecting her. The knowledge that those bastards hurt her only increased my fury and there was no stopping the carnage.

The sweet scent of her blood is what led me to her. Even through all the other overpowering scents in the city, I could pick out the scent of her blood with ease. Like an invisible thread, I followed it to the cemetery.

If I hadn't been staying in the Quarter like I have been, I never would have made it to her. Even as it is, I just barely found her in time before she was brutally raped. Attacked because someone has an unknown vendetta against me. Attacked because she was somewhere she was never meant to be. Attacked because I was naïve enough to think they wouldn't be watching my employees.

Her cotton shirt hangs in shreds off one shoulder. The pieces that once were her bra are tangled in the mess of fabric. Blood dribbles down her collarbone and between her visible breasts. There are other scrapes and abrasions, but those cuts are the ones that will need attention.

I can't stop the snarl that builds in my chest when my eyes lock on the open button of her shorts. I hadn't noticed that before. *Was I too late*?

Moving at a speed that's hard for human eyes to track, I move to stand before her, not caring that I'm intruding on her space. "Did they touch you?" My voice is harsher than I intend. The fury I feel is hard to conceal.

She staggers away from me; her shaking hand raises to silently stop me from coming closer. "W-wait," she stammers. "Just wait. *Please*. Stay back. I-I'm not... *ready*."

Even if I felt inclined to listen to her request, I couldn't stay away.

Her eyes drift to the bodies that lie in bloody heaps around us. She worked in a trauma room for years, she's used to carnage, but she's not used to seeing *how* it happens. No one has ever torn another apart in front of her. She's a healer while I'm a killer.

Gently, I clasp the side of her face in my palm. She flinches at my touch at first, her whole body going rigid. It hurts more than I'd like to admit that my touch is unwelcome, even if it's an expected reaction.

Just as I'm about to pull my hand from her, she surprises me by closing her eyes tight and leaning into my touch. She releases a long, shuddering breath before the tears slowly slide down her face. Her head shakes slowly before she whispers, "No, they didn't touch me. Not in that way."

The men got off easy considering, but had I arrived one minute later and found them assaulting Quincey, their deaths would have been drawn out for weeks. Each day I would have taken a hot knife and sliced off a piece of their flesh until their bones were visible. What happened to them tonight was an act of mercy.

She jumps and pulls back from me when my free hand wipes away the tears on her cheeks. The blood that coats my hands transfers onto her skin and I silently curse. "It's okay, love. I won't hurt you," I vow softly. "Never you, Quincey."

Big powder blue eyes meet mine and scan my face like they're looking at me for the first time. In a way, they are. She's finally seeing through the barrier she's slowly been breaking down since I brought her home.

She's seeing all of me for the first time and despite the ugliness and depravity of what I am, she never looks away.

"Are you scared?"

"Not as much as I should be," Quincey answers softly, her voice hoarse. "You've never scared me as much as you should. I don't know if that makes me crazy or—"

"Fearless," I answer for her. "It makes you wonderfully and recklessly fearless. If you were wise, you would be running far, far away from me."

"If I wanted to, would you let me?"

The predator in me would never allow such a thing, but that's not the reason I shake my head. "No," I reply simply. "No, I wouldn't. You could try, but I assure you that you will not get far. If I learned anything tonight, Quincey, it's that I'm not ready to let you go just yet. Regardless of the debt you owe and against all common sense, I'll hunt you down and bring you back to me if you run."

Anyone who got in my path or helped keep her from me would end up like the dead men tonight.

"What do you want to do? Do you want to run from me now?" I take a step away from her, allowing her the space to get around me if she chooses. "I'll give you a head start, but there are many hours until sunrise. I have all the time to find you again if that's what you chose. Or will you let me care for you now? You're bleeding and exhausted, I can help you if you'd only let me."

Her eyes dart down the open path behind me as she contemplates her options. If she wants to try to run tonight, I will do her the courtesy of allowing it, but it won't be long till she's back in my possession.

"No more running," Quincey says, her voice sounding stronger. "We've both been running enough lately, don't you think?"

She's referring to my two weeks of evading her. *Hell*, the majority of our weeks together have been spent with us failing to avoid each other. She asked me once if I was tired of all the anger that fuels my soul. I'm not yet tired of the anger, but I am tired of running from her.

I return to stand in front of her. This time she doesn't flinch when I hold her face between my hands, my thumbs rubbing across her cheekbones softly. "Yes." I surrender to her while also surrendering to the connection I've been denying for weeks.

Quincey's breath hitches when I press my lips to her forehead. I inhale her scent as I kiss her. The lingering stench of fear and anxiety that clings to her clammy skin makes me snarl internally. She never should have been out here. From this moment forward, Quincey will never be permitted anywhere alone. That's if I lift the ban of her leaving the four walls of the house. Right now, I'm even less inclined to grant her such freedoms.

Pulling away, I drop my hands to her shoulders. "Come on, love, we need to get these rags off before we leave." It may be a standing tradition in this town for women to flash their breasts, but I will become murderous if anyone eyes Quincey's exposed chest. After what she's been through tonight, she doesn't need any more unwanted attention.

As if she's just now noticing she's been partially naked in front of me this entire time, her arms cross in an attempt to cover herself. "I loved this shirt," she comments exasperatedly. "I'm slowly running out of clothes." She laughs softly, but it sounds forced. An ill attempt to lighten the mood.

I've seen her closet, she's not wrong. She owns less than ten outfits—if that.

"Don't worry over a shirt, it's easily replaceable. *You*, however, are not," I promise her as I undo the buttons of my shirt. It's blood-stained and ripped, but it's in better shape than the shirt she wears. Everything in my life is replaceable. Access to endless amounts of money means I can afford to replace anything, and the gift of infinite time ensures that nothing is everlasting. I learned long ago it's best to not get attached to things or people, but I am failing on all accounts when it comes to her.

As gently as I can, I pull the fabric from her body. Her hands grasp at the shreds of her shirt to keep herself covered causing me to shake my head softly at her. "You never need to hide yourself from me. Let me help."

Reluctantly, she drops her hands and allows the shirt to fall from her body. Blood is smeared all over her breasts and dirt is caked on her arms and legs. Probably from where she fell in the street.

I've just pulled my own shirt off my body when I hear him approach. "Jesus *fucking* Christ, Silas," Duke scolds when he sees the massacre. "What a mess, what were you—" The rest dies out when he spots Quincey standing shirtless in front of me. "Q! Shit, darlin' you okay?" He takes a step toward her, worry crossing his features.

With a meek squeaking sound, Quincey shifts closer to me, her small hands holding my sides as she hides her bare body from him.

Instinctually, my arm wraps around her. Her warm skin searing me to my core as I press her closer to me.

The furious look I send him over my shoulder must convey my message because Duke staggers to a stop. "You have one second to turn around before I pluck your eyeballs from your skull." I do not care that he's my best man and the only person I can consider a friend, him seeing Quincey partially naked is not an option.

The shirt falls to Quincey's mid-thigh once we get it on. Even ripped in places, it covers everything I need covered on her. She stands still, staring up at me with big eyes as I roll the too-long sleeves for her. Quincey has never been overly compliant, but right now, the shock of what's happened has made her docile.

I need to get her home and cleaned up.

The adrenaline and fury I'd felt when I first showed up at the cemetery had distracted me just enough that her blood didn't call to my beast. But now it's becoming the only thing I can focus on. The cut on her neck has a thin stream of succulent blood falling from it and flowing down her chest. I can't seem to get myself to look away from it.

Quincey follows my gaze and when she grasps what I'm staring at she wisely takes a step away from me. Her trembling hands move to cover the cut, but that does little to stop the bleeding.

"Silas." Duke's voice is low, an unspoken warning. "Maybe I should take Q and get her fixed up. I'll bring her back when—"

I don't let him finish. My response comes out like a feral snarl. "*No.*"

He shifts forward, eyes darting warily between both Quincey and me. "It's okay, I won't let anything happen to her. I'll bring her back to you when the blood is gone."

Grinding my teeth, I bite out, "I said no. I can bear it." Even as I say it, I don't know if it's true, but for her, I'm going to try my damnedest. "Call a team, get this shit cleaned up. Find out what you can from the bodies before you get rid of them."

Duke reluctantly nods, the concerned look never leaving his face as he watches Quincey. "I'll go get the car and drive you two back while I wait for the team to show up." I don't have to worry about how he'll keep tourists from wandering onto the grisly scene in the meantime, Duke always has a trick up his sleeve. He turns to leave, but Quincey's soft voice stops him.

"The case is in an empty grave a couple rows over." Her blue eyes flick to mine. "I'm assuming it shouldn't be left behind considering the… *contents* of it."

She was able to open it, meaning she knows what she was foolishly protecting with her life. Blood is easy to come by, there is always more of it. No doubt she thought she was protecting something more valuable. She should have just dropped it and let them take it, but how was she to know that was an option?

"I'll grab it when I come back," Duke reassures her. "You did good, Quincey."

She chokes on a sardonic laugh and shakes her head at him as he walks away.

No longer needing to hide my speed and strength from her, in one very fast, fluid movement, she's swept up into my arms and cradled to my bare chest. She gasps and her arms loop around my neck to steady herself. "I don't think I'll ever get used to that," she mumbles, but she doesn't fight me. A sense of calmness washes over me when she rests her head against my shoulder. "I have so many questions, Silas."

My lips brush across her forehead before I answer. "I know and I'll answer as many as I can, but first, I need to get you away from here."

CHAPTER 28

Silas

I don't put her down until we reach the bathroom in my apartment. The short ride home I held her in my lap and even though she argued with me, I carried her inside the building and the entire elevator ride up to the top floor of the building. I keep waiting for the reality of what just happened to crash through her stunned mind, but she's yet to come unhinged. Quincey just stares up at me, like she's still trying to come to terms with the fact that I'm real.

Learning about the existence of vampires is never an easy thing for a human to wrap their mind around. They've been told since birth that creatures like me are nothing but folklore and tales used to scare children, it's hard to accept they've been wrong this whole time. She's handling it better than most. Ira was the last person who handled it as well as her. He'd simply shrugged indifferently, telling me he'd known for years. When I'd questioned him on why he'd kept his mouth shut for so long, he'd simply stated that '*it was none of his damn business*'.

Somehow, Quincey knew as well.

I leave her on the bathroom counter so I can turn on the faucets of the large glassed-in shower behind me and grab some fresh towels from the cabinet. Without a word, I press one of the black towels into the wound on her neck.

"We need to get the bleeding under control." My voice sounds pained, even to my own ears. The level of control I'm having to exercise now is agonizing. If it were anyone else's blood, I would be able to remain composed, but Quincey's blood appeals to the deepest, darkest parts of me.

Her hand covers mine over the towel "I've got it," she tells me. "Don't do this to yourself, I can see it hurts you."

My head shakes stiffly as I refuse to move my hand. "What hurts me is you were injured because of me. I tried to keep you from my world—keep you at a safe distance—and yet, here you sit, *bleeding*." I want to kill those fuckers all over again.

She ponders my words for a second before asking, "This is why then? You disappeared for weeks because you were afraid to hurt me? Because you're a" —she struggles to say the word— "vampire?"

This is the first time she's said it aloud. It's almost as if saying it made it real for her.

"My level of restraint is something that has been revered by many for centuries. Self-control is something many like me struggle to ever learn, whereas it came naturally to me. There's only been one instance in all my years alive that I lost control and it was a devastating event. When it was over, I vowed it would never happen again. For over three hundred years, I've not acted impulsively or rashly, everything I did was meticulously thought out. That all changed when you came along." I haven't been the same since I met her. "My first act of thoughtless behavior was the night I killed Gallo's man. The scent of your blood and those terrified—*beautiful*—eyes of yours, made something in me snap. My fist was through his chest before I even noticed I had moved."

Her eyes widen and recognition fills them. "That's what happened to him? I knew you killed him. I just didn't know how; it'd happened so fast. Which now makes sense, I guess."

"It was hasty and unnecessary, but I couldn't stop myself." Duke had the situation under control, there had been no reason for me to linger around once he showed up, but I couldn't walk away. "I was supposed to keep my distance from you, you were just there to do a job that I couldn't do myself, but you found a way to sneak between the barricades I'd put up to keep you at bay. When I kissed you that night and you bled? It took every ounce of my crumbling control to not kill you right there. You have no idea what your blood does to me, Quincey. So yes, I kept my distance from you because I'm a *vampire* and was a danger to your life—I *still* am. I'm trying my best to hold on to the remaining threads of my resolve because the idea of causing you any more pain is an unbearable thought."

Slowly, as if she's still unsure of what boundaries still remain between us, Quincey places her warm hand over my chest. The contrast of our complexions is glaring, just like everything else, we are opposites in every sense. "You've given me a million reasons to be afraid of you but they're not working. So, stop telling me about how you could kill me, because I don't believe you will. I've been bleeding all over you tonight, if there ever was a time to lose control, it would be now, but you haven't."

In a second, I've torn my hand from her neck and moved feet away from her. "You have an aptitude for being able to see the good in everyone, you cling to it until the good is all you're able to see in that person. It's an admirable gift, but foolish at times, like now for instance. You think I'm a good man simply because I haven't killed you yet? That doesn't make me a good man, Quincey. You have no idea—"

"Don't think for a second that I don't know who you are, Silas." Indifferent to my change in attitude and tone, she jumps from the counter, tossing the towel into the sink as she slowly closes the distance between us. "I know exactly who you are. I know that you are as cold and ruthless as you seem, if not more so. Just like I know you're capable of doing truly monstrous things without so much as batting an eye. I've never for a second been in denial about that side of you. It's been clear to me since the start." She comes to a stop in front of me but makes no move to touch me. "But I also know there is a side of you that is still capable of caring. A side of you that is still *human*. You've made this obvious to me by how you've gone through great extremes to care for Ira. If you didn't give a shit about him, you would have gotten rid of him the second he was diagnosed. If you didn't care, you wouldn't have paid off a *very* large debt and kidnapped someone to look after him." If anyone else got in my face like she's doing, I'd never tolerate it. Even though I don't enjoy it, I allow it because there's truth in her words. She's wise beyond her short years. "You came for me tonight." Her voice becomes less abrasive, softening as she scans my face with her gentle eyes. "I've caused you nothing but trouble since I arrived. It would have saved you the headache if you'd just left me out there, but instead you saved me. And I think you did because you care about me too."

"*Quincey*," I plead, swallowing hard. She's dancing with the devil without knowing the choreography.

"You can be the heartless monster that makes people shake in fear to everyone else, but not me. I see past it." Her blood-covered hand tenderly takes mine and I don't stop her. "I see all the sides of you, Silas. Some of them I enjoy more than others, but I *accept* all of them. Granted, there will need to be a period of grace as I adjust to the whole—*vampire thing*—but even that..." She pauses and shakes her head in disbelief. "Even that I'll be okay with because I *care* about you too, Silas." Her chin lifts as she stands up straighter, as if bracing herself. "So, keep trying. Keep trying to scare me away. It's not going to work, but I dare you to keep trying. I clearly don't scare easy. If I'm standing in front of you now after you literally tore people to shreds in front of me, I'm not going—"

I move so fast she gasps into my mouth as I silence her with it. Her hands fly up in shock, but as my tongue brushes against the seam of her lips, they reach up to grab my bare shoulders. Quincey holds on to me so tight, it's almost as if she's afraid she'll lose me if she doesn't. I don't have the words to tell her that she's captured my heart—*my soul*—even when I wasn't aware I still had one to give her. So, I show her instead.

My mouth shows her that I care with how I devour her with hungry kisses, my tongue caressing against hers when she finally parts her lips for me. My hands show her as they tenderly smooth over each one of her curves as they trail softly down her body. The heat of her sexy body and the soft moans that come from her as I worship her mouth makes my cock desperate for her warm touch.

Her mouth never leaves mine as I back her into the glass and black marble rain shower behind her. She squeals in delight, smiling against my mouth as the warm water washes over our partially dressed bodies. I can't help the smile that tugs at my lips. The last time I truly smiled is unknown to me, but I know I've been fighting them more frequently since she's been here.

Quincey's back collides with the cool stone of the shower and she makes a low grunting noise at the force of how hard I slam her against it. My shirt she still wears clings to her body. Water floods into our shoes, but we don't stop. I don't think we could stop if we had to. Weeks of pent-up emotions and feelings have brought us to this moment. The barricade built of secrets has been blown to pieces, leaving nothing but our clothes between us.

Her hands work frantically at the buttons of the shirt, but she's not removing the ruined piece of clothing fast enough for my liking. Pulling away from her lips, I smirk as I tear the shirt from her body without remorse. The shredding fabric falls to the shower floor. She grins gleefully at me before pulling me back to her by my belt. With each lick into her mouth, my body relaxes. The tension I've been carrying around for hundreds of years melts off me. I can't always let my defenses down like I am, but inside the four walls of this apartment—inside this shower—I can be the man that Quincey needs.

My fingers thread through hers at her sides before forcibly bringing them above her head, holding them hostage against the marble. With an annoyed snarl, she tries to pull her hands free, making me smirk. "The only way you're getting free is if I allow it, and that is not happening. I have you exactly where I want you—completely at my mercy," I tell her as I roll my hips against her, grinding my growing erection against her.

Her chest heaves as she pants. "I want to touch you."

"Soon," I promise, as I place kisses along her jaw. "When I'm done touching you."

Her skin tastes of salt from the sweat that developed as she fled from her attackers, but despite that, she's as sweet as ever.

As I kiss from her jaw down the beautiful column of her neck, Quincey's breath hitches and her heart rate spikes. Just to test how fearless she is and how true her words are, I scrape my blunt teeth against the sensitive skin. My gums burn, my fangs threatening to descend at any second, but I hold them at bay for now. The water that streams down her chest runs red from the knife wounds. The whole steamy shower reeks of her blood, but I manage to stay in control.

"Are you scared now?" I murmur against her neck.

She gives a jerky shake of her head. "No." Her voice is breathy, full of desire, but there isn't a single ounce of fear in it.

Letting go of her hands, I pull back just far enough from her neck so I can look her in the eye. "Do you trust me?"

Heavy powder blue eyes stare at me. "I want to."

I want to. That's good enough for now, I will earn her undying trust with time, even if I don't deserve it. My eyes dart to the blood that spills from the cut on the other side of her neck and then to the one between her breasts. "Do you trust me in this very moment to not hurt you?"

Inquisitiveness crosses her features, but she whispers, "Yes."

Taking the hands she's left above her head, I place them at her sides.

"Keep these here," I order. I'm afraid that if she puts her hands on me while I do this, her pleasant touch will make me lose control. Instantly, as if she can't help herself, she lifts a hand toward me. Growling, I press it back harshly into the marble. "I mean it, Quincey. Keep them there."

Caging her to the wall with my arms, I lean down. Her breasts heave, she's breathing hard, as I lower myself to the cut. Her eyes never once leave mine as I swipe my tongue across my bottom lip. My saliva can make bleeding stop almost instantly and help wounds heal faster. This is one of the ways vampires have been able to keep their existence hidden for so long. They're good at covering their tracks.

"Don't move," I warn as I slowly drag my tongue across the wounds. She doesn't look away or close her eyes as she watches me swipe up all the blood between her breasts with my tongue. Her heart beats so hard, I can feel it against my tongue.

The exquisite taste of her blood explodes in my mouth. Nothing I've ever tasted has ever compared to what Quincey tastes like. For the rest of my days, nothing will ever come close to her. Like an addict chasing that first high, I will be searching for blood that is just as delectable as hers. I know in an instant that I'll fail in my search.

No one will ever rival her. In all my years, I've never met another like her.

The wound stops bleeding quickly, allowing me to move onto the one at her throat. This time, as I lap at the blood, I can't stop myself from placing my mouth over the wound and sucking ever so slightly.

Her whole body jerks, her hands flying forward like she intends to touch me, but she finds the strength to put them back where I ordered her to keep them. "Silas," she groans, her head tilting to the side to allow me more access

She truly isn't afraid of me, and that knowledge fills me with pleasure. I don't want her fear, I want her acceptance. I want those smiles she gives so freely to Duke and Ira to be directed at me. I want the moans that escape her as I touch her to belong to me. I may own her because of a debt, but I want her body and trust to be freely given.

Leaving her neck, I kiss her roughly once more before dropping to my knees in front of her. While she steps out of her shoes, her hands are tearing at the button of her waterlogged shorts before I can reach for them myself. Batting her impatient hands out of the way, I take over. In seconds, the shorts are yanked down her legs, red panties included.

She stands completely bare in front of me, not a single thing keeping her hidden from me. I've been around to see some of the most beautiful art pieces made, but Quincey's body is the most stunning piece of artwork I've been able to view to date. Each curve, each freckle, each scar a masterpiece.

And all for me.

"*Mine*," I snarl before, without any warning, I hook her leg over my shoulder and bring my mouth to her cunt. Her gasp ricochets off the stone and glass, appeasing the hungry beast in me. Her blood and arousal feed the same monster—he's starving for both.

My tongue swipes through her slick folds. She's soaked, not just from the water spraying over us, but from her need for me. When I flick over her clit, her hands delve into the strands of my hair. Whether it's in an attempt to steady herself or keep me in place, I don't know or care. Either way, I don't stop.

I feast on her, licking and biting until her thighs are shaking and my cock is aching painfully in my wet slacks. Just like the night I listened to her get herself off, her noises spur me on, but this time they're so much sweeter because I'm the one causing them. Not just the vague thought of me is bringing her closer and closer to the edge, this time it's my tongue spearing in and out of her pussy while my thumb rubs in circles around her clit.

Just as she's about to come, I pull away from her hot center and drop her leg from my shoulder. Quincey cries out in desperation, but when I spin her around so she faces the wall, the noise stops as she figures out what I'm doing.

Her hands lay against the stone as I pull her hips back toward my face. Slowly, almost agonizingly slow, I drag my tongue through her center before I dip a finger inside her slick heat. Muscles clench around the digit as I slowly work it in and out of her.

"*More*," she pleads with a rasp.

"More what?" I taunt as I nip at one of the perfect globes of her ass. "What do you need, love? Tell me what you want from me."

I'd probably give her the keys to my kingdom right now if she asked.

"I need more of you," Quincey begs. "Make me come, Silas."

Gladly.

Reaching around her, I return my attention to her sensitive nub. Her hips buck as I strum it with my fingers while I add an additional finger inside of her. I rap my fingers against the spot inside of her that makes her knees weak, and her world tilts.

Selfishly, I don't want to stop. The way her body reacts to my touch and the lovely sounds coming from her lips are addicting. I want to play with her little body, teasing her until she's screaming at me in frustration. She's like a toy that only I get to play with, a sweet treat that only I get to savor.

I pull my fingers from her drenched pussy, needing to taste her on my tongue again, I suck them clean, but it's not enough. Returning my mouth to her hot center, I stab my tongue inside her, once, twice, before licking a trail backward.

As my tongue passes over that forbidden ring of muscle, her body goes stiff, her breath hitching in her throat. Am I the first man to touch her here? By her reaction, it would seem so. A pleased rumble forms in my chest knowing this, that I'm the first man to touch her in such a place. I go slow, easing her into the unknown. Her uncertainty is short lived, because as I lick and circle her asshole with my tongue, I pinch her swollen clit between my fingers.

The cry that escapes from her sweet mouth as she comes will live with me the rest of my days. Her whole body shakes as the orgasm washes over her. It's a truly magnificent sight to behold, and to know I caused it is even better. It's so intense, her knees begin to buckle, but I'm able to keep her upright when I wrap my arms around her middle.

"Oh my god," she gasps as she struggles to bring oxygen into her lungs. "*Silas*."

CHAPTER 29

Silas

Her forehead rests against the stone wall as she struggles to catch her breath. If I was a true gentleman, I would allow her to recover before continuing on. But all of New Orleans knows I'm many things, but a gentleman is not one of them. Even if I felt inclined to grant her a reprieve, my swollen cock would never allow it.

I kiss each of the globes of her ass, causing a contented sigh to come from her. Before rising to my feet once again, my blunt teeth bite down on one of her ass cheeks, making her jump. Instead of being scared, she giggles softly between panting breaths.

Her skin prickles with goose bumps as I drag the pads of my fingertips up her thighs and then her sides when I stand to my full height behind her. The air is hot and humid, the scent of her arousal filling every inch of the glassed-in shower. The long strands of her golden hair cling to her perfectly arched back. Because I can, I drag my tongue up her spine, counting each of her vertebrae as I go.

When I reach the top of her back, my hand roughly grabs her chin, forcing her to turn her head toward me. I don't wait for permission as I slam my mouth into hers and thrust my tongue into her mouth, forcing her to taste herself. She groans, sucking the flavor of her pussy off my tongue.

Quincey gleams up at me wickedly when I pull away from her. She turns to face me as she licks the remaining taste of herself from her lips. My skin shivers as she drags her fingers down my toned abdomen until they reach the buckle of my belt. Not once does she look away from me as she undoes the buckle and then the zipper of my water-sodden slacks.

I stand like a piece of stone as she boldly dips her hands inside. My throbbing cock jumps at the first brush of her fingers. My teeth bite down painfully into my bottom lip as she rubs her palm agonizingly slow up and down the shaft. Like the little minx she is, her swollen lips pull into a smirk as she watches my face for a reaction, almost as if it's a challenge of sorts to make me break my composure.

"You're playing a dangerous game, love," I rasp. "I can have you on my bed, flat on your back with my cock inside your pretty pussy in less than five seconds. Do you really want to tease me?"

Her thumb swirls the bead of precum around the crown of my dick, with the faintest amount of pressure. It's just enough to make my hips buck ever so slightly. The movement doesn't go unnoticed by her, it makes the smirk on Quincey's face grow even cheekier. "Oh, I really think I do. Let's see how long it takes the cruel king to beg for it."

I take her chin between my thumb and index finger and tilt her head back, so I know she's truly paying attention to me when I say, "You said it yourself, Quincey. I'm a fucking king. I don't beg or bow to anyone."

In a fashion that couldn't be truer to her strong character, Quincey looks me dead in the eye and declares, "It may not happen tonight, it may not happen this week but one day I will make you beg for me. You will get on your knees and *fucking* beg for me." To drive her point home, her fingers finally wrap around my length and squeeze.

"That mouth is going to be the end of you," I snarl in her face, baring my teeth.

I'm sure there's a witty comment dying to be released on the tip of her tongue, but I don't give her the opportunity to say it aloud. Before she can comprehend what's happening, I'm lifting her into my arms and whirling us around to the opposite wall of the shower. Her legs wrap around my waist tight to keep herself steady and her arms snake around my neck. Her back has just barely connected with the black marble before I've lowered my slacks enough to free myself from the confines of fabric. Without a warning, without a second of hesitation, without trepidation, I thrust fully inside of her.

Quincey's back bows and the gasp that starts to form becomes trapped in her throat at the abrupt invasion into her body.

My muscles lock as heat rushes through every single one of my nerves. It's been a long time since I've felt the heat of the sun on my skin, but the glorious warmth that radiates off of every inch of her body makes me feel as if I'd been thrown directly into the sun. The coldest places of my soul heat and come alive as I stretch her pussy.

"So quiet, Quincey. That smart mouth of yours has nothing to say now that my cock is in you?" I rumble into her ear once I'm finally able to speak myself. "If I'd known all it took to keep you quiet was to fuck you, I would have done it sooner."

As slowly as I can muster, the thin veil of restraint so close to shattering, I pull an inch out of her body before thrusting back inside. I repeat this motion over and over until a frustrated mew comes from her.

"Silas," she all but whines my name. To think there was a time I refused to allow her to say it. Just another failed attempt at keeping her at a safe distance. "*Harder*."

Nipping at her bottom lip, I smirk. "I knew you'd be the one that ended up begging."

The fire in her eyes sears me to the bone, but it's quickly put out when I finally give her what she wants. Slowly I pick up my pace, sinking as deep into her as I can. Her body is tiny and she's human, one wrong move could be the end of her.

Her head tilts back, her lips parted, teeth bared as she pants short breaths. At this angle her neck is on complete display to me, the blue veins that sit under the skin call to me and my hunger. I lose the fight against them, and finally my fangs descend at the lovely sight. It would be so easy, so perfect, to feed from her, but I can't risk it. Licking the streams of blood from her body is different than feeding from her. If my fangs sink into her flesh, there is a high probability I won't be able to stop.

"Fuck, Silas," she cries out as I thrust harshly into her. Her muscles clamp down on my cock, making my world spin momentarily.

"So tight," I bite out, careful to keep my head bent just right to hide my fangs from her. Quincey assures me she's not afraid of me—of what I truly am—but I want to ease her into it. Seeing my fangs as I fuck her is bound to be off-putting and all I want is to make her feel good. She deserves to feel good. "So tight, and all mine." Mine to hold, mine to keep, mine to ultimately destroy. "My Quincey, *mon soleil.*" The nickname leaves me before I know I'm going to say it. It's fitting, no, *perfect,* for her.

"Yes," she hisses.

Dipping down, I take one of her rosy nipples into my mouth, before doing the same to the other. Her fingers delve into the strands of my hair, pulling hard as I bite lightly at the buds, careful to not break the skin.

Her tits bounce as I rut into her, her body slides up the smooth, wet, marble of the shower wall. The sound of our bodies coming together fills the space, along with our sounds of pleasure.

The walls of her pussy quiver and shake. "Right there," she cries. "Don't stop, please don't stop."

My fingers dig into the flesh of her ass, no doubt leaving a bruise. I don't like seeing her hurt or wounds on her body, but any marks left on her by how hard I fucked her will be admired. It's my way of leaving my temporary brand on her.

Quincey's hips lift and with each of my thrusts, she meets me with her own. Her fingers move from my hair to hold on to my shoulders to give her leverage. Nails dig into my skin, the prickles of pain send chills down my spine. I suck air into my lungs and my muscles tense. I'm close, but she's there.

"Ah," she moans. "I'm coming!"

Her body locks and she falls silent as the orgasm crashes into her, but then she throws her head back and cries out loudly. I can't keep myself from kissing her again as she comes, regardless of my fangs. Quincey pants into my mouth as she rides out the waves of her release. When the muscles of her cunt tighten around my length and when she sucks on my tongue, I'm lost.

"Fuck!"

My release is blinding as my body tenses and I spill inside of her, coating her walls with my seed. She swallows my groan greedily while I thrust into her over and over until I have nothing left to give her.

Exhausted, Quincey drops her forehead to my shoulder as my cock continues to pulse inside of her.

We both come down from the euphoric high. While she catches her breath, I press chaste kisses along her shoulder and up her neck. She shudders at my touch, sighing contentedly.

My little ray of sunshine isn't as innocent as she seems. She may look like an angel, but she fucks like a demon.

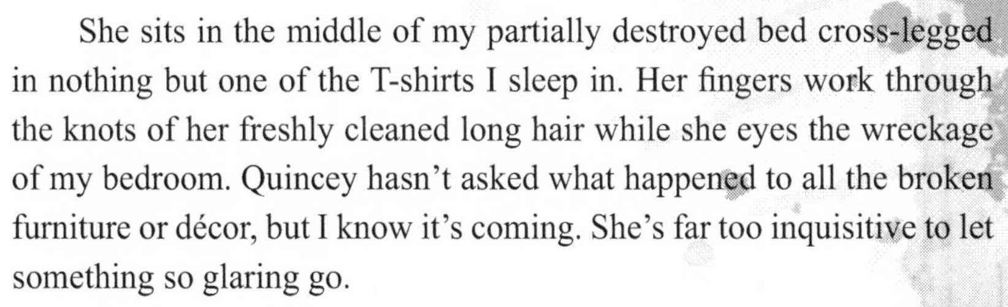

She sits in the middle of my partially destroyed bed cross-legged in nothing but one of the T-shirts I sleep in. Her fingers work through the knots of her freshly cleaned long hair while she eyes the wreckage of my bedroom. Quincey hasn't asked what happened to all the broken furniture or décor, but I know it's coming. She's far too inquisitive to let something so glaring go.

My bedroom, though a disaster zone right now, is my sanctuary.

It's where I go to decompress after a long day and it's one of the few places I can go where I don't have to hide who I truly am. This is why I don't allow others in here. No other women have ever been permitted in my house, let alone my bedroom, but here Quincey sits.

I keep waiting for the regret to come, for the reality of what I've done to crash into me, but it hasn't happened. The guilt I always thought I'd experience if I developed… *feelings*… for another woman isn't as insufferable as I assumed it would be. The unease that sits uncomfortably in my chest stems from the unfamiliarity of the situation. It's my biggest rule; I don't enter into things unless I know how they're going to end, and with Quincey, I have no idea what the fuck I'm doing. The whole thing is unknown to me, but that being said, the new sensation of contentment is greatly outweighing the discomfort.

I stand by the fireplace halfheartedly listening to what Duke has to say, but I'm more focused on the woman across the room. The part of the conversation I'm dreading is coming. It's unavoidable, no matter how much I wish it were. Digging up my past isn't something I enjoy, but there is no way around it with her.

Quincey deserves answers, no matter how much I wish pieces of my history would stay dead.

"I've got their names and their addresses; I'm going to head there after I'm done looking through the security footage at the Quarter. I want to see what hole these fuckers crawled out of. I'm going to trace their steps backward to see what I can find," Duke explains, the sound of a car door shutting comes through the line. "I'm at Blackwood now, I'm going to have Rory help me get into the feeds that I don't already have access to. As much as it pains me to admit, she's better at the computer stuff than I am."

Very few are better than Rory, that's why when she tried *and* succeeded at hacking into Blackwood's network, I hired her instead of killing her. Skill like hers doesn't come around every day. She's a diligent worker, and despite her edgy appearance and criminal background, she's a trustworthy person I'm glad to have on my team. Rory doesn't know all my secrets, but she knows that Blackwood Technologies, while a legit tech company, is also a corporation I run millions of dollars of illegally earned money through yearly.

"Ask about Ira," Quincey reminds me from the bed. The second we left the sanctuary of the shower, she got antsy, worrying about Ira. Even after everything that's happened tonight, her first worry after the adrenaline and emotions eased was her patient.

"Do you have an update on Ira?"

She perks up in bed when she hears me ask, waiting intently for news.

"Constance is staying with Ira tonight and tomorrow morning, so you and Quincey will have some time with each other." I elect to ignore the knowing tone in Duke's voice. "He's upset because he hates Constance's stuck-up guts—his words not mine—but he's as good as he can be at this point. He's grown accustomed to having Q with him and she's the best, so I get why he's bitter."

When I give her a reassuring nod, Quincey relaxes once more.

"I'll have you bring her back before sunup." There's still business I need to attend to in town before I can return to the estate. The idea of sending her back without me is unsettling, but I make a mental note to instruct Duke to up the security at the house. While I could tell him now, there is no need for Quincey to overhear the order. If she knows I'm worried, she'll worry and there is enough on her mind right now.

"No surprise, but Della's a complete wreck over what happened. Feels guilty—"

I cut him off instantly.

"As she fucking should be. If she thinks there won't be repercussions for what happened today, she's wrong." Never in her thirty years of service to me have I been as disgusted and disappointed in Della as I am now. She almost cost Quincey her life because she couldn't be bothered to do her damn job. The anger that had subsided springs to life inside of me once more. "She's incredibly lucky I made it to Quincey in time, because if I hadn't..." I don't bother finishing the statement, my threat is clear in my tone.

"*Silas*." Quincey's eyes narrow at me and she shakes her head. "Enough, it's fine. I'm fine." Aside from the bumps and bruises from her fall, physically she's fine. It's unknown how this will scar her psychologically moving forward. The only solace I can offer her is that no one will ever get close enough to hurt her like that again. "It's probably for the best I was there anyway instead of Della," she offers glibly over her shoulder at me as she climbs off the bed to get a better look at one of the paintings on the wall.

My entire body turns to stone, and rage creeps into my veins at her dismissive tone. I don't bother telling Duke goodbye. The call is disconnected, and I'm across the room before Quincey can fully leave the bed. Her blue eyes widen in confusion when I cage her in place with my larger body. "What—"

"Don't ever tell me again that you believe it's for the best that *your* life was the one at risk," I warn closely to her face. "Your life is worth more than gold to me, and I won't tolerate you speaking so flippantly about it, *mon soleil*."

She silently repeats the name of endearment I'd inadvertently given her, her lips moving as she tests the name out. "What does it mean?"

I ignore her question completely, continuing to stare hard down at her. "If you continue to be reckless with your precious life, I will take you over my knee and leave a permanent outline of my handprint on your ass. Do I make myself clear?"

Instead of her eyes filling with concern or trepidation, heat and lust fill them. At this point, I've decided it's pointless to assume how Quincey Page will react to something, she always does the opposite of what I'd expect. "I just let a vampire fuck my brains out, Silas. I think it's safe to say that I enjoy living recklessly." Boldly, she tilts her head up just enough for her to ghost her lips across mine. "I'm not saying it's okay that I was chased and almost raped, but had Della been there, she never would have been able to get away. They would have killed her." Her fingers trace along the hard lines of my face. "Just remember that when you see her next. In the end, everything worked out okay. Don't you think?"

"You saw me rip those men apart," I remind her. "You watched me kill people tonight." *That*. Is not okay. She needs to be shielded from the bloodshed of my world.

Her face hardens. "We don't mourn the lives of rapists, Silas. We dance on their graves and celebrate that there's one less evil person on this planet." My mouth opens but the finger she presses against my lips promptly silences me. "And before you spew some bullshit about you also being evil, just know I don't want to hear it. I've heard enough of that tonight, there are much bigger things I want to talk about."

Sighing heavily, I place one last kiss to her temple before moving to sit on the bed beside her. "I suppose there are some things you would like to discuss."

"That's putting it mildly." She sits back on the bed, her bare legs crossing under her.

"Where do you want me to start?"

"We can start at the beginning, but you should know something first. I found the room in the basement."

CHAPTER 30

Quincey

Many things have been confirmed for me in just a span of a couple hours. First, my mother's drunk ramblings were right. Vampires are real and Silas is one of them. Two, they're as deadly as the lore makes them out to be. Silas ripped a man's head clean off with little to no effort. Three, Silas fucks like a god. It doesn't matter how many different ways I've imagined what it'd be like to sleep with him, nothing my mind could conjure up would compare to the real thing.

There isn't a drug on the market that could recreate the euphoria that filled my every cell as Silas fucked me. Much like a drug, I'm hooked on him. I just had him, but I already need him again.

Now isn't the time to be thinking about sex, but my brain can't help but wonder.

Silas's face hardens, his lips flattening into a stern line when I admit I went searching through his office and subsequently his shrine in the cellar. There was no point in keeping it a secret from him. He would have found out eventually, besides it's better this way. This way he can't try to keep me in the dark on certain things that I already know about.

"When?" he finally asks after a moment of tense silence.

"A couple days ago," I tell him honestly. "I could sit here and tell you that I'm sorry I snooped through your private quarters, but we both know I'd be lying. We also know you don't like liars, so let's push past it and keep going. You can be mad at me later about it."

Silas swallows hard. "Did you touch anything? The items are irreplaceable and *delicate*, Quincey. They're not to be handled."

My hand reaches out to touch his thigh reassuringly. I find that I don't enjoy the way he stiffens at my touch, but at the same time, I know he has a right to be upset with me. No matter how desperate I was for answers, I still betrayed him by invading his privacy and going against his explicit orders to not ever enter his wing of the house. "No, I promise I didn't touch anything. It was all so old I knew I'd damage it if I did." I pause for a beat before asking, "Just how old are we talking, though?"

"Are you asking about the age of the items in the cases or my age?"

I bite my lip nervously. "Both I suppose."

"The items vary in age, but most of them date back to the seventeenth century." I knew they were old but hearing just how old is still shocking. "The same century that I was born."

My eyes widen. "That would make you—"

"Almost four hundred years old," Silas answers before I can finish. "Three hundred and eighty-seven, to be exact, but there's no point in keeping track anymore. Age is irrelevant to me. I will remain the same for the rest of my days."

He's over three hundred and sixty years older than me. I've always been attracted to men older than me, but this takes it to a whole other extreme. He's lived through so much of history. My measly twenty-four-years of life mean nothing in the grand scheme of his life. My decades of life are a mere blip in time to him.

I want to react, want to jump up from the bed and ramble on about how insane this all is, but I remain seated next to him. "How…" I clear my throat nervously. "How long have you been like this? A vampire?" That word still seems absolutely ridiculous to speak aloud now that I know they're real.

"I was turned just after my thirty-first birthday," Silas explains. "It wasn't my decision to become what I am. It's a life I never would have chosen for myself."

I knew this without him having to tell me. Who in their right mind would choose to be a vampire? Being bound to the night and feeding on nothing but blood does not seem like an idealistic life. "It seems incredibly lonely."

"It is," he admits. "Getting attached to humans is never wise. If you're in a location too long, the whispers and speculation start when you don't age with time like the rest of them. Plus, human lives are so short and watching people you grow fond of die year after year when you will never know the peace of death yourself is taxing." His midnight black eyes lock on to the painting across the room. It's more modern than the pieces in his cellar or at the estate. "For many vampires, they take mates. It's less solitary to go through this life when they have someone by their side."

"A mate?" I repeat. "Is that like a wife or something?"

Too antsy to sit, Silas stands from the bed so he can move freely through the expansive—albeit *destroyed*—room. I haven't gotten around to asking him what happened in here yet. It looks like a tornado went through the room. "No, it's not the same. When you're married, you're joined by law. A simple piece of paper declares that you belong to another. It's also easily broken by a divorce. Taking a mate binds you to them by blood. The connection is permanent. The only thing that can break the bond is death."

"So, the '*death do us part'* thing is very literal for vampires?"

Silas scoffs under his breath. "And a vampire's life is very long, taking someone as your mate should never be taken lightly."

The woman's things preserved in the cellar come to mind. Awkwardly I ask him about her, "Did you ever have a mate?"

Silas's pacing screeches to a halt, a pained expression crossing his devastatingly handsome features. I think he's going to say yes, that she was his mate, but he shocks me by shaking his head. "I've never taken a mate because I had a wife." He doesn't look at me as he talks, it's almost as if he can't. "She died shortly after I was turned."

She's been gone for over three hundred years, but the grief in his voice makes it sound as if he'd just lost her yesterday. I'm torn between wanting to hug him for his loss but also feeling jealous of a woman that's been dead for centuries. "She's the woman in the painting, right? It's her stuff that is preserved in those display cases?"

He gives me a curt nod. "Yes. Those items belonged to Cecily, but I don't wish to talk about her with you Quincey." He turns from me, leaning on his hands on the back of the couch.

"Why not?" I frown. "She obviously meant the world to you. For God's sake, you've carried around random trinkets that belonged to her for *centuries*, Silas. She *still* means a lot to you and that makes me want to know about her."

With his insane vampire speed, he whirls around to face me, his dark eyes full of frustration. "I can't talk to you about her because I made a vow to Cecily when I married her that I would never so much as look at another woman, let alone *care* for another. I've broken that vow many times over the years, but it was only sex. Meaningless fucks with women whose faces I hardly remember. *You* aren't a meaningless fuck to me Quincey, you're so much more and because of that, I can't talk to you about my dead wife. I have to keep you two separate, or the guilt will grow to be insufferable."

My heart breaks a little hearing this. "You feel guilty being with me?" I question softly. "It feels wrong being with me?"

He kneels in front of me, his hands grab my hips and pull me toward him. "No, *mon soleil*. It doesn't feel wrong, it feels right and that's what makes me feel guilty. Each time I think of you, each time I touch you." His thumbs caress back and forth over my bare skin. "Each time I kiss you, it feels *right*. It should feel like the ultimate betrayal against her, but it doesn't."

Understanding settles in me. He doesn't feel guilty because he's cheating on her. He feels guilty because of his *lack* of guilt. I cup his face in my hands. "I don't know much about her, but I do know she loved you and that makes me immediately like her. If she loved you the way I think she did, she'd want you to be happy. She wouldn't want you to be miserable for the rest of your life, Silas." Very few people—if any—have had the honor of seeing the vulnerable look on Silas's face right now. I feel incredibly lucky he's dropped his impenetrable wall for me, even if it is only for a second. "I'm not telling you to erase her from your heart, she's part of the reason you're the man you are and for that I'm thankful to her. All I ask is you make a little room for someone else, it doesn't have to be me, but allow someone else to love you the way Cecily did."

Even if Silas wakes up tomorrow and decides I'm more trouble than I'm worth, I hope he'll open himself up to someone one day. No one should go through their life without feeling loved, Silas deserves someone too.

His hands engulf mine, pulling them from his face gently. "A little room?" he repeats, his voice just a rasp. "Fuck Quincey, can't you see that I've already given every piece of my heart that I can to you? She'll always own a piece of it, but the rest is already yours." My own heart thuds painfully in my chest, filling with joy as I absorb his words. "I know I shouldn't. I know being anywhere near you will only put you in danger, but I can't bring myself to stay away. Not anymore."

"Don't run from me," I whisper my plea, anxiety that he'll leave creeping into my bones.

"I couldn't if I tried." Silas kisses my knuckles tenderly. "This is new to me, Quincey. I don't know how to do this—I don't know how to have you in my world. I ask that you're patient with me as I figure this out."

"As long as you're patient with me as I get used to this whole *vampire* thing," I counter. "There's bound to be a learning curve."

His lips pull ever so slightly. "Indeed."

The smile disappears, and his face grows serious once more. "I need you to promise me something, love. I need you to promise that if I ever tell you to run from me, that you will do so, no questions asked. I need you to promise you'll get as far away from me as possible, as fast as you can. If I lose control and you're around, I will kill you before you can beg me to stop."

"But—"

"No buts, I need you to promise."

Stiffly I nod. "I promise."

CHAPTER 31

Quincey

"While the plague ran rampant through London in sixteen sixty-five, another unknown killer was also taking lives. Almost a quarter of the population died in just over a year. Many of those deaths weren't from the black death. They were from vampires. Or *one* vampire." He lies next to me in bed staring at the ceiling while I stare at him, memorizing each of the angles of his face. "Andreas was the first vampire in existence. How he came to be is still a mystery, but there are a lot of theories that it was a virus of sorts. For hundreds of years, he was the only one of his kind. Andreas was smart, one of the smartest men I've ever known, but he allowed emotions to dictate his actions. When the plague hit London hard and people started dropping dead, he decided he was going to save them."

I grimace, knowing where Silas is going with this.

"He didn't save them because he felt like it was the right thing, he was simply *lonely*. Very few survive being turned, the process wreaks havoc on a human body. Vampire blood more times than not turns into a poison when a human ingests it. The body decays from the inside out as it eats through healthy veins and muscles. It's a horrifying sight. The poor people who died were written off as other casualties from the plague. Those who survived were forever altered, changed to be just like *him*."

My hand takes his, squeezing gently.

"When the change is complete, many don't come back with their humanity. It's as if the change burned away anything that made them human. There is no sense of right or wrong, the only thing they know is they're starving and anything that gets between them and fresh blood is as good as dead. These—*creatures*—are the ones the stories are based on. These are the true monsters." He swallows hard before continuing. "We'd just moved away from France the year before to London. We left in hopes of a better life, but unbeknownst to us, it would be the thing that ruined us. Cecily got sick first, she urged me to leave her, to save myself, but I refused to leave her side. I fell ill shortly after. Andreas found us on our literal deathbeds. With the fever, I was disoriented and unsure as to what was happening, but I remember him telling me he was going to save us. He forced his blood down both mine and Cecily's throats. The pain of the blood moving through my system was excruciating, but as my heart slowed and my body turned cold, the pain left. When I opened my eyes for the first time as a vampire, I'd never felt stronger—*healthier*—in my life. I felt invincible, because to an extent, I was."

"What happened to Cecily?" I ask.

"She wasn't next to me when I woke up. I found her hours later with her fangs in a little boy's throat. She killed him and threw his body to the side like a piece of trash. When I looked into her dead eyes, I didn't recognize her. The gentle look that had permanently resided in them was replaced with something evil. The Cecily I married had a bleeding heart that rivaled yours. She would cry for the pigs and chickens in the cages at the market, but she killed the boy who couldn't have been older than ten without a single ounce of remorse. Her only concern was feeding. I was famished myself, but I still had restraint. Cecily never got enough. For days, I watched her rip through people and never grow full, and each day that passed it became clearer to me that my wife was gone."

"Oh, Silas." My heart breaks for him. No one should have to see the person they love turn into a monster like he did.

"No matter how hard I tried, I couldn't reason with her. She was completely lost to me and when she attacked a mother and daughter next, I knew I couldn't sit back and watch any longer. The Cecily I loved would have been devastated to learn that she'd caused such destruction." He pauses. The next words he speaks are low but so clear, devoid of any emotion. "I killed my wife with my bare hands because I knew if I didn't, she'd never stop taking innocent lives. As I sat there on a dirty London street with my dead wife in my arms, something broke in me and I've never been the same. The anger I used to become the man I am today corroded my soul that day, the darkness crept in and I welcomed it with open arms. I wouldn't have survived if I hadn't."

It makes so much sense to me now, how he's been able to hold on to that fury for so long. An event like he went through would have broken a weaker man, instead, he let it fuel him and make him stronger. It also corrupted him at the same time. The devoted husband became the ruthless king.

"Killing her was the hardest thing I've ever done, but killing Andreas was the easiest. He was moving through Europe, going town by town, turning sick people. I followed behind him, leaving a trail of dead in my wake. I was no better than Cecily, the only difference was I wasn't being fueled by an uncontrollable hunger, it was rage. I only had one goal in mind, and I killed anyone who stood in my way. By the time I finally caught up with Andreas, the blood of hundreds was on my hands," Silas explains, still staring up at the ceiling. I wish he'd look at me but understand why he can't. "Other vampires followed Andreas like he was their king, all because he granted them immortality, but I knew the truth. I knew he was a selfish bastard and the power had gone to his head. He never saw it coming. His arrogance made him foolishly believe I was another one of his sheep. He believed I would be thankful to him for *saving me*, so when I ripped his head from his shoulders, the surprised look still remained on his face as it rolled through the dirt. He almost killed me in our battle, but I prevailed. My fury made me stronger. Just like that, I dethroned the king."

Understanding hits me. "And that's when your reign began."

Finally, his head turns, black eyes full of years of anger and pain peer into mine. "It was never my intention. I'd planned on killing Andreas and then walking into the bright morning sun so I could be reunited with Cecily, but I knew if I didn't take control, vampires would run rampant through the world. A plague would be the least of their worries. Humans would never stand a chance. My word became law amongst the vampires. It was understood that if you stepped out of line, you died. I was the judge, jury, and executioner. Nothing has changed in almost four centuries, it's just easier now with modern technology to keep track of things."

I scoot closer to him until our chests are touching. The tension in his body caused by having to relive the worst days of his life is obvious, but as I run my hand soothingly up his arm and kiss the corner of his mouth, his body relaxes. "Thank you for telling me," I whisper close to his lips. "I know that wasn't easy for you, but it helps me understand you better."

"Does my past make you see me differently? Do you still believe I'm a good man?"

"If you were a bad man, you wouldn't have killed the woman you loved to save the lives of others, Silas," I assure him. "You haven't scared me away just yet."

"I may not scare you, but you scare me, Quincey." His admission has me shocked in place. "I have no idea what I'm doing with you."

"We'll figure it out," I promise him, swiping my thumb back and forth over his cheekbone. "I know this is a hard thing to believe, but you don't actually have to have all the answers all the time. Sometimes you just have to close your eyes and leap into the unknown."

He ghosts his lips across mine before whispering words that will play on repeat for the rest of my days. "Leap with me, Quincey."

"I've already leaped and now I'm falling." *Falling so fucking hard.* "Are you going to catch me?"

"Always."

CHAPTER 32

Silas

I've lived almost four hundred years without her, but two days apart from her feels like an eternity. I loaded her into a car two nights ago, sending her back to the estate without me, and it was shockingly harder than either of us expected.

She'd wrapped her thin arms around my waist, squeezing me tight before reluctantly climbing into the car. Like a lovesick fool, I'd stood on the sidewalk watching the black SUV drive away until I couldn't see her anymore. Duke, who'd watched the whole exchange, looked at me with such a dumb look on his face, I'd almost broken his nose. I'd somehow found the restraint to not maim the cocky fucker.

I've been doing my best to focus on the mess at hand with my mystery enemy, but my mind wanders to Quincey more than I should allow. She's asked for a period of grace as she learns to adapt to what I am, but I need to remind myself that I too am going through a change. For a very long time, there was nothing important enough to distract me from my work. It was my priority, the only thing I concerned myself with, but now I worry about her.

My body has been on edge for two days because I'm away from her. I've hired some of the best security teams in the country to guard the property, but it doesn't feel like it's enough to keep her safe. After the events the other night, the only way I feel like I can keep her safe is by guarding her myself.

And that's not realistic. I can't cart her around with me to all my meetings. If too many people see her with me, it will be the equivalent of painting a bright crimson target on her back. I have to be smart about where I'm seen in public with her. The dark corners in the city I frequent are no place for her.

"Are you even paying attention to a word I'm saying?" Rory looks at me blandly over the screen of one of the two laptops sitting in front of her.

Duke pops another one of the chocolates he'd promptly stolen from her when we arrived in his mouth. "Don't mind him, *Morticia*, he's all bent out of shape because he misses his woman," he tells her from the black leather couch he sprawled himself out on across the room. "You'd think that he'd be in a better mood now, but *nope*. It's just opened up a whole new can of worms of new things for him to be stressed about." Duke kicks his feet up on the table in front of him.

Rory glares at him, her dark brows pinching. "Who the hell raised you? You'd think all those years in the military should have instilled some fucking manners in you. Get your feet off my coffee table before you scratch it." She growls at him like an angry younger sister. "And I told you to stop calling me Morticia."

"Why? The name fits so well? You've got that sexy goth vibe going on." Duke waves a hand in her direction. "If you'd just dye your hair like I've been telling you, it'd be perfect, but you insist on keeping it purple."

Rory's shoulder-length hair is dyed a pale purple color and right now it's tied up in two buns on top of her head. She takes Blackwood's dress code as a mere suggestion, just like Quincey wears whatever the hell she wants. Though today Rory is wearing a black blazer, she still wears a distressed, revealing tank top with a faded design on it. The black and gray gothic moth tattoo that covers almost all of her chest is on full display. A majority of her skin is covered in tattoos and her ears are riddled with different piercings. There's a hoop through her nostril as well and she's only just recently removed the one in her lip. If she was anyone else, I'd never allow them to work for me, but Rory is the best hacker out there and I'd rather her be on my side than against me. I can tolerate her attire and unpleasant hair color.

"I don't have time for this pointless conversation," I interject before Rory can fling her words back at Duke. They're like siblings, constantly arguing over the pettiest shit. "Repeat what you were saying before, Rory."

With one last snarl in Duke's direction, she types away at the laptop in front of her. "I tracked the men who chased what's her face—"

"Quincey," I supply stiffly.

She waves me off. "Right whatever, *her*. I tracked their movements that day, trying to see if they could lead me to any clues as to who they were working for. Clearly, these idiots aren't the brilliant masterminds that almost hacked you and blew up your shit. They didn't even bother trying to hide from the security cameras on the streets, it was really easy to follow them."

"What did you find?"

"I followed them back to the airstrip they flew into twenty-four hours before when they went after Quincey." She flips the screen around so I can see the men I killed descending the stairs of a private plane. "And that is where my intel ends."

I scowl at her. "What do you mean ends?"

"Whoever they work for is good at covering their steps. It's going to take some more digging to find where this plane came from and who owns it. From what I can find, the plane is listed under some bogus company based out of the Caymans. Any idiot with a computer could find that information. Just give me a little more time and I'll dig up what I can for you."

My hands flex tensely at my sides. "I don't have more time to give, Rory. I need these people found and I needed them found yesterday. I'm tired of being in the dark and them being two fucking steps ahead of me!" I boom at her, it's not fair she's getting my wrath, but I'm struggling to keep it at bay right now.

Rory leans farther back in her chair to create additional space between us, the feisty look she's been wearing when talking to Duke slips away and wariness replaces it. "I'm working as fast as I can, Mr. Laurent. I'm good at what I do, but so are they. It's just going to take some extra steps to beat them."

"Make it happen, Rory." With a nod of my head in Duke's direction, I head to the door. "Let's go."

He jumps up, waving flippantly at Rory before following me. "Back to the apartment?"

"No, I need to go home."

I need to see her, to touch her.

For once, I'm starving for something other than blood.

"About fucking time, man."

The entire estate smells like her.

She's permeated every inch of the six thousand square foot house. The sweet scent of her floods me as I enter the front door. The house that used to feel dark and devoid of much life seems brighter than usual even in the middle of the night.

It's small changes. Lamps are turned on in rooms that usually are permanently dark—untouched. Freshly cut roses sit in a glass vase on the entryway table and somewhere in the house, soft music plays lowly. For the most part, it has nothing to do with the physical changes she's made, it's just her presence. Her energy exudes life.

Like a predator tracking its prey, I move silently through the house following her scent. I should have known I'd find her still in Ira's room, curled up in the chair she'd moved closer to his bed.

He's awake, but each time I see Ira, the sickness has eroded more and more of him. The only thing keeping him upright is from the pillows she placed behind him. He looks so frail, but at least the pain has been well managed by Quincey.

She sits with her knees drawn to her chest, staring out the open windows at the night sky. I should go in and let her know I'm home, but I find myself wanting to watch her from the shadows a moment longer.

"Did you ever figure it out?" Ira asks her, drawing her attention away from the moon.

She smiles softly but looks confused. "Figure what out, Ira?" She rests her hand comfortingly on his arm.

He coughs, his whole body heaving with the movement. Once settled, he elaborates. "Did you ever figure out why you couldn't rid your mind of thoughts of Silas? Why no matter how much he pissed you off, you couldn't stop?"

My body jerks, my muscles seizing at Ira's words.

Quincey spoke about me to Ira?

Quincey dips her chin, trying to hide the tinge of pink that grows on her cheeks at his question. The smile however that splits her face does not go unnoticed.

"I'll take that as a yes." Ira laughs hoarsely.

Clearing her throat, she nods her head at him. "Yes, I think I figured it out."

"Are you going to leave a dying man in suspense? Spit it out, dear."

"I couldn't stop thinking about him because deep down I didn't want to. While I was busy hating him, I was falling for him. It just took me a little while to realize that under the anger there was another emotion growing. By the time I figured it out, it was already too late.

Silas has engraved his name in my heart and there is no erasing it. It's his now."

Ira's face fills with joy, his eyes shining happily behind his crooked glasses. "I knew you'd be good for him. When I first met you, I knew you were what he needed. I knew you'd accept him for what he truly is."

"You knew after my first night here?" she questions.

"No, dear." Ira shakes his head in a jerky movement. "I knew for a year before you finally got here."

A year? Wait. That's not what he told me when he came to me about acquiring her. He said he'd seen her at St. Sin, and he was drawn to her. He told me that after her shift, he'd followed her, and he'd watched as she took care of a head wound on a street performer. The young kid had done a flip in his dance routine and accidentally landed on his head. Quincey had run back to the bar and performed first aid on him. Was that story a lie?

"I'm not following what you're saying, Ira," she says slowly, concern crossing her pretty face.

"There was a team of oncology doctors in Boston I went to see last year. They thought there may be something else they could do for me, so I flew up there to have a consultation with them, but the cancer had spread. They were the ones who told me there was nothing else that could be done, that I was terminal," Ira explains.

I remember him going to see some doctors, but how did I forget that they were in Boston? The same town Quincey was living in. I should have put two and two together myself.

"Before my appointment, I watched a delirious drunk man, three times your size get in your face, but not once did you flinch. You were tough as nails. Even when he shoved you and you fell, you didn't back down. You kept your cool. That's when I knew you'd be able to handle Silas's anger. Then after my appointment, I didn't know what to do with myself. What does one do when they learn they're going to die? I sat in the waiting room for hours, staring at the black screen of a broken television as I contemplated all my life choices up until that point. You must have seen me sitting there because you came over and sat next to me."

Quincey's hand covers her mouth. I can smell her salty tears from here even before they fall down her face.

"You asked me if I was okay, I lied and told you I was right as rain. You smiled at me and told me you were going to sit there with me anyway. I didn't know just how much I didn't want to be alone in that moment until I wasn't anymore. You didn't say anything, you just sat with me for over an hour. That's when I knew I wanted you to help me die, that if you were there, I wouldn't be alone." His frail hand reaches for Quincey's free one. "I'm sorry you were brought here against your will, dear. It was selfish of me, but I don't regret it. You've been there for me in ways I'll never be able to repay, and now I can die knowing you'll be there for Silas too."

"Ira," Quincey chokes out, her shoulders shaking. "Don't apologize, it's okay."

"He's been alive for a very long time Quincey, maybe you can remind him what it's like to actually live. When you have the gift of immortality, you forget how precious life is." Ira's lips pull into a sad smile. "Just trust me on this, I know better than anyone how fast it can all be taken away from you."

Quincey wipes the tears away from her eyes. "I don't understand why he didn't change you." She sniffs. "He could have saved you."

"No dear, that was never an option for me," Ira tells her. "There's a strict law in place now about vampires changing humans. It hasn't been allowed in almost a hundred years."

"Surely exceptions can be made. Who enforces this rule?"

Ira's eyes cut to mine as if he knew I've been standing in the dark doorway this whole time. "Breaking a law that you created is usually unwise," he tells her while looking in my direction. "Isn't that right?"

Quincey follows where Ira's eyes stare. She does a double take when she sees me standing there. Her heart picks up the second she spots me, and her body starts to move in my direction of its own accord, but she stops herself before she can leave the chair. It's almost as if she can't fight the need to be near me. *I know the feeling, love.*

Slowly walking into the room, I nod my head solemnly at Ira. "The law is in place for a reason. Too many people were coming back without their humanity." Just like Cecily. "I couldn't tolerate such reckless behavior anymore, so I prohibited it. Like any law, it's still broken by many, but I always find out. Anyone who breaks the law is executed for their crime. I can't impose a law but break it myself. It doesn't work like that."

Regardless of the circumstances or *personal connection* I may have to them, it cannot happen. There are no exceptions. People in my past have learned this the hard way as they watched me ruthlessly dispose of their mistakes.

I didn't understand it then, I thought other vampires were being irresponsible and rebellious by breaking my law when they changed a human. Even when they claimed they did it because they loved the human and couldn't imagine living their immortal lives without them, I still didn't care. All I saw was insubordination and dealt with it accordingly. Now that I have Quincey, I find myself reluctantly understanding their motives.

"I wouldn't choose to be a vampire either," Ira adds as a way to comfort her. "I'm at peace with dying, Quin. Don't shed another tear for me, my old heart can't take it."

"I just wish there was more I could do for you." Her voice is thick with emotion.

"There is." Ira grabs her hand tightly with his. "Stop believing you're cursed. You had a bad string of luck is all, dear. Your touch doesn't take lives, it's time you stop listening to the ramblings of your mama. So many people would be lucky to have you be their nurse. You need to go back to doing what you were meant to do when this is all over."

I tuck a strand of her hair behind her ear, making her turn her attention to me. "I've been around for a long time, *mon soleil*. You can trust me when I say there is no such thing as curses." She turns her head into my touch when I caress the side of her face.

Ira watches the whole exchange, a thrilled look on his face. His grand plan worked after all. I'm sure he's feeling pretty pleased with himself. "I'm feeling tired. You two go on and spend some time together."

Quincey stands from the chair and points at the red button at the top of the remote that sits on his tray table. "Press that if you need anything, Ira."

"You tell me that every time you leave the room, Quin." He chuckles. "I think I know the drill."

She checks the levels of his IV bags and numbers on his monitors once more before allowing me to lead her out of the room by her hand.

Her hand in mine soothes the unease that's wracked my body for two days since she left. How am I supposed to get anything done with her in my life? I need to figure it out fast because I'm not planning on letting her go.

CHAPTER 33

Quincey

He leads us to his bedroom instead of taking me back to mine.

Just like the bedroom at the apartment, the room is dark. From the dark gray almost black wall color, to the dark wood furniture, to the black antique chandelier that casts just enough light for you to not run into things. Antique paintings hang on the walls. The scenes they depict are anything but bright and happy. The art is full of disturbing, haunting images that would cause nightmares if I slept in the same room as them every night.

Unlike the room in the city, it's pristine. The furniture is all the right way up and nothing is broken into bits. It's eerily neat in here, not a single thing out of place. In the middle of the room is a large bed with dark maroon bedding. My lips pull slightly at the sight of it. "I'm a little disappointed," I muse playfully. "No coffin?"

"No, I'm afraid I sleep in a bed like everyone else," Silas smirks at his giant bed.

His hand releases mine as I move about the room. There aren't many knickknacks in here like his office. No personal touches that would give you hints as to what kind of man sleeps in here. There are no half-read books on the nightstand, no articles of clothing thrown over the accent chair in the corner, no signs the space is lived in. "You really sleep in here?" I double-check, looking at him over my shoulder.

"Yes," he insists while giving me a weird look. "Why is that so hard to believe?"

I wrinkle my nose at him. "You're such a neat freak, no one would ever know that you spend any time in this room. My bedroom in Boston would have driven you crazy with all the random stuff thrown about. My closet was so small, I had to keep clothes in bins under my bed, which of course meant things were always sticking out from under it."

"I'm not a neat freak," he argues. "It's not as if you're a slob yourself. Your room here is very orderly."

Cocking my head at the morbid painting of a man staked to a stone table, I tell him distractedly, "I don't want Della reprimanding me about making a mess. Besides, I had to sell the majority of my things to pay off Gallo. I don't have enough belongings to have clutter lying about." Grimacing one last time at the painting, I turn and smile at him. "It's okay. I'm looking at it as a way of wiping the slate clean, starting over. I can do anything now, nothing in my past is holding me back."

"You'd let go of your past that easily?" His dark brows furrow, the corners of his mouth tipping down.

"I won't ever forget my past, it made me who I am today, but I won't hold on to it so tight it keeps me from moving forward. If I'm going to be happy in the now and excited for the future, I can't let my past consume me like that." It doesn't do me any good to be upset about my past or resentful of my upbringing. I can't go back and change anything. I can't make my parents be the wholesome parents I always wanted them to be. "I won't ever be able to forgive my dad for selling me like a piece of meat and I won't be able to forgive my mom for taking my childhood away from me, but I'm ready to let go of the anger."

My dad is dead, I will never have to hear another one of his lies and my mother... well, as for her, I see no reason as to why I would ever see her again. One of the joys of growing up and becoming an adult is you figure out pretty quickly that just because you're related to someone by blood, it does not make them your family. Sometimes family is the people you choose to have in your life. Like Lucy. Lucy is my family.

"I'm not sure how to let go of the past," he shocks me by admitting.

Moving across the room, I cup his face in my hand. The man who stands before me isn't the one who rules these streets with an iron fist. His guard has dropped, allowing me to see the man I'm falling for. "Letting go of the past doesn't mean you forget it, Silas. You'll never forget, no matter how many years you're alive. You'll never forget the things or the people that brought you to this point, but the pain you're clinging to isn't doing you any good anymore."

His dark eyes soften as he scans my face with a look of wonderment. "How did you become so wise in so few years on this earth?"

"I'm not sure," I muse. "But according to Ira, you could learn a few things from me."

I'm still in shock that Ira, sweet little Ira, was the puppet master this whole time. That he was the one pulling the strings behind the scenes. I'd already gotten over Silas forcing me here, but had I known Ira was the one who requested me from the start, I may have gotten over it faster.

I wish I could say that I remember the day in Boston when Ira first met me, but I can't recall it for the life of me. My time at the hospital is a blur of high-stress moments as the different traumas came in. Even though I don't remember that day, I'm glad I took the time to sit with Ira. The fact that I could offer him a bit of comfort on one of the worst days of his life makes all the other bad days at that hospital worth it.

His lips tip up. "Like what?"

Smirking slyly, I push playfully on his chest. "For starters, I can show you how to relax."

I know my halfhearted shoves do little to actually sway his strong body, but he's a good sport and allows me to push him backward until the back of his knees hit his bed. Quirking a brow at me, he challenges, "Is that so?"

"I don't care that you're immortal, surely all the stress you carry around can't be good for your heart." I turn on my soothing nurse voice that I usually reserve for ill patients. I swore I'd never do the sexy nurse thing, but here I am feeling little to no shame.

"My heart hasn't beat in a long time, love," he rasps as he falls onto the low-slung bed. "Though there have been a couple times as of late that I could have sworn I felt it beat once more."

With my hands on his spread knees, I lean forward to brush my lips teasingly against his. "Really? Like when?"

He remains still as I continue to tease him with barely-there kisses on his mouth and along his jaw. "When you were attacked and I couldn't get to you, I thought the fear was going to make my chest split open. I loathed that feeling. I destroyed my bedroom because of it." My kisses come to a stop and I pull back to look him in the eyes. Now I know why his bedroom looked like a tornado blew through it. The guilt for making him feel that way eats at me. "And then later that night, I swear it beat again as you came around my cock and your heat became my own."

I'm kissing him before he barely gets the final word out. What a lonely, cold existence he's lived. In a way, I think he's been punishing himself for what happened to Cecily. That deep down he thinks he doesn't deserve to feel happy because she no longer feels anything because of him. I want to show him that it's okay to move on, that his endless supply of time will go to waste if he doesn't.

His hands grip the fabric of my loose cotton shorts as he drags me down to straddle him. I need very little coaxing. I climb onto his lap freely and eagerly. His tongue runs along the seam of my mouth, seeking entry. My lips part, allowing him access to sweep his tongue inside. I groan as the flavor that is just him hits my tastebuds. It's intoxicating. I could kiss him for hours and never get sick of it. A thousand years could pass, and I'd never tire of his touch. He's got me hooked on him.

Impatiently my hands shove his impeccably tailored jacket from his shoulders. He lets go of me just long enough to shove the offensive garment off to the side. It looks wildly out of place splayed out in the middle of the floor in his pristine room. It's barely hit the hardwood before my fingers begin undoing each of the buttons of his shirt. I'm thankful he doesn't wear a tie with daily suits. It's one less thing I'd have to tear from his body.

I tear my mouth away from his so he can pull the hoodie over my head. His eyes light up when he discovers I'm not wearing anything under it. As if he can't stop himself, Silas's head dips so he can suck one of my taut nipples into his mouth. A hissing breath is released from between my lips as he scrapes his blunt teeth across it.

When he trails kisses up my chest and then sucks softly at the juncture of my neck, my heart leaps in my chest. Not in fear, but in anticipation. I shouldn't want him to bite me, it should be my biggest fear, but the idea of him sinking those fangs of his into my vein sends waves of need through my system. "Would it hurt?" I breathe out my question as I tilt my head to the side, allowing him better access.

"No," he answers against my skin. "Not at all. If done right, it's very pleasurable."

"Will you do it one day? Will you bite me?" I ghost my fingers down his now exposed chest, the muscles feel like cools stone under my touch. "I want you to drink from me."

One second I'm sitting on his lap straddling him, the next I'm on my back pinned under his immense weight. Wild, angry eyes glare down at me as his fingers lock around my wrist like a vise. "Don't ever say such a thing again, Quincey," he seethes close to my face. "If you tempt me like that and I grant your request, there's a chance I won't be able to stop. I warned you about being reckless with your life, what the consequences would be if you were again. Do you really want me to take you over my knee?"

I grin up at him wickedly. "I'd rather you bite me, but I'll take what I can get." Feeling bold, I roll my hips up, grinding myself against the growing dick still confined by his slacks. The anger melts from his eyes, pure need replaces it as I do it again. "What would you rather I give you, my blood or my ass?"

His hand leaves my wrist only to lock around my neck, his thumb presses into my pounding pulse point. "I don't need you to *give* me anything. If I want it, I'll simply take it from you, *mon soleil*." This time when I roll my hips, he matches my movement, making me gasp at the glorious friction. "I'll claim your ass as mine one day soon, but I want to leave my mark everywhere else first. I'm going to brand you from the inside out with my cock."

"As if you haven't already done just that." I stretch lazily beneath him, spreading my legs wider to accommodate his hips. "But if you insist on staking your claim again, I suppose that's fine with me."

"Devious," he murmurs. "You enjoy playing with fire, don't you?"

"Not usually, but you seem to bring it out of me." His hand relaxes enough on my throat to allow me to rear up and capture his mouth with mine. "Now take off your fucking pants, Mr. Laurent."

The rest of our clothes are torn off in a hurried frenzy. Within seconds, I'm once again straddling the six-foot, four-inch vampire that is built like a goddamn god. His body is the most beautiful piece of artwork in the entire estate, it's a preserved masterpiece in its own right. Each defined muscle looks as if it'd been carved by hand.

My fingers wrap around his thick length, and with languid movements, I work my hand up and down. His dark eyes watch with such intensity my skin burns. His hips buck under me when I spread the drop of cum around the head of his dick. The low sound he makes in the back of his throat is like music to my ears. His fingers dig into my hips, leaving fresh bruises over the two-day-old ones, but I don't care. I'll wear his marks proudly.

Biting my bottom lip, I hold his gaze as I bend at the middle to take him into my mouth. Silas groans as my wet, hot tongue slides over him. I take him as far back as I can. His eyes flare, heating with pleasure when I can't stop the small gagging sound I make. He's struggling to let me take the lead. I can see the internal battle written on his face.

"Quincey, fuck," he breathes out.

Wanting him to lose control, I pull back, sucking shamelessly on the tip.

The growl that comes from between his bared teeth is my only warning before I'm pulled off him. My head spins as I'm moved at a pace my brain struggles to keep up with. My vision is still fuzzy when I feel his mouth clamp down on my swollen clit.

"*Ah*!" I gasp, rearing up onto my elbows to find his broad shoulders spreading my thighs as he feasts on my pussy.

His big hands hold my ass, tilting my pelvis up toward his eager mouth. He licks and sucks at my sensitive flesh. When I writhe beneath him, the sensation too much to stay still, his arm moves to lock down over my hips, ensuring I stay right where he wants me. My short reprieve comes when he turns his head to bite down at the juncture of my thigh. His blunt teeth hurt but in a way that makes my skin prickle with pleasure. He doesn't bite down hard enough to break the skin, much to my unexplainable annoyance. Silas licks over the tender spot, salving the ache.

"Silas, please," I whine, sounding unbelievably needy to my own ears, but I don't care.

"I've got you, love," he soothes, mistaking what I'm truly begging him for. This is clear when he returns his mouth to my center instead of biting me like I want. I want him to make me bleed.

Silas's free hand snakes around to tease my opening before two thick fingers sink inside me. That's what I need to send me over the edge. The muscles in my stomach and thighs shake before my back bows as I come.

He never lets up. His mouth continues to torture me as I ride the waves of my orgasm. He doesn't stop until I'm still, panting beneath him.

With one last, leisurely lick through my folds, he rises above me.

I see them even though he dips his head in an attempt to hide them from me. The tips peek out between his slightly parted lips. They must have descended while he was making me come.

There is something so unbelievably *hot* about seeing his fangs in this moment. I take hold of his chin, turning it so he's forced to look at me. "Stop hiding them from me," I order him.

Silas narrows his eyes at me, a look of uncertainty in them, but he stays still when I slip my finger through his parted lips so I can run it along the sharp canine. Without giving him a warning, I press the fleshy part of my fingertip against the point. It takes barely any pressure to break the skin. The pain makes me wince, but it's endurable.

"What the fuck, Quincey!" He jerks away from my hand, allowing my wounded finger to leave his mouth. Bright crimson blood drops blossom at the tip before slowly dripping down the digit. "What were you thinking?"

He wants to yell at me more, I can tell, but he falls silent. Pitch-black eyes lock on my finger. His whole body goes rigid on top of me as they track the perfect droplet of blood. My chest heaves with anticipation. Starting at my top lip, I drag my finger over my mouth, down my chin. I paint a line of fresh blood all the way to my navel.

He doesn't move an inch until I smear my finger along his bottom lip. His tongue follows behind, lapping up the blood. Silas's eyes squeeze tightly shut when I dip my bloodied finger back inside his mouth. Just when I think he's about to shove me away, his fingers lock painfully around my wrist, holding me in place as he laps at the cut. The muscles of my pussy clench when he sucks eagerly at the wound, drawing as much of my blood into his body as he can.

With an almost animalistic snarl, his eyes fly open, the inky black orbs burning me to my very soul. He lets go of my fingers and rasps the question, "What are you trying to do to me?"

Even if I had the words to answer him, I'd never get the chance to speak them. In one fluid move, he's lifted my leg over his shoulder and his cock, hard as steel, is buried deep inside of me in one stabbing thrust. As he bottoms out at my cervix, I lose the ability to think let alone breathe. My back arches, my fingers clutch the maroon bedding so tightly I'm surprised it doesn't tear, and my lips part with a silent cry.

I can feel him in every single one of my nerve endings. Every inch of my body is aware of him. As the sudden brain fog clears, the first thing I'm aware of is his mouth on me again. He laps up the trail of blood I'd painted on myself. As he makes his way up my throat, he pauses at my ear to whisper darkly, "Your cunt is almost as sweet as your blood. *Almost*." Silas's teeth nip at my earlobe. "I'm now thoroughly addicted to both."

His mouth stays on me, either suckling at my neck or devouring my lips, kissing me as if his life depends on it. In this moment, my need for him is so intense, it feels as if I would die if he left me right now. My nerves are on fire for him, my muscles shake with exhaustion and my heart pounds so hard in my chest he must feel it in his own.

I hold on to him, fingers scraping up and down his muscular back before digging into his shoulder as he fucks with ruthlessness. He grunts with each thrust The muscles of my pussy squeeze his length, desperate to keep him inside. "No one touches you but me," he says against the skin of my neck, his breath hot. "Do you hear me, Quincey? If anyone else touches you, I will set the world on fucking fire. You're fucking mine." His pace is angry, unbridled. "Say it. Tell me what I want to hear."

I move my hips with his, meeting each of his thrusts. "I'm yours," I choke out between moans. "I'm yours, Silas."

The orgasm I'd been barreling toward builds faster. Sensing it, he pulls back from my neck. "Look at me when you come, I want to watch as you fall apart."

His words set me off. Silas fucks me into the bed until my world explodes and I come, screaming. My thighs quiver and I thrash beneath his large body. He captures my mouth once more as he shudders, filling me with his cum.

CHAPTER 34

Silas

The sweetness of her blood still lingers on my tongue as she curls into my side, her head resting over where my heart should be beating. It's something I hardly think about anymore, but when I first woke as a vampire, I missed the sound of my own heartbeat. It doesn't matter how much life Quincey breathes into me; it will remain forever still in my chest. Her heart will just have to beat enough for the both of us for however long we can continue to do what we're doing.

A human and vampire relationship will always have a looming expiration date on it. It doesn't matter how much I care for her. My time with Quincey is limited. If I was ever willing to, Quincey would be the one I'd break the law for. She'd be magnificent as a vampire, but I can't take the gift of life away from her. I'd be stealing her sunshine from her, dooming her to a life of darkness if I turned her. I could never do that.

This is what happens when a vampire falls for a human. The desperation to keep them alive causes reckless decisions. I've seen it happen firsthand, just never thought I'd experience it myself, but here I am with a human I'm not willing to give up.

Fuck.

"Whatever you're thinking about, stop." Quincey's warm hand soothes me, brushing lightly across my chest. "I can feel you growing tense."

Trying to force myself to stop thinking about what's to come, I take her hand in mine and bring it to my mouth so I can kiss the pulse point in her wrist.

"Tell me about Ira," she insists groggily. I took her two more times, taking everything from her until the beast inside of me finally got its fill. I'd tenderly cleaned her up before tucking her into my bed with me. It feels so right to have her in a space I swore I'd never fill. I've never shared a bed with anyone, but now I can't imagine my pillows not smelling like her as I fall asleep. "How did you meet him?"

"He tried to pickpocket me when I was walking the streets one night." I smile fondly at the memory. He was a scrappy little kid, his shirt two sizes too big, his pants too short for his lanky legs. "He was starving and looking for a way to survive. Little did he know he was trying to steal from a vampire who heard him coming from two blocks away. Instead of punishing him, I bought him a meal and started paying him to do odd jobs for me. Eventually, he became my driver for a short time, but it was too dangerous to have him out there with me. It was safer for him to just work here at the house, so he became the groundskeeper. His real job, though, was being my moral compass when I was lacking my own. He's been my confidant in some capacity for sixty years."

"A whole lifetime you've known him," Quincey murmurs. "I can't imagine how hard it is watching the people you care about age while you stay the same. It must be so hard to keep your secret."

"I work in the shadows; very rarely do I broker business deals in person. This allows my face to remain a mystery to different connections. I'm able to stay in one place longer if I do that. New Orleans has been my home since I left London, I always find a way to come back. There're plans put in place that ensure that." I hesitate, not sure I should be telling her this, but decide she should know. "I've been training Duke to take over for me here, to become the face of the operation. My time here is almost up for this lifetime, I was planning on leaving after Ira passed."

My mystery assailant has also put a hold on those plans. I'm not going anywhere until they're taken care of.

She springs up, pulling the dark sheets to her naked body to cover herself. "*What*? You're leaving New Orleans?"

"I'll come back in a few decades when the people who know me have died," I explain to her. "This is how it works, love. I can't stay in the same place too long. It draws unwanted attention."

Her fingers anxiously shove her long hair away from her face. "Where will you go? How soon after Ira dies will you leave" —she catches herself before she can finish the sentence— "This house and *Della*. What about Della?" Quincey asks instead.

"I was thinking I'd go back to Europe, maybe France. It's been a long time since I've lived in my home country." I haven't been there since I originally left it with Cecily. It never felt right to return home without her, but now I think it may be time. "Or New York is always an option, so many faces there, it's easy to blend in." She doesn't smile at my attempt to lighten the mood, her brows remained furrowed, lips turned downward. "As for Della, she has family here she would never leave." A schizophrenic son that refuses to take his medication, is her family. He prefers to live on the streets with the voices in his head as his only company.

I recently learned the reason she'd been running late that day and had sent Quincey in her place to the drop. She was coming from the jail where her son was being held. *Again*. Connor is an artist and the medication that keeps him stable destroys the creative part of his brain. He's miserable when he's not able to paint and Della knows this. She fought it for a long time but ultimately couldn't force him to take medication that made him despondent.

"Europe," she repeats. "You'll go to Europe, for *decades*? But what about us, what about what we have? Does that mean you'll just leave without—"

I reach up, taking her stunning face in my hands, halting her words. "Please, let's not worry about this right now. I haven't finalized plans yet as there is still unfinished business I must put to bed before I can even think of leaving New Orleans."

Big, powder blue eyes that I'm positive now own my soul look into mine. "Promise me you won't just leave, Silas. Promise me we'll work this out together and you won't just make the decision for both of us."

It's a lie but I say it anyway because making her happy has become a priority in my life. "I promise." I pull her back down so she's resting on my chest once more. "Close your eyes, *mon soleil*. Sleep with me at least until the sun comes up."

I don't want to leave her any more than she wants to be left. The void where my heart once sat aches at the thought of it.

She is, without a doubt, making me fall in love with her and I'm afraid it may be the end of us both. My arms hold her as tight as her human body can withstand as she falls asleep on my chest, every fiber in my being telling me not to let her go.

She prefers to sit on the counter instead of the perfectly good kitchen table. It's not the proper thing to do, but I've found I quite like her at this height. Means I don't have to lean down to kiss her.

Her lips taste of the strawberries she's been snacking on while she watches me cook her dinner.

After spending the whole day away from each other, the bright sun in the sky keeping us apart, I woke up to find her pacing the length of her bedroom like a caged animal. Her shoulders were tight, her teeth nibbled anxiously on her bottom lip as she moved. The second Quincey's eyes landed on me in the doorway, the tension left her body and she launched herself at me with a smile that could break the hearts of many. She'd declared our opposite schedules weren't going to work for her too much longer, and I couldn't agree more.

She's not sleeping as much as she should, the dark circles under her eyes are evidence of that. Despite the exhaustion she feels, she smiles happily at me from her spot on the counter. I have things I need to attend to, pressing matters that require my attention, Rory has information she needs me to come to her office to see, but my need to spend a few fleeting moments with Quincey is stronger than my sense of duty right now. She'll be fast asleep by the time I get home later tonight.

"This '*hobby*' of yours is absolutely hilarious to me now," Quincey chuckles after taking another bite of fruit. "A vampire who enjoys cooking food he can't eat. It's like a vegan who only makes steak. Why torture yourself?"

"I enjoy the process of cooking. I can get lost in it and forget for a second about the demons that wait for me in the streets." Many of them are demons of my own creation, but that doesn't make the burden of them any less. I chose this career, I knew what I was doing when I was building my empire, but some days I wish I could go back and just do something simple. I say this but know that the boredom of a monotonous job would eat me alive. "Besides, this food," I stir the sauce in the pan, "it doesn't appeal to me anymore. My body doesn't crave it like it does blood." Putting the lid back on the pot, I move to stand between her thighs. "Though I don't think I'll ever crave anything more than I crave your blood, love."

She licks the sticky fruit residue off her fingers, smirking at me. "Hey, I offered. You're the one who turned me down, remember?" Quincey pushes her bottom lip out dramatically.

Pushing her thick hair off her shoulder, I run my thumbs along the pulse point in her neck. "You're really sitting before me pouting like a child because I won't bite you? There you go, crossing the line between brave and foolish again."

"I don't think it's foolish." Her arms loop around my neck, pulling me close to her. "I have something you need, and I'm freely offering it to you."

"You're freely offering to let me accidentally kill you, Quincey." I wish she would realize this. Last night when she cut her finger on my fang, my beast raged inside of me, banging against the steel doors I keep him behind. I've never seen something as beautiful as Quincey painted in her own blood. "Why do you want me to hurt you?"

"That's the thing, Silas. I don't think you'll hurt me." An immeasurable amount of trust sits in those blue eyes as they stare up at me.

I trace the lines of her face tenderly, memorizing each of the freckles that sit on her sun-kissed skin. No longer wanting to discuss this, I change the subject. "I want to take you out." Precautions will need to be made and I'll need to be smart about it, but I want to spend time with her outside of the house.

Her brows pinch in confusion. "Take me out... like a hitman? Or a date?" she clarifies painfully slow. "If literally anyone else on this planet said that to me, I would automatically just assume they meant date, but with you, I really feel like it could go either way. So, I just need to be sure—"

My finger presses against her lips. "You haven't angered me enough yet to justify the cost of a hitman, love." Her lips lift and the corners of her eyes wrinkle with humor. "We won't be able to spend the whole night away again, but you've earned a few hours away from the house. Constance will be able to sit with Ira for a little while so we can..." I trail off, the term feeling completely foolish. I don't do this. This is another foreign thing to me.

"Go on a date?" she supplies.

"Yes," I concede. "I suppose it would be a date."

She pushes my hand away so she can lean forward and press a kiss to the corner of my mouth. "Sounds fun, just tell me when and what I need to wear, but first" —she pulls away from me and points at the food on the stove— "you need to feed me now. I'm starving."

"So demanding," I scold.

"I learned from the best."

CHAPTER 35

Quincey

There's a soft knock at my bedroom door when I climb out of the shower. I know it's not Silas. He never would have bothered knocking, he would have just waltzed right in. The sensor that would alert me of Ira being out of bed or in distress sits silently on my dresser as well. Securing the plush towel around my torso, I pad across the room.

Della stands there, a weird look on her face and a garment bag over her arm. "You sure do know how to keep someone waiting," she huffs before pushing into the room. "I was knocking for five minutes."

I twist the strands of my wet hair, squeezing out the excess water. "I was in the shower. What's going on?"

She tosses the contents of her arms onto the bed and turns to look at me with her hands on her hips. "I went shopping."

"Okay?"

"The clothes you own are fit for a bowling alley or a dingy bar. Both establishments are places Silas isn't going to take you for your... date."

She chokes out the last word like it's a forbidden one. "I wanted you to look nice for the occasion, for him. And I figured I still owed you for putting you in the position that I did."

Ugh. People really need to let that go.

Silas says he's no longer upset with Della, but I've seen the way his eyes narrow in contempt when she enters the same room as him or when her name comes up in conversation. He still blames her for what happened.

Della hasn't been any better. She's been overly nice and accommodating since I came back with a few bumps and bruises. I'm not sure how much Duke or Silas told her, if she knows that I was almost assaulted, but I really hope they kept that part of the story to themselves. She doesn't need to feel guilty for something I'm not upset over. I still stand by what I told Silas, I'm glad I was there. Della would be dead if she'd been there like they planned.

"Della, stop. You don't owe me anything," I plead with her. "You didn't have to buy me anything."

Her mouth purses, her eyes narrowing behind those cat-eyed glasses she wears. "Fine, don't look at the dress as an apology gift, look at it as a thank you gift."

I sit down on the bed, crossing my bare legs so I don't accidentally flash the old woman. "A thank you gift? What could you possibly be thankful to me for? I haven't done—"

"You've done more than I ever thought you could do, Quincey," Della cuts me off, holding her hand up to silence me. "Despite being blackmailed into it, you take care of Ira with a tenderness that has been lacking from this house for a very long time. You didn't hold what Silas did against Ira; you've gone out of your way to make him comfortable. I wish I had come up with the rose idea months ago, it's brought Ira so much peace to have them back in the courtyard." For the first time since I've met her, real emotion tears at her voice. "And then there's what you've done for Silas. Do you remember what I said that first day about Silas not dating? He's never allowed someone to get close enough to him before you to even consider dating them. He'll never admit it—he has a reputation to uphold after all—but I think he keeps people at bay because he's afraid of losing them. It breaks my heart to know he'll spend lifetime after lifetime alone because he insists on keeping everyone at a safe distance. I'm not sure what the future holds for you two, but I'm thankful to you for making him brave even if it's for a short time."

As my heart soars, it also starts to break. The harsh reality of what Silas and I are doing will always be looming around the corner. The stopwatch is running and each minute that passes we come closer to the inevitable end. My throat tightens when I ask, "How am I supposed to love someone when I know it's going to have a painful end?"

Yeah, I said it. Love. I'm falling in love with this man. It's painful, like a knife twisting in my chest, but it's there, reminding me of its existence with each heartbeat.

"You love them hard, you love them fast and you appreciate the time you do have. Don't focus on the ending when it's only just starting, Quincey." Della tips my chin up to look at her when my head falls. "That won't do any good for either of you. Silas and you are both resilient, together you'll find a way to make it work." She wipes the lone tear that escapes off my cheek. "Now, go make yourself pretty for my boy. He deserves to see you in something other than clothes that make you look like a bum. I'm leaving here shortly, but you have a great time tonight. Tell me all about it tomorrow." She pats my face once before leaving me alone in my room, a million different thoughts swirling through my head.

I get up from the bed and stare at myself in the mirror that sits in the corner of the room. Closing my eyes, I shake off the feeling of impending doom. I told Silas he needs to stop living in the past, so I need to stop worrying about the future. We both need to be present in the now and that means I have a date with an incredibly sexy vampire to get ready for.

Della is a fabulous chef, but she's an even better shopper. The dress is made of dark red, almost maroon, satin fabric. Thin spaghetti straps hold up the deep V neckline. It's shorter and more revealing than anything I'd expect Della to purchase, but I love it. I love it way more than the very high, matching stilettos. My hands smooth the fabric that flares at my hips as I contemplate whether or not I can get away with wearing my checkered *Vans*.

Deciding Della will have my head if she finds out I didn't wear the heels, I slip them on, bending down to fasten the ankle straps. Rising back up, I stare into the same mirror I looked in just a little while ago, this time the sorrow is gone from my eyes. I look better than I have in almost a year, at least more put together and less frumpy.

Della was right, I'm glad she bought me this dress. I wouldn't have wanted to go on a date with Silas in my usual wardrobe. He's always so immaculately put together. The woman on his arm should look like she also put some effort into her appearance. And I did tonight. Each piece of my waist-length hair is curled to perfection, falling down my back and I spent extra time on my makeup instead of just my usual simple coat of mascara.

Smiling one last time at my reflection, I leave the room like I'm floating on a cloud of happiness. Who knew the man who caused me so much anger would make me the happiest in the end?

Silas slept in the city today, said he had some things to take care of but will be here shortly to pick me up. I need to check on Ira before I leave. He was unusually okay at the idea of spending a couple of hours with Constance earlier when we talked. I know he's just taking one for the team by not being bitter about her, but I'm thankful he's putting on a brave face for me.

I think the man is just happy that his grand plan is working.

Knowing I'll be there for Silas after he's gone gives him peace. The fact Ira set this whole thing in motion still makes me smile. His probing questions about Silas and begging me to be patient with him now make so much sense. He was busy orchestrating all of this from his deathbed.

Ira thinks I've given him comfort, but he too has given me something I'll never be able to thank him enough for.

He gave me Silas.

But like they say, it doesn't matter how much time you have, it will never be enough.

The smile that breaks out across my face is short-lived. The deafening gunshots that split through the night air outside burst the happy bubble I was floating in just seconds ago. On instinct, I drop down, curling into myself to become the smallest target possible. My arms cover my head, as if they will do any good to stop an incoming bullet.

Adrenaline rushes through my blood. My heart pounds wildly against my chest. I'm frozen in place, unable to move as the symphony of gunfire continues outside the windows. Silas upped the security on the property after the incident in the city. But I have no idea if it's our security team firing their guns at an unknown threat or if they're out there being gunned down.

I need a plan. Sitting in this hallway is not an option.

With a steadying breath, I call upon all the training that was ingrained in me while working in the trauma unit. I couldn't let my anxiety and fear slow me down then or people would die. If I do that now, I will die, and then who will help Ira?

Ira. I have to get to him, drag him somewhere so he isn't a sitting duck.

Staying as low as I can, I run down the hallway to his bedroom. Each time the high heels I wear click against the hardwood floor, I silently curse. There isn't time to take them off. I need to get Ira to safety and then find a way to call for help. My phone is charging in the kitchen.

I'll find a way to sneak down there once I have my patient secured.

His room is pitch black when I push the door open. Odd since I always leave a low light on in the event there's an emergency and I need to rush inside. The curtains are pulled shut, blocking out any light from the moon. Something is wrong. Alarm bells go off in my head and fear creeps down my spine, leaving a trail of goose bumps in its wake. Ira never wants the blinds closed, he likes to be able to look outside at all hours of the day. This is one of the first things I learned about him.

The dim light from the hallway only streams in so much, I can't yet make out his sleeping form from where I stand. The room itself is eerily quiet. This room is never quiet, between the constant beeping of his machines and the oxygen… What the hell? All of his machines are turned off, nothing but black screens sit there. I fly across the room at the realization.

"Ira!" I call his name while I fumble at the lamp on his nightstand. "Something's happening, we need to get out of here!"

I almost wish I would have left the light off, then I never would have had to see the horrifying sight in front of me.

His wrinkled, weak, sunspot-covered hands grasp at his neck. Green eyes stare up at me from behind his crooked glasses. Fear and tears seep from them. His mouth moves like he's trying to form words. Nothing comes out but choked breaths. The sheets that were once sterile white are stained bright crimson red as the blood that pours from his neck spreads through the fabric.

"Oh my god, Ira!" There's only a second of hesitation before my hands shove his out of the way. Hot, sticky blood oozes between my fingers as I apply pressure. His body trembles beneath me, his feeble hands cover mine in a hopeless attempt to help stop the bleeding. How did this happen? "It's okay, I've got you. It's going to be okay!" I promise him, even though years of medical training are telling me that it's not. "You stay with me, Ira!" I haven't gotten a good look at the wound, but it feels jagged as if something ripped through his throat.

His mouth opens again to say something, but the only thing that comes out is a spray of blood as he coughs. It sprays across my neck and face. "It's okay, it's okay," I repeat over and over while turning my head to wipe some of the blood from my face. "You're not allowed to die, not like this."

As they get closer, each gunshot outside makes my whole body jerk in fright. Is the security team shooting at the person who did this? How did they get inside without anyone hearing them? Is this my fault? I was so busy making my hair look perfect for my date that I left Ira unattended. I should have been in here. If I was here, I could have stopped this.

Hot tears run down my face. My throat burns with sobs that are dying to be released. Weakly, I smile reassuringly down at him. "I'm going to make it better, Ira. I'm going to fix this and you're going to be okay."

Desperately, I look around me for something I can use to stop the bleeding. As fast as possible, I keep pressure with one hand as the other reaches for the robe that lays across the end of his bed. It matches the light blue pajama set I'd put him in earlier. He always insisted they match, and I'd tease him about it constantly.

I ball the fabric and hold it against his neck. Not once does he look away from me. "Quin—" he chokes out, blood pouring from the corners of his mouth.

"Shh," I soothe. "Don't talk, keep your strength."

His mouth moves silently as he struggles to form words. "Q-Quin… run."

I shake my head down at him. "Nope, not happening. I'm not leaving you here. I'm going to stop the bleeding and you're going to be fine. We're going to leave together."

His eyes flick over my shoulder. "Be—"

I wish his heart monitor was on so I could see his vitals, see if what I'm doing is helping him at all. Maybe if I'm fast, I can get them turned back on…

"Q-Quin." My name comes out as a gargle. "No—"

"I've got you, Ira," I talk over him. "I'm going to make it all better and you're going to get to see Silas again. We're going to finish reading the book we started. You're going to be able to see your roses again because I'm going to stop the bleeding."

The sobs are no longer able to be kept at bay. My chest shakes as they fall freely from me. My bloody hands shake on his throat as they make my body heave.

The hands that I swore were cursed won't be able to save him. Even if the best surgeons came through that door, they couldn't do anything for him. Nothing can save him. Most of his blood volume has spilled out on the bed and is dripping onto the floor and on my shoes. His already weak heart is going to stop because there isn't enough blood in his body for it to pump.

With as much strength as he can muster, his fingers wrap around my wrist and squeeze. I look away from the wound and into his panicked eyes. "Be—behind you."

"Wha—" Turning my head, I find someone standing behind me. Ira's blood still staining their chin.

"He was a tasty treat." Hateful eyes flick to Ira before returning to me. "I'm sure you'll taste even better."

I'm so stunned to find them standing there, I'm not paying attention to what's in their hand. The syringe goes unnoticed until it's being plunged into my neck. The effects are almost instant. My vision blurs and my muscles go weak. I try to fight it, keeping as much pressure on Ira's neck as I can, but it's no use.

"No," I gasp.

My hands slip from his wound first before my knees give out and I crash onto the wood floor. I barely feel my body hit the ground. I can't move, can barely blink as I watch Ira. His hands try to cover his wound himself, but he's too weak. They fumble hopelessly at his neck. I want to scream, want to fight, but darkness is starting to form at the corners of my vision. The overwhelming sense of uselessness sets in.

I told him I'd help, but now I can't fucking move.

Ira turns his head just enough to look at me. The words he tries to tell me will forever remain a secret, but the look of forgiveness that shines in his eyes will remain with me forever. His lips wobble as they tip up in the slightest smile. Ira spends his last breaths reassuring me.

With blurry eyes, I watch the last bits of life leave Ira's body.

His face goes slack, his hands fall limply at his sides and his chest stops struggling to fill with precious oxygen. He wanted me there when he died, but not like this. It wasn't supposed to be like this. He was supposed to peacefully drift off in his sleep in a room full of freshly cut roses, with the fireplace lit and crackling while I sat beside him reading from the book we'd started together.

It wasn't supposed to end like this.

The tears fall from my eyes and I have no choice but to let them stream down my face in angry rivers.

My attacker bends down beside me, a malicious smile plastered on their face. With false tenderness, they push the strands of my hair off my face. "Let's see how strong the King is once he loses his Queen."

"Do you hear me, Quincey? If anyone else touches you, I will set the world on fucking fire. You're fucking mine."

Silas's promise repeats in my head before I'm greeted with nothing but darkness.

CHAPTER 36

Silas

They finally succeeded in getting what they want.

The cargo container that had been moved to a different secure location with twenty-four-hour security sits before me, completely empty of the product that it's supposed to be filled to the brim with. Product that had already been sold and promised to my buyers. Buyers who will start to cause problems if they don't get exactly what they've purchased from me.

All of it, *gone*.

The container's only contents are the bodies of the team that were hired to guard it. Louis lies on top of the pile of corpses. His lifeless eyes stare at me, his mouth still gaping open in a silent scream. The bodies are mangled. No doubt these men were tortured for information before they were finally put out of their misery. A waste of time, considering these men didn't know a fucking thing about my empire. They were simply hired as glorified guard dogs to watch over my shit.

I shouldn't be dealing with this right now. I should be heading back to the estate to pick Quincey up for our date. Plans have been made to ensure she has a good time. *I* was even looking forward to it. Now there is no way in hell I'm getting within five feet of her tonight. The anger coursing through me like wildfire is making me too volatile. I don't trust myself to not hurt her. She'll be upset, but I'll make her understand it's for the best that I don't show up tonight.

I'll find a way to make it up to her.

My fingers just brush against the phone in my pocket to call her when Duke's concerned voice comes from the other side of the container. "What now?"

It can't get any worse, can it?

The words written in blood on the side of the empty container tell me I may have spoken too soon.

Duke runs his finger through one of the letters, smearing it further. "Still fresh. This didn't happen too long ago. This twisted fucker wants to watch as you lose everything." He points his thumb toward the writing. "*Clearly*. I would bet money he's somehow watching us right now. He wants to see how you react to what he's taken."

I don't respond, an object pinned to the bloody metal by the writing holding all my attention. Unease slithers into my chest, constricting it to the point of pain. Moving so fast Duke jumps back in surprise, I rip the photograph off the wall. Blood drips over the image, but it's still clear as day.

It was taken the night Quincey was attacked. Her bloodied body is held tightly to my chest as I carried her to the waiting car. My lips are pressed to her hairline in a comforting gesture, and the look of utter relief is clearly written across my face.

My hand vibrates with rage as I look down at the photograph in my hand. The message written in blood holds so much more weight now.

You took everything from me… I'll do the same.

I should have seen this as a possibility. They're trying to take everything I care about from me. Up until recently, that was just my business. They must have figured out there is something else I care about more than anything.

Quincey.

"Duke," I snap. "We need to leave. *Now*." I move in the direction of the car without bothering to wait for him. I need to get to her, hide her away somewhere safe. We'll take Ira with us. It will be harder to travel with him, but I can't leave him behind.

Duke pauses. "Shouldn't we wait for the cleanup team? I don't want someone to accidentally come across this."

"*No*."

He runs up beside me and clamps his hand down on my shoulder in an attempt to stop me, but I violently shrug him off. "What's going on?"

I shove the picture into his hand wordlessly.

It takes him a second to figure it out but when he does, he curses harshly. "*Fuck*! Okay, let's go."

"I don't give a fuck if someone finds this mess, I need to get her out of the city. Tonight, Duke. Start making preparations. Make sure the pilot is on standby and the jet is fueled enough to get us out of the country." I bark orders at him. I'd planned to flee to Europe alone, but now, it's not safe for me to leave her here. My enemies know about her.

I shift restlessly in my seat again, counting each mile in my head until we reach the estate. Who are they? Why are they coming after me now?

If they were a true enemy of mine, I would have disposed of them a long time ago. I'm not reckless enough to allow the people who wish me dead to walk away breathing. I usually take care of them on the spot, it's how I've lived this long at the top of the food chain. If someone challenges me, I quickly remind them why I'm in charge. This also acts as a deterrent for those who also have the ill-advised idea to take me on.

The shrill sound of Duke's phone fills the tense air of the vehicle.

"Now isn't a good time, Rory," Duke answers the phone, the stress he feels evident in his tone.

"I don't care. Laurent needs to hear this," Rory's voice comes through the speakers of the car.

I sit like a piece of stone, waiting for more bad news to come from her mouth.

"You're on Bluetooth, he can hear you," Duke tells the hacker.

"I did some digging like we talked about. I've basically been awake for forty-eight hours searching through this information. Each company I found that was connected to the plane just led me to a different shell company. Whoever these people are, they're going to great extremes to keep their name off the public records."

The annoyed growl that escapes me has Duke side-eyeing me with worry. "Get to the fucking point, Rory!"

"The point is, I finally found a name," Rory announces. "I had to search through many companies and a million different documents. It took me in circles for days, but then I saw a name on a form that was filled out literally over a hundred years ago. It was filed with the city clerk in London to start a new business. I'll save you all the boring details, but I followed the name and company all the way back to today and get this… It's the same company that has been trying to buy Blackwood Technologies for thirty years. Just earlier this year, they made an offer the board of directors debated accepting until Silas put the kibosh on it *real* quick."

I have no intention of selling Blackwood off. Even if I can't run it myself anymore, it's a proprietary I never plan on giving up. Technology will continue to grow and change as the years pass, and I want Blackwood to spearhead those advancements.

"Laurent, do you recognize the name Gideon Rolfe?" The name washes over me like a bucket of ice water, fear chilling me to the bone as the pieces that had been missing snap into place. "His name isn't on the company documents anymore and *hell*, the company name isn't the same anymore either. It's changed multiple times over the years as bigger organizations acquired it, but his name was on the original document one hundred and twenty years ago. He's dead. But maybe you know someone else with the Rolfe name? Someone in his family tree could be coming after you?" Rory theorizes.

No, it's not a descendant of Gideon.

I haven't thought of that man in a very long time, our business was finished a long time ago, there was no reason for me to even consider him as a threat, but in hindsight, it appears I shouldn't have been so lenient with his life.

Duke, noticing the fury on my face, quickly tells Rory we'll call her back and ends the call. "Who is he and how bad did you fuck him over, Silas?"

The anger gets the better of me, and I slam my fist into the dashboard repeatedly until there are sizable dents in it. It does little to soothe the raging inferno in me. "Gideon was an ally of mine for forty years, a very long time ago. He played a role similar to yours until he did something foolish, and I had to clean up his mess. I… *dealt*… with it accordingly, or I thought I did, and I never saw him again."

"What happened?" Duke yells at me. "What did you do to him that has him coming after Quincey now?"

I rub my hands over my face as the memories I thought were long dead come rushing back. "He fell in love with a human and as humans do, she got sick. She was dying and he couldn't live without her. So, he changed her to be like us, but Margret didn't come back like herself." She came back the same way Cecily did, all the humanity had been stripped from her. "She was uncontrollable, killed over a dozen people in her first day, twice that the second day. Gideon was too weak to do what needed to be done, so I did it. I tore her head from her body and then set it on fire while two of my enforcers held him back." The pained screams that came from him as he watched echo in my head now just as loud as they did over a hundred years ago. "It wasn't a law punishable by death then and I allowed him to walk away, but after that day, I put the law into effect. I never wanted what happened to Margret to happen to another, the world would never survive the bloodshed if it continued to happen."

Gideon fled after that, and I never thought about him again. Until now.

While I was busy forgetting his existence, he's been sulking in the shadows, biding his time until he was able to ruin my life as I did his. I was right, this whole thing is personal.

"I stole his sun from him and now he wants to take mine," I say lowly to myself. "I took Margret from him, he plans on taking Quincey from me,"

"*Fucking hell*, Silas," Duke mutters while his foot presses harder on the accelerator.

"I should have just killed him when I did her. It would have been a mercy." He's walked this earth alone for the last one hundred years because of me. At the time, I thought I was doing him a kindness by allowing him to live, now I'm learning my leniency may have done more harm than good.

A loud alarm blares through Duke's phone making him swerve on the road as he dives for it. "Shit! Something's happening at the house, all of the security sensors have been tripped." He puts the phone to his ear and tries to call someone, who, I'm not sure, I'm too distracted by thoughts of Quincey.

The dread I felt the night Quincey was missing has nothing on what I feel now. It's not just helplessness I feel, but physical pain racks my body as a new level of terror rips through me.

If I'd just been strong enough to stay away from her, none of this would be happening. She wouldn't have become a target if I'd kept my distance, but now she's being punished because I love her.

With a roar that vibrates the whole car, my elbow slams into the glass of the window, making it explode into hundreds of pieces.

Duke drops the phone, shaking his head. "No one is picking up," he tells me solemnly. "I tried everyone, even Quincey, but she never answered."

"Let me out," I order.

"What?"

"Stop the fucking car and let me out." We're on the winding back road that leads to the secluded estate, no one would see me. Plus, I don't give a fuck if anyone does right now. "Let me out of this fucking car, or I swear on your dead sister's life I'm going to—"

I never finish the threat.

There's a deafening explosion and a blinding flash before the car is sent airborne. My ears ring from the blast, but the crunch of metal as we slam into the nearby trees will be something I never forget. My unrestrained body is thrown about the car as it repeatedly rolls. My ribs crack as my torso crashes into the dashboard and my skull splits when my head slams against something hard. A vampire's body can withstand a lot, will heal from almost everything, but it's not impossible to break.

There's nothing I can do to stop my body as I'm thrown through the destroyed windshield. My body screams in pain when I land yards away from the wrecked car.

Bloodied and broken, I lie on the forest floor staring up at the moon and stars above me. They taunt me with their beauty as I slowly begin to lose consciousness. A woman who's made of sunshine and braver than anyone I've ever met is my final thought before my head wound pulls me under.

"Are you going to catch me?"

"Always."

I made a promise to her, and I intend to keep it.

Quincey, *mon soleil*.

My sun.

THE END… FOR NOW

Silas and Quincey's story continues in *Midnight Queen*, coming summer 2021

MIDNIGHT QUEEN

KAYLEIGH KING

ACKNOWLEDGEMENTS

Thank you for reading Bloody Kingdom. Whether you loved it or hated it, as always, I'm thankful you took a chance on my book.

These characters came into my head and refused to leave until I put their story onto paper. They didn't give a crap that I was supposed to be writing another book at the time. They screamed at me until they got their way. I'm glad I listened to them because this story poured out me so fast.

As always, I want to thank my readers. Without your support, I wouldn't be here. Without you I wouldn't be able to follow my dreams. When you guys are excited about my books, it makes me excited.

I want to thank my beta readers, Greer, Ash, Bre, and Cat. Thank you for reading through my garbage-fire first drafts. Thank you for telling me how to tell a better story and thank you for telling me 'pretty words' when my poor author ego needs a boost.

Thank you, Cat Imb at TRC Designs for literally saving the day with my cover. You have this insane ability to read my mind and know what I want when I can't put it into words. Thank you for always fitting me into your hectic schedule. You are magic.

To Ramzi for being my twisted sister and soulmate. Thank you for helping me with anything and everything. Thank you for holding my hand and showing me the way through this crazy 'book word'.

Thank you to my life saver Greer. When I tell you this book wouldn't exist without her, I mean it. Every time I feel like walking into traffic or need someone to tell me everything will be okay, Greer is there. Doesn't matter what time of day either, she's there. Everyone needs a friend like Greer. I'm lucky to have her in my life.

Thank you, Christina. Your ability to deal with my bullshit

should be celebrated. I want to tell you that I'll be better organized next time, but we both know that will be a lie. I can disappear into my writing cave because I know you'll be there to pick up the slack in my absence. You're a rock star.

To my street team, this is my first time having a true team. I've been going at this author stuff alone for some time, but I can say now that I prefer to have a group of people behind me cheering me on. Thank you for taking the time to share and read all my things!

To Ellie and Rosa at My Brother's Editor. Thank you for always dealing with my last-minute nonsense and endless errors. Thank you for making my words pretty.

Lastly, to my family. Thank you for supporting me in everything I do. Without your support and grace, I wouldn't be chasing my dreams. Also, PS: Dad, please never read these books.

ABOUT THE AUTHOR

Kayleigh lives in Denver Colorado, just two hours away from some of the best skiing in the world. A luxury completely lost on her considering she avoids snow at all costs. Well, she avoids *outside* at all costs—she's what you'd call an 'indoor cat'. She much prefers to sit inside on her computer all day drinking massive amounts of caffeine. She'd have an IV drip of the stuff connected to her if she could. When she's not writing, you can find her binge-watching Netflix like it's her job. Or at the local Mexican restaurant, because the girl loves tacos and margaritas.

ALSO BY KAYLEIGH KING

The White Wolf Prophecy

Wolf Bound

Soul Bound

Shadow Bound

Fire Bound (coming soon)

Made in United States
Orlando, FL
08 April 2022

16599321R00183